'This great big flowery scrawl, this is my mother-in-law's writing? This is Daisy?' Lindy was flicking through to the end of the book. 'Has Orlando read it?'

'No,' said Victoria, 'it's for women only.'

'But Daisy was his mother. He worshipped her. He never stops talking about her.'

'Precisely. And I can imagine what he's been telling you. You and I might have to have a talk about that one day. But the fact that he adored her is exactly why he mustn't ever see The Visitors' Book. You do understand, don't you Lindy? Would you want to read about what your mother got up to when you were asleep upstairs as a child?'

Caroline Upcher has worked in film, publishing and journalism. She wrote two novels under the name Carly McIntyre, *Next of Kin* and *Saskia*, as well as Naomi Campbell's *Swan*. *Falling for Mr Wrong* was her first novel written under her own name. Caroline Upcher lives in London and Long Island, New York.

The VISITORS' BOOK

CAROLINE UPCHER

ORION

An Orion paperback
First published in Great Britain by Orion in 1997
This paperback edition published in 1998 by
Orion Books Ltd,
Orion House, 5 Upper St Martin's Lane,
London, WC2H 9EA

Third impression 2003

A CIP catalogue record for this book
is available from the British Library.

Printed and bound in Great Britain by
Clays Ltd, St Ives plc

For Steve, Amanda and Ned Lay,
who go to The Cottage at weekends.

I would like to acknowledge the help of the following people:

> Louise Allen-Jones
> Kari Allen
> Anne-Louise Fisher
> Carolyn Mays
> Kathy van Praag

and I would also like to acknowledge the invaluable help and advice of a mother of two profoundly deaf children who has asked not to be named.

Some people live their whole life and never see anyone die, but she was only four years old when she witnessed two people drown.

She should have been asleep. She had been tucked up in bed for hours. The curtains were open and because the moon was almost full she could see everything in her bedroom as if it were day.

She heard voices outside. Shouting. She struggled to push aside the bedclothes and stood up on the bed. Now she could see out of the window to the house next door.

She saw three people she knew running across the grass, chasing each other. One of them was a woman and she had no clothes on. They pushed and pulled each other and all the time they were moving closer to the river. They reached the back and seemed to be fighting. As she watched two of them fell in.

The next day everyone was talking about it, ignoring her, dismissing her if she tried to say something. So she kept quiet and listened instead. They talked about two of the people she had seen and how terrible it was that they were dead.

But they never mentioned the third who was still alive.

Maybe she had imagined it.

PART ONE

I

Victoria Hissey was in a state.

Her beloved godson Orlando, whom she adored and thought of as her own son, had swanned off to the Caribbean and returned less than a month later with a brand new bride whom he claimed to have met on a beach. And he expected Victoria to behave as if nothing untoward had happened. Life would go on as usual.

Well, it wouldn't. Not a chance.

Lindy. For some reason the name irritated Victoria. It sounded frilly. It was not the name of someone who could be taken seriously. At least not by Victoria. She'd met Lindy only once, briefly, in London. Pretty, in rather a shy way. Not frilly as it turned out. Mousy-brown hair, dead straight but well cut in a shiny bob. Safe, classic, inexpensive clothes, a Benetton angora sweater, a Marks & Spencer skirt. Well, that could change with Orlando's money. But the girl was on the small side with rather short legs and there was nothing Orlando's money could do about that.

And now Orlando had brought her down to The Cottage at Laybridge for the weekend with the assumption that Victoria would show her what was what. Except Orlando had no idea what that entailed. Nor, although it was something that went with The Cottage, did he have a clue as to the existence of The Visitors' Book. But Lindy, as his wife and the woman now in charge of The Cottage, would have to be told about it.

Victoria picked up the phone.

'Lindy? Hello, it's Victoria Hissey. I wondered if you'd like to come up to the house and have a cup of coffee with me? Don't bother with the car. There's a short cut via the Bluebell Walk. It's so pretty at this time of year. Just go out of The Cottage, turn left and follow the lane until you see the house. Shall we say eleven?'

Five minutes later it began to rain. Victoria stared out of her bedroom window at the meadow across the river and wondered how the sheep could be so oblivious to the wet as to go on chomping away at the grass. She watched them moving closer and closer to the riverbank, bumping into each other. God, they were stupid! A massive empty field all around them and they had to huddle together and fight for one small area of grass. If they moved any closer to the river they would undoubtedly fall in, and if there was heavy rain for days and the river rose and there was flooding, they would all be swept away.

Victoria allowed herself a secret smile of satisfaction at the thought. She had not been raised in the country. She had come to live at Laybridge as a result of her marriage, and while she had adapted to country life with relative ease, she remained eternally irritated by sheep.

Victoria was a widow, merry when she'd had a few but otherwise rather solitary by nature, which suited her life as a writer. She wrote long historical novels setting them all at Laybridge House in Wiltshire and basing her characters on the ancestors of her late husband, Hugh Hissey. Laybridge had been built in the latter part of the sixteenth century with magnificent views over the river Lay.

Victoria was currently embarked upon a book whose story was based on the week in 1651 when Charles II had taken refuge at Laybridge and was kept secretly for six nights before riding on to Shoreham and taking ship for France.

Guilt had been the reason Victoria had remained in the country following Hugh's untimely death; guilt and, later, her plant centre. Two tumours, one on the brain and the other on the spine, had been discovered in April 1984 and he had been dead by the end of June. They had been planning a small party to mark their twentieth wedding anniversary. He had been only forty-four. Now, seven years on, Victoria still missed him even though he had driven her mad. The hero of her latest book was, she realised, Hugh inasmuch as one could imagine Hugh as Master of Laybridge in the seventeenth century. All Hugh's pedantic neuroses and excessive caution were played out in the character of Henry Hissey (she kept the family name even though her books were fiction – it was good for publicity, her publishers told her), who was totally against the idea of harbouring Charles II for a week. Henry Hissey worried and fretted and whined in Victoria's book, just as Hugh would have done, and remained impervious to the romance and excitement of playing a part in helping his king. It was his wife, Kate, who masterminded the whole thing in defiance of her husband. Kate, Victoria realised, was based on her mother-in-law, Hugh's mother Sarah, who had risen masterfully to the occasion during the Second World War when Laybridge had been requisitioned by Salisbury Hospital.

And, in truth, Victoria delighted in Laybridge and its magnificent gardens. After Hugh's death when she had discovered exactly how much it cost to keep Laybridge going in the style to which she had become accustomed, and how utterly useless Hugh had been at harvesting the family money, Victoria had looked around for a way to avoid delving further into her capital. She had her writing but after fourteen books her sales were mysteriously dwindling. Ironically it was her publishers who came up with the solution to her potential financial problems. Victoria's long-standing editor had finally retired and a new one was proposed. This time it was to be a man and a rather young one by the sound of it. They had telephoned with news of his double first in history at Cambridge and listing endless credentials which Victoria had interrupted with: 'Don't bore me with all that rhubarb. Why don't you send him down to have lunch with me?'

The young man, Toby, had been too nervous to go on his own and had requisitioned another young editor, Lucia, to accompany him. The lunch was a huge success. Not because Toby impressed Victoria. He didn't much, but she knew she could see off any editorial argument he might attempt about her work and, these days, that was really all that mattered to her. After fourteen books she couldn't be doing with anyone taking a pencil to one of her manuscripts. She knew what was wrong with them and she knew she was the only one who would be able to fix it. It was Lucia who had surprised her. Victoria was fascinated by the pair of them. They were clearly having an illicit affair and she began to ply them with wine in the hope of loosening their tongues so that she could prise the details from them. Victoria was not a gossip. In fact she was proud that she could be relied upon to be discreet. But she was forever torn between her natural inclination to be anti-social and her desire, as a writer, to be party to the secrets of other people's lives. But Lucia was not forthcoming with details of her sex life. She asked instead for a tour of the gardens and as Victoria led her along the avenues of apple trees, through the rose garden and down to the River Walk, Lucia suddenly asked: 'Why don't you start a garden centre here, a plant centre?'

'I am not a plantswoman –' Victoria began, only to be cut short by Lucia's enthusiasm.

'But it would be so wonderful for your novels. Think of the publicity! Everyone would flock to buy plants and wander round the gardens and all your books are set here. They could be on sale. Buy a copy of your latest book and get a free plant. Plus there's you and the Hissey family history all tied into the books. You could have garden fêtes with celebrities to open them. You could even write a gardening book for me …' Lucia was getting quite carried away.

Victoria took advice. She hired someone to establish and run the plant centre for her. She exercised her charm to its full extent on Harold Farley, head gardener at Laybridge for thirty-five years, and finally won him round. Victoria knew perfectly well that Harold's had been a token resistance. At seventy, he would welcome taking more of a back seat. He had done little more than oversee the work done by other gardeners for years and provided he retained the nominal title of head gardener, he wouldn't really care what happened.

A year later her publishers launched her new book at the opening of the Laybridge Garden Centre and once again she began to sell, although, as Victoria well knew, it was all cosmetic. The new book was no better than the last. There was only one thing – or, rather, one person – that would free her to write again with real passion.

At the opening, Victoria made a speech beginning with the words: 'I am not a plantswoman but …'

It became her catchphrase. She became obsessed with the garden, interfering wherever she could, much to Harold Farley's annoyance, heralding any suggestion she made with the words: 'I'm not a plantswoman but … don't you think the laburnum arch is becoming just a bit too intrusive?'

Laybridge and Victoria prospered. Such a venture as the Laybridge Garden Centre could never have seen the light of day had Hugh lived, Victoria realised. Hugh would have worried the idea into the ground, old misery that he was, instead of allowing it to blossom and bear fruit.

And then she would remember the other reason she had stayed buried in the country. Bruno Manners and the guilt she harboured about her relationship with him, an affair that had begun long before Hugh's illness and continued until his death. It was ridiculous, she knew, but remaining at Laybridge and continuing to maintain Hugh's home as it had been in his life time helped to assuage the pain she feared her obvious love for Bruno must have caused her husband. For Hugh had known all about her and Bruno. Of that, she was certain.

Hugh Hissey's best friend, Guy Manners, had been just like him: unassuming, pedantic, cautious, nervous and kind. They had differed only in their choice of wives. Daisy Manners was dark and lithe and brittle.

Guy's brother Bruno was the black sheep of the Manners family. He hadn't exactly been expelled from

Radley but once he had sat, and failed, his A levels, it was made clear to his father that they were no longer interested in accommodating Bruno as a pupil. He went to London and found himself a job on a newspaper. Guy went up to Cambridge where he met Hugh and they read history together. It was 1959. Four years later Guy, trembling with pride, brought a beautiful dark-haired girl home for Christmas and Bruno, playing the role of smooth young journalist to the hilt, had seduced her by New Year's Eve. Hugh, who had been invited to stay with the Mannerses for the New Year's Eve celebrations, witnessed everything when he walked into the bathroom he was sharing with Bruno. Bruno and Daisy were lying on the floor. By the time they had realised someone had come in, Hugh was gone. They never knew who had seen them and Hugh never mentioned it to Guy.

Two months later Guy proposed. Daisy was twenty. It was all rather messy, and the only time in Guy and Hugh's friendship when they had words. Hugh begged Guy not to go ahead with the marriage. Daisy would make Guy's life utterly miserable, he said. Hugh knew that it really didn't matter to Daisy whom she married. She would continue to sleep with whoever took her fancy. Marriage wouldn't make a jot of difference. A husband would be expected merely to provide her with financial security. But to Guy, Daisy was an exotic butterfly he had captured against all odds. He couldn't let her get away. He would never find anyone like her again.

It was in the first year of Guy and Daisy's marriage that, estranged from Guy and feeling particularly vulnerable, Hugh met Victoria. Many years into their marriage he was able to look back and ask himself if he had fallen for the tall, moody girl because she had been the opposite of Daisy. She was not a flirt like Daisy. She did not smile easily, but when she did it was worth waiting for and that, Hugh decided, was why he fell in love with her. He liked to make her laugh. That he rarely did, since his talent to amuse was almost non-existent, entirely escaped him.

When Daisy gave birth to a boy and insisted he be called Orlando, Guy terminated the rift between himself and Hugh by asking Hugh to be Orlando's godfather. At the christening, Victoria, by now Hugh's fiancée, saw Bruno Manners for the first time and although he never said a word to her she understood what it was to fall in love and that what she felt for Hugh was merely affection.

She didn't see Bruno again for twelve years.

Now, just when Victoria had finally decided it was high time to bury the memory of her affair with Bruno and settle down to a life of relative calm in the country, it looked as if that fool Orlando was going to cause chaos by bringing home a totally unsuitable bride. What Orlando had done was unthinkable: met a perfect stranger in the Caribbean and married her without apparently giving it a second thought. Under different circumstances Victoria would have been titillated by the romance of it but this was a little too close to home. She would be the one who would have to pick up the pieces when it fell apart.

Victoria adored Orlando Manners. He was completely irresistible to all women unless they were allergic to near impossible good looks, exceptional charm, a degree of endearing helplessness and a large private income. His grandfather, like Hugh Hissey's father, had been a landowner who had invested shrewdly to safeguard the family's security. And because his father and his uncle, while having entirely different personalities, had borne an uncanny resemblance to each other, and because Orlando was the image of his father, he also reminded Victoria of Bruno.

It always came back to Bruno.

After Orlando's christening, and to cement their renewed friendship, Hugh Hissey had offered Guy Manners the largest house on the Laybridge estate as a weekend bolthole. It was Guy's in perpetuity until Hugh died. Victoria knew perfectly well that Hugh's real intention had been that Guy should use it as somewhere to go to escape from Daisy, somewhere where he, Hugh, could enjoy Guy's company exclusively. But Daisy would not be put off that easily and, to Hugh's horror, every weekend The Cottage had been filled with her London friends. Victoria, knowing she could retreat to Laybridge whenever she wanted, had been intrigued by the wild weekend parties and, leaving Hugh grumbling into his whisky in the library, she often wandered down to The Cottage to see what was going on.

She never told Hugh what she witnessed, the joints being passed around, the multiple activity in the bedrooms, the sad, patient expression on Guy's face as he indulged Daisy by trying to make her wanton friends welcome. She did not want Hugh to be aware of the chaos in which his godson was being raised. Hugh would only fret. He wouldn't do anything about it. It was always Victoria who acted when there was a problem to be solved, and when she saw what was happening down at The Cottage, she took to inviting Orlando up to Laybridge to spend the night away from the noise and the people bursting drunkenly into his room in search of a bed in which to have sex. Hugh began to see his godson every weekend and, in everyone's eyes, became much more of a father to him than the hapless Guy.

And so when Guy and Daisy Manners fell into the river Lay in mysterious circumstances in the middle of the night and drowned, Orlando, twelve years old and home from his prep school for the weekend, was up at Laybridge and never saw a thing.

2

Hugh astounded Victoria by inviting Bruno Manners to Laybridge for Guy and Daisy's funeral. She knew what it cost him to allow Bruno to enter his home. Hugh couldn't very well bar Bruno from his brother's funeral but it was another thing to invite him to spend the weekend with them. He was doing it, Hugh said, for Orlando. As Orlando's uncle, Bruno was the only family he had left.

Even though it had been twelve years, Victoria had never forgotten the effect Bruno Manners had had on her at Orlando's christening.

He had arrived late at the funeral.

As she stood between Hugh and Orlando in the front pew of the little church in Laybridge village, clasping Orlando's hand tightly in her own, Victoria decided that he was not coming.

He had never been near Laybridge. In a rare indiscretion Hugh had told Victoria about the time he had come upon Bruno and Daisy, and Victoria had assumed that Bruno hadn't had the nerve to come near Hugh since Guy's marriage to Daisy. Maybe he wouldn't have the courage to show up today. It wasn't as if he could slip in unnoticed without people knowing who he was. Bruno Manners was almost a household name. He was a writer like she was, only he wrote bestsellers. He had given up journalism pretty quickly and turned to writing thrillers with instant success. They had ludicrous premises in the 'What if?' area (the first had centred around a plot by the Germans during the Second World War to capture the Little Princesses, Elizabeth and Margaret Rose, only the kidnappers took the wrong children), but they were intelligently written with enough accuracy in the political and historical research surrounding the fictitious aspects of the story to attract a solid middlebrow following. He was hailed one minute as the new Frederick Forsyth and the next as the new Jack Higgins. Victoria had bought every book he had written and gazed in secret at his author photograph on the dust-jacket.

He arrived as Hugh was walking up to the pulpit to speak about Guy and slipped into the pew beside Orlando. Victoria turned and found she was looking straight into his eyes. Hugh, reaching the pulpit, climbed the steps and looked down at the congregation. He saw Bruno and paled. He opened his mouth a few times but nothing came out. Oh, Christ, thought Victoria, he's dried and I can't help him. He always loathed Bruno. I could have told him this might happen.

Victoria was far from calm herself. Bruno's presence was disturbing. It wasn't as if he was devastatingly handsome but he emanated immense sexual power. He wasn't particularly tall, around five eight or nine, but he was well built. His mass of unruly black hair stood out among the other well-trimmed heads of Guy's friends and the men of Laybridge. Daisy's louche London friends had not bothered to show up for her funeral. The mourners were there for Guy Manners, not his wife.

She had forgotten Orlando. Daisy had been his mother.

He was clutching her hand and she could feel him shaking. Speak, Hugh, you idiot, speak, Victoria silently implored him. Give us the boring speech you've been preparing all week. Put an end to this confusion.

Orlando's control snapped. He brought his hands to his face to hide his tears and pushed past Bruno to run out of the church.

Bruno followed him.

Somehow, with Bruno gone, Hugo was able to begin his address and Victoria knew she could not leave now.

When the pallbearers brought out the coffins Bruno and Orlando were standing by the open graves. Bruno stepped aside and allowed Hugh and Victoria to stand by Orlando. Afterwards, back at Laybridge, Victoria was kept busy dispensing tea and giving Orlando plates of cake to hand round while Hugh offered whisky to those who wanted it.

Bruno intercepted Victoria on the way to the kitchen. 'You write too, don't you?'

She nodded. 'Yes, historical novels set here at Lay-bridge. Now, please, I must –'

'I've just seen all my books in the library. Good old Hugh, didn't know he was a fan.'

'Actually he isn't. He doesn't read fiction.'

'So who bought them? You? Christ, how embarrassing. I've never read anything of yours.'

Victoria looked away. Why wouldn't he let her through?

'Were you friends with Daisy?'

'No. Not really.'

'Why not? Didn't you like her?'

His bluntness was beginning to unnerve her. All these direct questions. It was time she asked one of her own.

'That time you spent with Orlando, when you followed him out of the church, what were you talking about?'

'Boys' talk. Nothing that would interest you.'

This was too much. She brushed past him but he came after her, overtaking her down the long passage.

'What happened that night? How did they die?'

'Accidental drowning, according to the inquest.'

'Do you believe that?'

'Why shouldn't I?'

'Were they fighting? Were they arguing about me?'

Victoria stopped in astonishment. 'Why on earth should anyone fight about you?' she asked, as dismissively as she could. 'Why should you always be the centre of attention?'

Then he touched her for the first time, holding her by the wrist. 'I'm sorry. I can't ask Hugh. There's no one else. Guy was my brother.'

She was shaking. His hand was hot on her wrist. His heat was coursing through her.

'I know,' she whispered, 'but please let go of me.'

He didn't stay the weekend, after all, but left that night. Victoria wondered if it would be another twelve years before she saw him again.

It was less than twelve days.

Hugh astounded her yet again by offering Bruno The Cottage as a place to come and write. Victoria knew what he was really doing and again she felt a surge of affection for him. Guy Manners had left a request that in the event of his death Hugh Hissey should be made Orlando's legal

18

guardian. From now on Orlando would live at Laybridge. But Hugh, knowing that Bruno was Orlando's only blood relative, had found a way for them to meet regularly where he could keep an eye on them.

The first weekend Bruno went down to The Cottage, Victoria told herself she was just popping in to make sure he had everything he needed. She knocked on the front door but there was no reply. She walked round to the side and peered through the kitchen window but could see no sign of life. The kitchen door was locked but the front door was always left open.

Victoria let herself in. 'Hello!' she called. 'Bruno, it's Victoria Hissey. Just want to make sure you're all right.'

Silence.

His car was outside. Maybe he'd gone for a walk. She wandered through to the sitting room and wondered why the curtains were drawn. Then it dawned on her. From here the lawn sloped straight down to the river. Maybe he didn't want to be reminded of the river.

What should she do? Should she wait?

It was the first time she had been in The Cottage since the accident. Without thinking what she was doing she wandered upstairs. When she walked into the main bedroom he was standing there in the process of pulling off a T-shirt over his head. When he turned towards her he was naked.

'Do you normally go snooping through other people's houses when they're out – or when you think they're out?'

'Do you normally tear all your clothes off the minute you hear someone coming?'

'Yes,' he said, holding out his arms. 'Come here.'

3

Unlike his uncle Bruno, Orlando Manners was not vain. He knew he was attractive to women only because they never missed an opportunity to throw themselves at him. Until they did so he often failed to notice them, and his less attractive male friends knew that this only added to his allure.

Orlando liked women. He enjoyed their company and seducing them was not the first thing he thought of, even when he was attracted to them. And when he did get round to taking someone to bed, his own passion always surprised him.

His friends teased him about his work. As the owner of a successful photographic agency he was surrounded by beautiful models and they assumed he used the business as a knocking shop. His attempts to deflect the never-ending stream of nudge-nudge wink-wink innuendo only increased their conviction that he got his end away nightly, if not several times a day.

Nothing could have been further from the truth. Only if a woman's mind interested him did Orlando begin to notice her body rather than the other way round. The minds of the models that drifted through his agency on their way to castings with his clients rarely engaged him for longer than the two minutes it took to greet them, enquire how their work was going and wish them luck at the casting. The over-groomed blondes (why were they always blonde?) he met on the London party circuit smiled too much and, even though they appeared to be listening intently, invariably missed both the point and the irony of anything he said to them.

The realisation had dawned on him that he might never meet a woman who could mean anything to him within the rather narrow confines of his social circle. One girl, aware of his lack of interest in her, had accused him of being in love with his mother. He had photographs of Daisy all over his house in Elgin Crescent. Some unsuspecting women imagined her to be an ex-wife or even a current girlfriend, so strategically placed were the silver-framed portraits. They were all head shots and Daisy's face was dark and bewitching. The pictures could have been taken a year or two ago. There was no clue that this was a woman who had been dead for fifteen years.

. It was Orlando's best friend Peter McGill who took him aside and told him how off-putting Daisy was to potential girlfriends. Peter and Orlando did not have a great deal in common. They had been at school together. Peter worked as a financial adviser and worried constantly about money. He priced everything mentally, and often verbally, as soon as he saw it. 'Nice car' (jacket, tumble-dryer, house in the Dordogne, whatever) was automatically followed by the words 'must have set you back, let's see now …?' It made no sense at all to Peter that for a living Orlando dealt with flighty models and long-haired freelance photographers. He lectured Orlando often. But Orlando was fond of Peter, as he was fond of Lily, Peter's irritating nanny of a wife. At least they were real and leading normal lives, not like the affected, insincere people with whom he seemed to be constantly in contact. Still, he couldn't quite believe it when Peter tackled him about his mother.

'Orlando, you've got to let up a bit.'

'On what?' They were having a drink round the corner from Orlando's agency near Liverpool Street.

'You've got to stop going on about your mother, about how beautiful she was.'

'Well, she is beautiful.' Orlando rarely used the past tense when talking about his mother. 'You've only got to look at her photographs.'

'They're part of the problem. Having them all over the house like that. It puts girls off.'

Peter was embarrassed to have to say anything but Lily had insisted. They both wanted to see Orlando settle down but no girl seemed to have a chance against Daisy.

'But, Pete, surely you remember her? Didn't we always have the best time with her? Do you remember how she always used to ask your advice about her money even when you were only ten years old? I can hear her asking you: "What shall I invest this in, Peter? You tell me. Do."'

'Orlando, you don't remember. You think you do but how can you? It was so long ago.'

'But she's fun. Isn't she? She's dazzling. She's sharp.'

'People have told you that.'

'I remember. I was twelve when she died. Who taught me backgammon? Who taught me to dance? Who taught me the Peppermint Twist? Who taught me about photography? How do you think I got into this business? I might have been only a kid but she introduced me to all those big-time sixties fashion photographers. I met Bailey when I was seven. I've always loved photography. You remember how I called all those people she knew and they helped me get started. I had to work with photographers. It was ordained.'

'Fashion photographers.'

'Oh, all right, but what's wrong with them? I'm not pretending they're art.'

'Just as well,' said Peter. 'That new lightbox in your office, must have set you back, what …?'

There were moments when Orlando wished he had never bought the photographic agency that bore his name. He didn't have to work. He could have lived perfectly comfortably off the interest from his investments but the memory of the glamorous picture Daisy painted of sixties London was slow to fade. Young, rich and anxious to be accepted, Orlando had bought the agency because he was able to and because he was not required to be there very much. It came fully staffed with a ready-made client list. All he gave it was a new name. Still, he made an effort to go there two or three times a week, to keep abreast of what was happening, possibly out of guilt. He had always wanted to be one of the crowd even if he had to buy his way in.

They tolerated him and he could tell they even rather liked him and he took care not to interfere too much. But he knew they were mystified as to why he had insisted he go along on this shoot in the Caribbean. OK, the client was new and the photographer was fairly young and inexperienced, but the job wasn't particularly important. There was nothing about it that suggested Orlando's presence was vital. But the location was St Lucia and when he was eight he had come to St Lucia with his mother for a holiday. Just the two of them.

Except sitting here on the beach he couldn't remember a thing about it and he couldn't bear it. Was it true what Peter had said? Were his memories pure fantasy of the beautiful woman who was forever laughing? He was going to start crying again. She had told him it was OK to cry, it was OK to be emotional, it didn't make him any less of a man. She had told him that. Hadn't she?

A woman was coming along the sand. Though he was the only other person on the entire beach she almost fell over him sitting there with his arms wrapped around his knees.

He raised his head, aware that his eyes must be red. What would she think of him, a grown man blubbing by the sea?

'Are you all right? Can I help?'

'Not very original but what else could you say?'

Lindy watched him as he leapt to his feet and began to brush the sand off himself. His skin was almost black in places, he was so tanned. He was easily six foot with floppy black hair and a thin boyish face. His nose turned up and his dark blue eyes were encased in a spread of fine wrinkles like spider's legs as he squinted against the sun. He wiped his eyes, brushing away tears, and cursed. His hands were sandy.

'Ow! Jesus! How could I be so stupid?'

'Blink. It should make your eyes water naturally and wash out the salt and sand.'

'I might just as well go on crying then.' He laughed. 'Do you cry a lot?'

'I do, actually. I'm emotional.'

'Really?'

'I can tell you think I'm a complete wimp but I'm not. I

24

just think it's perfectly natural to cry. But you need a beach like this, somewhere isolated where you can settle down to a good blub and be sure no one's going to hear you. I couldn't let Victoria see me crying.'

'Couldn't you? Victoria's your wife, is she?'

'God, no. I'm not married. Victoria's my godfather's widow.'

'Are you about to recite your entire family tree?'

Orlando blinked again. This woman had an edge to her but she was pretty in a quiet kind of way. 'What's your name?' he asked suddenly.

'Lindy.'

'I'm Orlando. Shall we walk back together? You're out here on holiday obviously.'

He could see she was a bit miffed at being taken for an obvious tourist.

'And you live here?'

'No, no, no. I'm here for work.'

She didn't ask him what he did.

'You're awfully self-contained, if you don't mind my saying so. You don't say much, do you?'

'I don't have to,' she replied, smiling, 'not with you around.'

'OK. Fair enough. Where are you staying? The Aquamarine Club? Yes? Nice place, don't you think?'

'It's fine, but then I'm not being too critical. I didn't have to pay for this trip.'

'Hubby treating you?'

She ignored him.

'OK, sorry. None of my business. I'm a photographer's agent, or rather I own a photographers' agency, and one of my clients is out here with a journalist who is doing a story on the Aquamarine Club. It's quite new, you know.'

'And you're just along for the ride?'

'Well, yes, I suppose I am. But I did get my client the job, after all, and I have quite a lot of say about what goes into the piece.'

'What kind of a magazine is it?'

'Oh, it's sort of a giveaway. I mean it goes through people's doors and they make the advertisers pay through the nose. It's food, restaurants, holidays, books, films, usual sort of thing.'

'Circulation?'

'Oh, God, I don't know, about two thousand, maybe.'

'But what's the point of running such a non-profitable venture? How on earth can they afford to fund trips to the Caribbean? Oh, I get it. You're paying for the whole thing?'

How had she put that together so quickly? She was sharp.

'Well, sort of. I really believe in this photographer but he's just not getting the breaks. This is one way of getting people to see his work. Now, I've had a brilliant idea. Why don't we have you in one of the shots? Then you'll have a souvenir of your holiday. With your hubby, of course.'

'On one condition.'

'Anything. What?'

'You stop going on about my hubby because I haven't got one, and you tell me why you were crying.'

'That's two conditions. Looks as if you'd better have dinner with me tonight.'

He didn't know what made him pour out the story of

his parents' death as soon as they'd ordered their food. Was it because she seemed such a good listener? He never usually talked about himself like this.

Over coffee she held up her hand. 'Permission to speak?'

'Five seconds.'

'Thanks. It's just a quick question. Do you do this little-boy-lost routine every time you meet someone? You're not the only orphan in the world, you know.'

'How many other people do you know who were orphaned at twelve?'

'Fourteen.'

For a second he wanted to cry again but not because of anything to do with Daisy. He wanted to yell with sheer elation at having found someone so down-to-earth, someone who apparently was not going to be thrown by anything he said.

'I'm not used to it. People don't generally tease me. They creep around me with kid gloves. Ever since I can remember there have been all these things that must never be spoken about in front of me. Nobody understands how fucking lonely I am. I get away with murder, always have done. I milked it for all it was worth, this orphan caper. "Don't be nasty to me because my parents fell into the river and drowned and therefore I'm damaged and I can have anything I want."'

'You sound as if you must have been perfectly repellent.'

'You see? There you go again.'

'I wasn't teasing you that time.'

'No. I know. But you were being straight with me. You weren't afraid to hurt my feelings.'

'I couldn't care less about your feelings. I care considerably more about this ice cream and about the fact that I shouldn't be eating it.'

Orlando studied the woman across the table. He said slowly, 'I like the way you look. You have lovely hazel eyes and when the light catches them they go green. And your hair is good. It's dead straight and very fine and I know that's hell to deal with but there's lots of it and you keep it nice and shiny.'

'Gee, thanks. By the way I'm the only one who's allowed to be direct around here. Now hadn't you better get on with arranging this photo session of me or whatever it is? I leave tomorrow.'

'Not a chance! Not in the middle of the night. We'll need the light. Stay another week.'

She looked uncomfortable.

'I couldn't afford to.'

'Oh, bollocks to that. The magazine will pay but there is one condition. I can tell you're really into conditions and all this negotiating shit.'

'Yes?'

'You have to go on bossing me about and being very direct with me.'

Two days later they were in his whitewashed stucco hotel bungalow on the edge of the beach. Lindy had plucked a bloom from one of the oleander bushes outside and was in the process of fastening it in her hair.

'Don't bother with that. I want to go for a swim. I'm just going to nip to the bathroom then we'll go. You'll never get that thing to stay in. Your hair's much too fine.'

She chucked it after him.

Ten minutes later he was still upstairs.

'LINDY!'

He heard her come into the bathroom. He was crouched down in a corner with his eyes closed, shaking.

'What's the matter?'

He pointed to the shower where a medium-sized spider was having a nap on the tiles.

'What?'

'The spider.'

'Yes, Orlando, I know it's a spider.'

'Well, could you do something with it, please?'

'What?'

'Oh, Lindy, don't be so maddening. I'm petrified of spiders.'

'Oh, don't be ridiculous.'

Oh, don't be ridiculous! It was what Daisy had always said.

Lindy walked over and picked up the spider. She dangled it between her fingers for a few moments then flushed it down the lavatory.

Orlando put his arms round her and backed her into the shower, raining kisses all over her face.

'That is the single best thing anyone's done since my mother died.' He kissed her again. 'At least for me.' Another kiss. 'No woman I have ever known has saved me from a spider. They've all been just as scared of them as I am. This is just a small token of my undying gratitude,' kiss, 'you saved my life,' kiss, 'you did, you saved me.'

'Oh, for Christ's sake, get a grip. If you're going to kiss me at least kiss me properly. Here, like this.' And she pulled his face round until their mouths met. He felt his lips open automatically. He moved his hands down her body, reaching up underneath her T-shirt to undo her bra and then down inside the elastic of her shorts to cup her buttocks and draw her hard against him. It was as if she'd pressed a button.

I'm going to marry her, he told Daisy silently. I've come here to remember you but suddenly I can't and here she is. I'm sitting on a beach searching for you and instead I find her. It's a sign from you, isn't it, Daisy? It's meant to be.

4

The truth was that ever since Hugh's death Victoria had been lying to herself, pretending that all was well with her life. Not that her life had been exactly devoid of duplicity when he was still alive. She had often wondered about the stipulation in Hugh's will that Orlando inherit The Cottage. Was it his way of telling her to get rid of Bruno? But if so why had he not spoken out before he died? As it was, she had been so riddled with guilt as Hugh endured his last few months in agonizing pain, barely kept at bay by the morphine, that she had asked Bruno to leave.

She was to blame. She had sent him away and even after seven years she still missed him. In fact it seemed to get worse and it was interfering with her writing. Her sales had been dwindling because her recent books had been below her usual standard. Her heart wasn't in them any more. She was the first to admit that Bruno, as a reliable partner, was a disaster area. He wasn't remotely interested in commitment and had always maintained he could absolve himself from criticism if he made it quite clear to any woman he went to bed with that under no circumstances would he ever contemplate marriage with her. He liked living alone. He hated having to account for his whereabouts to anyone.

Victoria knew all of this. The trouble was that she understood it perfectly because she was exactly the same.

She adored being alone. She had hated always having to be there for Hugh, fond of him though she had been. She liked her solitude and, if she was to continue writing, it was something of a necessity.

But she also wanted Bruno. Not only wanted, needed him. It was a strange way to feel standing, as she did at nearly fifty, on the brink of the menopause. It wasn't as if she craved sex *per se*. She wasn't about to make a fool of herself and rush out to find herself a young hot-blooded lover to satisfy her misguided middle-aged lust. She craved only Bruno.

About a year after his death some of Hugh's well-meaning friends started inviting her to dinner parties in the country where they would introduce her, with an extraordinary lack of subtlety, to a variety of divorced men and widowers whom they obviously felt were candidates for Hugh's replacement. Indeed one or two were uncannily Hugh-like in their earnestness and anxious expressions. What nobody realised, of course, was that she was looking for a Bruno substitute, not someone to take Hugh's place, and she soon became convinced that no such man existed. She allowed her London friends to do their bit – at least their parties were more fun – but after a while she began to thwart even their efforts by asking if she could bring Orlando with her. Orlando, at twenty-one, was the perfect walker.

If anyone came close to being Bruno's replacement, it was Orlando. He was tall where Bruno was not, but Orlando had the same shock of unruly black hair and the same piercing navy eyes and slightly olive skin. Both men lived up to their exotic names: neither looked entirely English.

Victoria had grown used to having Orlando around. When he had moved into The Cottage she had laid down ground rules at once. She was a writer. She needed privacy and quiet. Laybridge would not be used as a solution to the overspill of weekend guests at The Cottage. They could all come to lunch and dinner by invitation only but the bedrooms were not on offer.

Still, she enjoyed being able to wander down the Bluebell Walk and pop in on him for a chat. Orlando did not live at The Cottage: he weekended there, as the Americans said. She hadn't really thought about it properly but he would, she assumed, inherit Laybridge from her when she died. Meanwhile, he had The Cottage. It was hardly just a cottage, with five perfectly adequate bedrooms and three bathrooms, but compared with Laybridge House, which had twelve bedrooms, nearly all of them closed (though precious few bathrooms), it was always thought to be on the small side.

Victoria had hoped that the rest of her life would jog along like this: living quietly in a backwater, writing, going up to London for occasional visits to old friends. Little by little time would heal her wounds and her memory of Bruno would subside. And Orlando would always be there to remind her of what she had once had.

Now it was all going to have to change. Orlando was married and he was bringing home a bride. He would no longer be able to escort Victoria to dinner parties in London, nor could she continue to pop down to The Cottage and see him whenever she wanted.

She still felt so young. Was it pointless to go on living with just Bruno's memory? Of course it was. She had not had a man for nearly seven years. Orlando was married. It was the beginning of a new era. She would, Victoria resolved, let it mark the start of a new life for her.

And now, thought Victoria, I have to tell the new Mrs Manners, mousy little creature that she appears to be, about The Visitors' Book.

5

However much Orlando might believe in signs and portents, the fact of the matter was that Lindy had won her holiday in the Caribbean in a magazine competition, which she had completed purely to fill the time while waiting for her highlights to take at the hairdresser's. It was corny beyond belief. She had tossed the magazine aside when she left and the faithful Mandy had retrieved it and sent in her entry. Lindy was not a woman's woman. She had few girlfriends in whom she could confide. Instead she poured out her problems to someone who was relatively anonymous: her hairdresser. Now Mandy saw her chance to throw a dash of romance into Lindy's life.

It was a holiday for two.

'Going to take your boyfriend?' asked Mandy, when Lindy went to have a trim a few weeks later and told her the news.

'Haven't got anyone special at the moment.'

'Your mum, then?'

'No, Mandy, I'm going to take you.' Mandy grinned.

On the plane going out Lindy wondered what had induced her to invite Mandy, who talked non-stop about boyfriends throughout the entire flight. She took Lindy through virtually every relationship she had ever had, sparing her none of the more mundane details.

'I said to him, "Where we going tonight?" He goes:

"Mandy, I don't care, you choose." So I said: "Right, we'll go to that new wine bar that's opened on the High Street." So he goes: "Oh, we're going there, it's dead pricy." So I told him where to get off there and then. I can't stand a mean man – what about you, Lind?'

But when they arrived it wasn't half as bad as Lindy had expected. Mandy was out discoing every night and flaunting her wares at the poolside bar by day. Lindy slept late, read, and took long solitary walks along the beach.

'He wants a bit of nooky,' said Mandy knowingly, when Lindy told her about Orlando.

'I don't fancy him,' said Lindy.

But she did.

It all happened very fast. From the day they slept together, Orlando seemed to take it for granted that they were a couple. Not just a couple on holiday but he began to talk about what they would do when they got back to England.

'I'm in London during the week. I've got a house. Elgin Crescent. Notting Hill Gate. But we'll go down to The Cottage every weekend. You'll love it. It was my mother's. My father's too, of course, but it's full of Daisy's things. I always called her Daisy. She liked me to. It made her feel younger, I think. She was so beautiful.'

Every day Lindy held her breath and wondered when he would wake up and realise who she was. Men like Orlando didn't shack up with ordinary suburban girls like her. She must look different or something under the Caribbean sun. Then there was this woman Victoria he kept going on about.

'She's like my mother. I don't mean she's like Daisy.

They couldn't be more different. But I grew up in her house so it's as if she's some kind of relation. In fact she's my godmother. You'll love her.'

Lindy couldn't help noticing that he talked about his mother as if he could remember her vividly and yet he couldn't have been more than twelve when she died. And Lindy hated it when someone said, 'You'll love so-and-so.' It had the most perverse effect on her. She felt immediately that she *wouldn't* like that person.

She didn't remember him proposing marriage. All she knew was that one night they were standing on the beach dressed a little more formally than usual and some kind of preacher was performing a moonlit wedding ceremony. It was corny but at the same time it was breathtaking and there was no way she was going to do anything to stop it. She had never encountered a man like Orlando. That he should notice her at all was almost unbelievable, but that he should say something like, 'You have lovely hazel eyes and when the light catches them they go green,' transported her straight to heaven. All her life Lindy had been aware of what she did not have rather than what she did. She didn't have long legs – or arms for that matter. She was not tall. She didn't have a very good figure. She didn't have thick lustrous hair. However much she tried, she didn't have any natural style. She studied pictures of models in magazines and tried to put together the same looks but on her figure they never quite worked.

The only thing she was sure of about herself was that she was intelligent and ambitious. She was going to make it in spite of everything. When she worked out early on that her looks were not going to attract the kind of men who would give her a step up the ladder into the world she yearned to be part of, she resolved to get there via her brains. Never in her wildest dreams had she ever imagined she would get such a drop-dead gorgeous break as Orlando Manners.

And here she was, preparing for her first weekend as his partner – she still didn't dare say wife in case the bubble burst – at his country cottage. Country cottage! The closest she'd ever come to the country was her father's allotment. Now, sitting up in bed with the pillows piled high behind her, she found she could look out through the window and see the roof of the conservatory and the river running along the bottom of the lawn. When she had first awakened, the early-morning sun was throwing glints on the water and the trees cast long shadows over the fields on the other side of the river. Beige sheep with black faces grazed, a pair of swans glided past the remains of a stone landing. It had been completely still, save for a few discontented chickens up the lane.

As she watched, two ducks swam to the bank and picked their way over the fields in the pouring rain, waddling a path through the rather surprised sheep.

Lindy looked around her new bedroom. Someone else's furniture. A former female presence had been stamped. Was it Daisy's or one of Orlando's girlfriends? He claimed never to have lived with anyone, although she knew he had brought women down to The Cottage frequently. Had one of them overseen the decoration of this room? It looked a little too new to have been around in Daisy's time. Or maybe Orlando never came into this room because it had been his mother's. The view of the river might have been too disturbing. It would be awful to wake up each morning and be reminded of how your parents had died the minute you opened your eyes. Yet he had shown her to this room and spent the night here with her. Would she be able to banish Daisy's ghost for him? Because if he didn't stop going on about her, Lindy was not sure that she was going to be able to handle it. It was as if he'd been married before and was still bewitched by his first wife.

No, by the sound of her, this definitely wasn't Daisy's stuff. Not classy enough. Over in the corner stood a glass-topped kidney-shaped dressing table with a chintz double-frill. Matching chintz covered the kidney-shaped stool with yet another frill brushing the carpet. There was a wooden towel stand and a circular table with a blue floor-length tablecloth, pink-rimmed. The four-poster bed in which she lay reached the beams of the ceiling.

Lindy looked with distaste at the shiny pink and blue chintz scattered all over the room. Who was responsible for this decoration? A former girlfriend, maybe, trying to stamp the room with her presence? It was a bit naff and ostentatious when it should have been faded and ethereal. She didn't know how she knew that but she did. This room looked as if her own mother had got her hands on it, and Lindy knew she was probably reacting to that as much as anything else.

She was ashamed of her mother. In fact, she was ashamed of both her parents, and of her background, and she despised herself for it. Who was she to call something naff? She was naff herself, wasn't she? But then again, no, she wasn't any more because she had worked so hard to reinvent herself.

Her father had been an accountant and she had grown

up in a perfectly respectable semi-detached Victorian villa in West Norwood reeking of the S word: suburbia.

They could have had a garden but instead they had a patio and her father disappeared to his allotment ostensibly to tend to his vegetable garden but really, Lindy guessed, to get away from her mother. She had never been able to moderate the contempt she felt for her mother. To Lindy, utterly driven and self-motivated, her mother's total dependence on her father was incomprehensible. She loathed the way her mother affected helplessness: 'Oh, I'm so stupid, I don't understand the first thing about money, I leave all that to your father.'

The highlight of her mother's life seemed to be her classes where, along with several other 'I'm so stupid' women, she learned such vital things as how to make lampshades, patchwork cushion covers and quick 'n' easy recipes copied from magazines. If Lindy's mother could open two cans, mix them with a packet of Philadelphia cheese and come up with something she could call by a pseudo-French name, she would. Heaven forfend that she should actually attempt to be creative in the kitchen. Life could be made so easy if you didn't make the slightest effort and left other people to do everything for you. Why bother to try to control your own destiny when other people could do it for you?

When her father died unexpectedly of a stroke, aged only fifty-two, Lindy was devastated. Now she was trapped, living alone with her mother, who appeared to accept as a matter of course that Lindy would now take care of her as her husband had.

But Lindy had escaped as soon as she had passed her A levels. She went to live with her aunt, her father's sister, who had a poky little flat in Earl's Court. Lindy respected her aunt Mary: she had left her husband because, after twelve years of marriage, he bored her. Furthermore she had refused maintenance. Lindy's mother thought that her sister-in-law was a fool and was excruciatingly patronizing to her, but Lindy reckoned it was her mother who was the fool. Aunt Mary might have no money but she had control of her own life and that was worth far more. She worked as a receptionist at a publisher's and it was through her that Lindy had got her first job. Aunt Mary brought home all the books in her reception area once they were replaced with new ones and Lindy read voraciously. When a job became vacant as a secretary in the foreign rights department, Aunt Mary tipped her off and secured her an interview.

Lindy stayed put for eight years, learning everything there was to know about the selling of subsidiary rights in books, serial, translation, book club, mechanical reproduction, one-shot periodical, anthology – if there was a right to be sold, Lindy knew how to flog it. She could have moved on to become a literary agent but somehow the more shadowy role of foreign scout attracted her. She approached one of the German publishers to whom she had sold translation rights in several books, and who did not have a London scout, and put to them the notion of setting her up on her own. They bit. Within three years she had moved to offices in Covent Garden and hired an assistant and a secretary. She had her own flat, a car, independence but, above all, she had confidence.

And her mother had confirmed Lindy's opinion of her by selling the house and moving in with widow friend in the north of England. Lindy had visited her there once, long enough to see that her mother had her friend running after her all day long. 'I've one of those sofa-beds whenever you want to come and stay, be with your mother,' the friend told Lindy.

'That won't be necessary,' Lindy told her and could already hear the cries of outrage echoing through the neighbourhood about the selfish, irresponsible daughter who didn't care enough about her mother to come and visit. Nobody would ever stop to work out that it was because the mother had never cared about the child that the child no longer felt anything in return.

So much so that when she married Orlando Manners, Lindy didn't bother to inform her mother until she had been married for two months.

6

'Lindy! How many minutes for your eggs? Who was that on the phone?' Orlando shouted up the stairs, and immediately birds began twittering as if he'd woken them up.

Lindy came down to earth. The wedding had been heavenly, on the beach at midnight. She wasn't sure that it had been entirely legal but what did it matter?

She could tell that Oscar and Delia in the office were intrigued that their control freak of a boss had suddenly upped and got herself married. She wasn't going back to work for a couple of weeks. At the moment, preparing for her role as Orlando's bride and hostess to his guests – *their* guests – on her first weekend at The Cottage was uppermost in her mind.

'Lindy! Did you hear me? Eggs! How many minutes?'

They were supposed to be husband and wife but he'd known her such a short time he didn't even know how she liked her eggs.

'Three. I like them really runny. It was Victoria Hissey. She wants me to go up there for elevenses.'

'Nosy old bag,' he said affectionately. 'She probably wants to give you the third degree. Find out what kind of hussy I've married. She didn't really get much of a chance to quiz you when I whisked you to see her in London straight from the airport. I've never seen her so thrown.

Quite gratifying, really. Shall I bring breakfast up or will you be down?'

'I'd better wash my hair for the old bag, as you call her, then I'll be down. Don't put my eggs on till then.'

She took the car, ignoring Victoria's instructions about taking the Bluebell Walk – whatever that was. Squelching through rain and mud was for idiots. The five-minute drive allowed her a fleeting opportunity to anticipate another meeting with Victoria.

I'm going to have to work at this, thought Lindy. She didn't really take to me when we met at that restaurant in London, I could tell. She wants Orlando to herself and if she has to give him up she would probably prefer it were to some kind of trophy wife, someone she could show off. I won't do at all. I'll have to try really hard with her for Orlando's sake.

Victoria kissed her distantly on both cheeks and led her into the room where she worked. It was at the back of the house and rather gloomy with oak panelling, like so many of the rooms at Laybridge, but it had doors opening on to the south terrace and Lindy imagined it must be rather lovely in summer.

'Are you settled in?' Victoria poured coffee and pointed to a jug of milk.

'There's not much settling in to do. Orlando's stuff has been there for years, as you know, and I haven't brought much.'

'Good.'

Lindy didn't like the way she said it, the implication being: the less of you around the place the better.

'Who is your editor at Beeson's?' she asked Victoria, wanting to change the subject.

Victoria was caught off guard. Most people had no idea who her publishers were, let alone cared who her editor might be.

'Toby Marriott.'

'Oh, really? That's interesting. I suppose I thought of you as having someone older, more experienced.'

'You know Toby, do you? He's fearfully good.' Victoria was on the defensive now.

'Oh, I'm sure he is. I've heard wonderful things about him.'

'How do you know Toby?'

Typical, thought Lindy. Why would someone like me know someone she knows?

'I'm a scout.'

'What's a scout?'

'Someone who is employed by foreign publishers to go sniffing around British publishers to see what they have for sale in the way of translation rights. If, say, I tip off my German publishers early enough that there's a terrific book being published in the spring, and I get my hands on an early copy of the manuscript and send it to them, then they might be able to pip their competitors to acquire translation rights.'

'But don't the competitors have scouts too?'

Wily old bat, doesn't miss a trick. Lindy had to admire her.

'Yes, of course. I just have to get in first.'

'And do you?'

'I try.'

'So, tell me, what do your Germans think of my books?'

'More or less what we might think of German or Dutch historical novels with specific regional settings of little interest to foreign readers. The Germans like historical fiction but I'm not sure they're wild about tiny rural backwaters in Wiltshire. You set your books here, don't you?' Lindy was aware that she was prevaricating but what else could she do? She had never read a Victoria Hissey book. Should she come clean and admit it?

But when she looked at Victoria, Lindy saw that she was smiling.

'You don't have to pretend. You haven't read me, have you? It really couldn't matter less. I've never sold abroad and you've put your finger on the reason why. I'll let you into a little secret – before I let you into a big one, the reason I've asked you up here. When I've finished the book I'm writing now, I'm going to write my first contemporary novel. I'm going to set it here at Laybridge but it's going to be very different. Maybe your Germans will be interested in that.'

'Will you let me read it?'

'Give me time to write it first, then, yes, of course, you shall be the first to read it. Now, have you met all Orlando's friends?

'Not yet. He's rather kept me to himself in London, except for that meeting with you. There's a whole crowd coming down this weekend.'

'You poor child. Anyone I know?'

'Lily and Peter McGill. A photographer he represents, whose name I've forgotten. He's bringing his girlfriend.'

'Lily McGill might be a blessing in disguise. She's got a kind heart underneath all her fuss and bother. Peter was at school with Orlando, used to play straight man to Orlando's fool. I can't remember what he does now. He's the complete opposite of Orlando. Talks very slowly, fades into the background, agrees with absolutely everything you say, comes across as awfully dull but there has to be more to him than that if he's remained friends with Orlando for so long. Orlando doesn't suffer fools gladly, as I'm sure you know.' For this girl wasn't a fool as Victoria was rapidly discovering.

'What about Lily? She's about to have a baby.'

'Oh, god, I suppose she's due around now. Lily's a type. She's kindness itself and utterly infuriating at the same time. She's older than Peter, not much but I remember we all made a bit of a thing about it when they married. She was born to be a mother and they've been trying for about three years. She'll do anything for him. She's marvellous here in the summer, organises my annual garden fête for me. She should have married a vicar, really. Now I want to tell you about The Visitors' Book. It's the reason I dragged you up here on this miserable morning.'

Victoria leaned across the sofa and drew something out from under a cushion. It was a battered rectangular leather-bound book.

'My hiding place for it. The number of people who've sat on it without knowing anything about it. But now it's time to turn it over to you, or at least the next volume.'

Lindy opened The Visitors' Book, which Victoria had placed in her lap, and read the first line: 'Je m'appelle Marie-France Constant et je me trouve en plein air devant mon "Cottage". Willy est parti faire des courses. J'éspère qu'il …'

Lindy flicked through a few pages and looked up, bewildered. 'What is this? It's all in French.'

Victoria reached over and shut the book. 'Don't read it now. You may not even be remotely interested in what I have to tell you but it's a tradition that goes with The Cottage and it involves the women who live there. I don't know whether it's a tradition that you will uphold but at least you ought to know about it and make your own decision. Now where shall I start? Way back in the thirties, before the war, my late husband's father had a mistress. She was French. He met her God knows where, brought her home to England and employed her as a kind of governess for Hugh. She gave him French lessons. Didn't do a damn bit of good. Hugh's French was appalling. More coffee?'

Lindy nodded. It was rather hard to guess where this was all leading. What connection could there possibly be between a French governess and a Visitors' Book? She might as well enjoy another cup of coffee while she waited for Victoria to get to the point.

'Hugh's father, William Hissey, known as Willy, installed Marie-France Constant – rather a good name for a mistress – in The Cottage.'

Lindy looked up.

'Yes, your Cottage. Willy Hissey used to pop along the Bluebell Walk to visit her whenever he felt like a bit of hanky-panky. Only it seems Mademoiselle Constant wasn't really content with being Willy's bit on the side. Unfortunately for Willy she wasn't very French about the whole thing. She lived in hope of becoming the second Mrs Hissey but Willy wasn't having any. Poor woman, she obviously had a rather terrible time. Everyone in the area referred to her as "that Froggie" and never spoke to her. She couldn't go back to France because she'd left in a bit of a disgrace and, to cap it all, Willy invited his rather more louche friends to spend weekends at The Cottage, the people his wife wouldn't let him invite to Laybridge, so poor Marie-France had to put up with them as well.'

'And the Visitors' Book?'

'One of the guests brought it as a gift. Only Marie-France didn't know what it was and used it as a diary. It's sort of an historical document, a record of her life at The Cottage. Do you read French?'

'Yes. So what happened to Marie-France? And how do you know so much about it? Did you ever meet her?'

'No, more's the pity. I'd have liked to. She gave up in the end and left The Cottage. Once Hugh had grown up, there was really no excuse for her to be there any more. No one else around there had any use for a French governess and Willy had probably found himself a replacement for her. When war broke out she went to London and no one ever heard another word from her. But she left behind The Visitors' Book and it lay in a cupboard somewhere until it was found some twenty years later by your mother-in-law, Daisy Manners, when she moved into The Cottage at the beginning of the sixties. Possibly the most beautiful woman I've ever met. Totally decadent. Desperately unfaithful to Orlando's father. There was a letter inside it from Marie-France suggesting that the next woman who became chatelaine at The Cottage pick up where she had left off. I'll never forget the day Daisy first showed it to me and we discovered all about Marie-France. I couldn't look Willy Hissey, my new father-in-law, in the eye for days. Eventually he told me all about her. He liked me, and we became quite close – not like that! But he liked talking to women and went on doing so long after he had stopped being sexually active. But I never told him about The Visitors' Book.

Daisy carried on the tradition, she was always scribbling away in it. She was a terrible gossip, very bitchy. As you'll see if you read it, she used it to record what everyone got up to at her weekend parties. Some of it makes for pretty racy reading.'

'This great big flowery scrawl, this is my mother-in-law's writing? This is Daisy?' Lindy was flicking through to the end of the book. 'Has Orlando read it?'

'No,' said Victoria, 'it's for women only.'

'But Daisy was his mother. He worshipped her. He never stops talking about her.'

'Precisely. And I can imagine what he's been telling you. You and I might have to have a talk about that one day. But the fact that he adored her is exactly why he mustn't ever see The Visitors' Book. You do understand, don't you, Lindy? Would you want to read about what your mother got up to when you were asleep upstairs as a child?'

Lindy was beginning to think it was all a bit rum. She suddenly felt desperately sorry for Orlando. He clearly adored his mother, or at least the memory of her, but from what Victoria was saying the woman had been a prize bitch.

'I'm sure my mother never ... but, look, it ends in nineteen seventy-two. Isn't there any more? She didn't ... I mean, she died in seventy-six, didn't she?'

'Typical Daisy. I expect she just couldn't be bothered to start another one.'

'And there hasn't been a woman at The Cottage until me?'

'No.'

Something in the tone of Victoria's voice had changed.

She had become more guarded, less inclined to share a confidence. Lindy had the impression that if she pushed any further she would be overstepping the mark.

'And you think I should write in it like Marie-France did? Record my thoughts and my life at The Cottage for posterity?'

It was all a bit ridiculous, like being given a schoolgirl's five-year diary.

'You may do whatever you wish,' Victoria told Lindy. 'Marie-France obviously found it helped her loneliness to unburden herself in it. Daisy abused the legacy by using it to bitch about other people. Maybe I'm just a sentimental romantic novelist but I rather like the idea of the tradition being upheld. That's why I've bought you a new book. Here, take it.' She handed Lindy a brand new leather book, dark green with the words The Visitors' Book embossed in gold. 'Look upon it as a housewarming present. Do with it what you will. Look, the rain's stopped.' To Lindy's secret amusement, she could see that Victoria was rather embarrassed. 'Let me take you round the gardens before you have to go home and give Orlando his lunch. Tell me, Lindy, do you cook? Shall you be producing the meals for his guests this weekend?'

They're my guests too, thought Lindy, even though I haven't met them. She took the two Visitors' Books under her arm.

'Thank you for these. I can't promise to carry on the great tradition but I *am* going to have a go at cooking. Why? What else could I do?'

'Let's see how you get on this weekend. There's always Rose Farley. She's cooked for Orlando up till now.'

'Rose Farley? Who's she?'

★

Oh, Lord, thought Victoria, as she returned from walking with Lindy across the south lawn, around the mulberry tree and back to the start of the Bluebell Walk, he hasn't told her anything about Rose. I was wrong about this one. She's not a little mouse at all. She'll want to do things *her* way.

Later, in the privacy of her study, Victoria pulled out another Visitors' Book from its hiding place under the sofa. Lindy had almost caught her out, spotting that the first volume had ended before Daisy's death. But there was no way anyone was going to learn of the poisonous secrets littered throughout the pages of Daisy Manners's second volume. Victoria had discovered the book after the drowning and had kept it hidden ever since.

She heard her cook, Peg Farley, coming down the corridor. Oh dear, whatever would little Rose, Peg's daughter, make of Lindy?

7

It had always irritated Rose Farley that Orlando's house was known as The Cottage. She had grown up in a real cottage that had once been a peasant's hovel, consisting of only two rooms on the ground floor with ceilings so low you could barely stand upright, and two poky bedrooms above. It was known as Farley Cottage because her family had occupied it ever since it had been built in the seventeenth century.

It irked Rose when, in the spring of 1987, she looked out of the dormer window of her bedroom in the midst of her adolescence, her body bent almost double under the sloping roof, and saw that Orlando had had a brand new garden shed erected that was nearly half the size of Farley Cottage. She longed to go and live in that shed, away from the chaos of the Farleys. Sometimes, when Orlando was in London during the week, she crept into the shed and stretched out on one of the sun loungers he kept there. It was so spacious compared with her box-like cell at home. But then she would remember where she was and the proximity of The Cottage would stir her memory, causing her to run out of the shed in a panic to get home.

During her childhood Rose had led a solitary existence. Her father, Charlie, the gamekeeper at Laybridge, but in name only since Hugh Hissey didn't shoot, had had a short, superfluous life, a large part of it spent in the

Laybridge Arms. No one knew why he took to drink with such a vengeance in his mid-thirties but he was dead before Rose had barely had time to get to know him. She could remember trotting up the Bluebell Walk to the trout stews to watch him feed the fish and then she could remember her mother saying she was going to the hospital. Every day she said it: 'I'm off to the hospital now. Your grandfather's here. No need to worry.'

But there had been reason to worry. Charlie never came home and at the time all Rose had understood was that it had had something to do with her mother's visits to the hospital. Other children had a mother and a father. Rose had her grandfather, who lived with them, and her mother. But Peg wasn't like other mothers. She didn't go to an office in Salisbury or work in a supermarket. She seemed to have no interest in anything that happened outside the valley. She had had long white hair gathered up in a bun ever since Rose could remember. She belonged in another age. Unless she was in church or in bed, Peg wore an apron, large and floral-printed, that invariably obscured from view whatever else she might be wearing.

Rose loved her but there were times when she felt as if Peg were her grandmother rather than her mother.

Peg Farley was proud of her good firm skin, made faintly ruddy by the constant exposure to fresh air on her daily treks in all weathers from Farley Cottage to Laybridge House and back again. She had the plump figure and ample bosom easily associated with her work as a cook, but her piercing eyes were evidence of her natural high intelligence and perception. She prided herself also on being good-natured and not given to complaining about her lot. If she had a drunk for a husband and a temperamental daughter, she didn't give any indication that she let it disturb the simple but rewarding life she had carved out for herself.

Peg lived for food, whether it was growing vegetables in her garden, being up to her elbows in flour or delivering a perfectly risen soufflé to Mrs Hissey's candlelit dinner table. Providing she was thinking about, shopping for, growing, preparing or eating food, Peg was content. She lived food from the moment she rose at dawn to walk up to Laybridge to prepare Mrs Hissey's breakfast, to the comforting bowl of rolled oats and warm milk she prepared for herself at bedtime in place of the Horlicks or Ovaltine she saw advertised on her black-and-white television.

Peg was one of life's brooders, unable to confide in others, bottling everything up inside her. She did her brooding on her way to work, fretting up and down the Bluebell Walk, trying to work things out of her system by the time she reached Laybridge. While Charlie was dying she worked out her grief every morning, weeping as she passed the trout stews, smiling by the time she began to make breakfast in the kitchen at Laybridge.

And it was on these daily journeys that she worked out her confused feelings about her daughter. Rose had her father's jet black hair and black eyes, and his pointed foxy features. She was the antithesis of the English rose for which she had been named but that did not mean she was plain, thought Peg. My daughter is a wild, gypsy-looking beauty with a temperament to match, she told herself. But where had this temperament come from? Rose had inherited Peg's firm skin and high colouring and Charlie's angular frame. She grew tall and her feet extended over the edge of her narrow iron bed by the time she was twelve but Peg could not afford to buy her a longer one.

In the night, as Charlie snored beside her, and even after he was gone, Peg could hear her daughter tossing and turning, trying to make herself comfortable in the room on the other side of the staircase. Downstairs Peg's father-in-law, Harold, slept on the broken-down settee in the living room because Peg would not allow her precious walk-in larder at the back of the kitchen to be converted into another bedroom. When Hugh Hissey built them a modern bathroom, Harold continued to use the tin tub in the kitchen and began to sleep in the bath.

Peg often wondered where Rose got her spirit and determination from. Charlie had been a gentle man, not nearly as sharp as he looked. Peg hated having to admit it but Rose's personality was more like that of her uncle. Peg detested Charlie's brother, Mick Farley. He had done the unthinkable and left the valley, become a salesman for some firm in London – travelled all over the country, as far as Peg could make out. To her he had become a stranger but Charlie had remained devoted to his brother, slipping away to meet him in secret whenever he was in the area, defending Mick's wanderlust, his restlessness.

And that was what bothered Peg about Rose: she was restless.

Rose hated the ramshackle higgledy-piggledyness of Farley Cottage both in and outside the house. Orlando's garden had flowerbeds, a leaning quince tree, an old lawn-mower now used only as an ornament, and was surrounded by bluebells. It had trimmed box hedges, a stone bird bath, a rustic seat, a climbing rose arbour and a lawn sloping down to the river. Her family's back garden was a repository for anything that didn't fit in the house: broken chairs, a rusty iron mangle, a couple of old bicycles, plastic baskets under the sagging washing line, a defunct fridge, a pile of spare tyres, an old car underneath the lean-to.

Her mother had claimed the front garden as her own. Rose approved of its traditional garden gate and straight path flanked by hollyhocks running to the front door with its rose-covered porch. She loved the twisted apple tree and the neat rows of Peg's cabbages, runner beans and herbs. Anyone seeing Farley Cottage from the front could retain a romantic notion of blissful rural life, but to reach Orlando's house, his guests had to continue down the lane in their BMWs and Volvos and witness the appalling mess at the back of Farley Cottage.

Then there were her grandfather's chickens. Rolls of excess chicken wire lay propped up against the outhouse while the birds roamed free, having long since broken through the holes in their coop. Rose squirmed with embarrassment every time she heard a car screech to a halt outside Farley Cottage and looked out of her window to see someone shooing away chickens in the lane. Living with them severely tried her patience: they regarded Farley Cottage as theirs and frequently slept indoors, returning to their coop to lay eggs. Her mother collected the eggs each morning and took them up to Laybridge for Mrs Hissey's breakfast. Rose, to her eternal fury, had to make do with Rice Krispies.

Looking back, Peg decided that the trouble had begun

when Rose was four and she became aware of a boy running around in the garden of The Cottage next door. He was much older than she was but he had black hair like hers and, to Peg's amazement, Rose decided he was her brother. Peg caught her just in time as she was about to crawl through the hedge and play with Orlando. The Cottage was out of bounds to the Farleys, which was fine by Peg. Daisy Manners did not want her weekend rest interrupted by her son – which was why, Peg realised, he always played in the garden – let alone 'the Laybridge cook's brat' as Peg had once overheard Daisy refer to Rose. Besides, Peg didn't like the look of Daisy's weekend guests: 'City folk, spoiled rotten. They all smoke in bed and the place smells like a bus station. The women only ever bring high-heeled shoes. The men start drinking after breakfast. I'm not cooking for them. I've told Mrs Hissey.'

Peg was adamant. As a result Daisy brought a woman down from London to cook and clean, which only enraged Peg further. Boundaries were drawn and war was silently declared between the Mannerses and the Farleys.

Rose might not have been allowed to stray into the Manners' garden but she had an excellent view of it from her bedroom window if she climbed on to her bed. This was how she came to watch the events of a Saturday night in 1976 when Guy and Daisy Manners drowned in the river Lay. The noise woke her up. Peg, fast asleep on the other side of the house, never heard a thing.

Rose never understood why she was so frightened of The Cottage. Every so often she half remembered fragments of what she had seen. When her grandfather, Harold, described the drowning to her, 'Caught by the floods, swept away with the current and washed up on the banks like sheep,' Rose came back with, 'Not all of them.' But they couldn't make her explain what she meant.

When Rose accompanied her mother along the river-bank and up through the Bluebell Walk to Laybridge, she would avert her eyes as she passed the cottage. In her childhood nightmares, a witch-like Daisy Manners would rise up out of the river, smite a few chickens and enter Farley Cottage in the middle of the night, coming up the narrow staircase that divided the house, to get her. Rose would wake up screaming and Peg would have to go in and comfort her.

'Grandad's downstairs, lovey. You don't think he'd let anyone get to you, do you?'

And Rose would drift back to sleep, confusing the image of Harold Farley asleep in the bath with that of an old lion guarding them all at the entrance to a cave.

Rose met Orlando one morning when Mrs Hissey appeared in the kitchen at Laybridge and presented a scruffy boy with untidy hair and grubby knees to her and her mother. He was, Rose realised, the boy she had seen playing in the garden at The Cottage, the boy she had thought of as her brother.

'I've brought Orlando to meet you. He's going to be living here from now on. Orlando, this is Mrs Farley, who cooks for me, and her little girl Rose. Say hello.'

'Hello,' said Orlando. He grinned, and Rose fell in love with him.

Walking up to Laybridge the next morning, Rose pestered her mother about him. 'Why's he living with Mrs Hissey? Why, Mum?'

'Because he's an orphan now. He's nowhere else to go.'

'What's an orphan?'

'Oh, Rose, not now.'

But no sooner had Rose met him than he was whisked away to boarding school and she did not see him again until he was home for the holidays. Sometimes she couldn't make him out: he showed her affection one day, contempt the next. She would nod happily at every suggestion he made and then cry in frustration when she could not keep up with him. Once she followed him to the top of the rolling downs above the Lay valley and he ran away from her, leaving her sobbing beside a haystack, too tired to go any further. She begged him to read her stories, only to have him grow bored and abandon the book with the story half told. Sometimes they shared secret picnics stolen from her mother's kitchen and ate them on the floor of Orlando's oak-panelled bedroom or waded hand in hand into the river with their jeans rolled up to their knees and splashed each other until they were soaked. They had fun but Rose knew it was Orlando who dictated what kind of fun it would be. He picked Rose up and put her down when he was tired of her, which was often so she grew into an angry little girl who worshipped him but could not harness him.

She went to school in Amesbury and sometimes, when his holidays began before hers, he rode his bicycle to meet her.

'Who's that?' her classmates asked.

'My brother,' she lied, and for a while she basked in their admiration. Then her lie was discovered and it made her angry again.

Orlando teased her. 'I have a little shadow / That goes

in and out with me / And what can be the use of her / I really cannot see,' he taunted her as she followed him everywhere.

Rose was convinced they were engaged. 'Orlando's asked me to marry him,' she told her mother, very matter-of-fact.

Peg pretended she hadn't heard. 'I've got some baked beans for your tea and some sherry trifle I made for Mrs Hissey, only she's not back from London to eat it and Mr Hugh doesn't care for sherry trifle.'

'Nor do I,' said Rose, 'and when I'm married to Orlando we won't have it.'

8

Victoria was fascinated by Rose. Unlike Peg she didn't worry about her. Rose was a loner like herself. That she chose not to associate with the moronic video-crazy girls at her school and elected to spend her evenings at Farley Cottage, reading rather than hanging around the cinema with a gang of spotty youths in Salisbury, made sense to Victoria. Rose would be just fine.

She was intrigued, too, by the relationship between mother and daughter. Rose could be truculent, Victoria observed. She overheard conversations between Peg and her daughter in the kitchen, which indicated that Peg found Rose something of a handful. But Peg would never be drawn on the subject.

'Don't know what I would have done if I hadn't had Rose after I lost Charlie. Gem of a girl, my Rose.'

Gem of a girl! Peg came out with some ornate expressions sometimes, thought Victoria. Especially when she was describing a girl who had told her mother in Victoria's hearing only the other day to 'Stay out of my room, Mum. Give me my privacy, give me room to breathe, please.'

But Peg never said a word against Rose. Typical Peg, thought Victoria. Wouldn't make a murmur if the house was falling down around her. Suffer in silence. Look on the bright side. What will be will be. Victoria couldn't help wondering sometimes if Peg stayed on as her cook year after year to shelter herself from the outside world and all its troubles. God knows, it was easy enough to do at Laybridge. If the sun was shining you could drink in the beauty and turn a blind eye to everything else.

It was when Peg began to teach Rose to cook that Victoria could tell something special was being passed from mother to daughter and it was at about that time that she began to wonder if, like her mother before her, Rose would be content to stay in the valley. But it wasn't just the sense of peace and tranquillity of country life and the joy of preparing food that would hold Rose. As long as she stayed at Laybridge, Victoria began to realise, there was another attraction. Rose would have Orlando.

When Orlando inherited The Cottage, Peg was officially the Laybridge cook but, at Victoria's suggestion, she moonlighted for Orlando when he began to bring down guests from London. In the beginning Victoria did nothing as she noticed Peg begin to age before her eyes as her workload doubled at weekends. If Orlando had visitors when Victoria had a house party up at Laybridge, poor Peg could be found trundling back and forth through the Bluebell Walk from one house to the other, catering to the demands of both parties. Victoria recalled when Peg had once offered her services to Bruno while he was at The Cottage but he and Victoria had decided that this was too dangerous. For all they knew, the Farleys kept a log of each and every visit Victoria made to The Cottage to see Bruno, but it would have been a different matter altogether to have Peg walking in on them whenever she felt like it. In any case it was just as well – the poor woman would have been dead of exhaustion by now, thought Victoria.

After little more than a year, Victoria knew that something had to be done. Peg couldn't go on much longer and Victoria valued her too much to let her go. But Orlando was incapable of looking after himself. The answer presented itself one Saturday afternoon in Salisbury, when Victoria was browsing in a bookshop.

'Mrs Hissey!'

'Hello, Rose. What are you doing in Salisbury?'

'I've got a Saturday job. Round the corner. At the launderette.'

Victoria was appalled but tried not to show it.

'I thought you hated Salisbury. And what about your A levels?'

Rose shrugged. 'My gran says there might be a job on the farm next year. I've got to earn money. It's not so bad. When it's not busy I can read.'

Victoria couldn't bear it. 'Come up to Laybridge when you get home. We'll talk.'

'What about? I mean, yes, OK, fine, thanks.'

They sat in the kitchen because Victoria knew Rose loved it and would be more comfortable there than in any other part of the house.

'When's Orlando coming home?' Rose asked immediately.

'Well, he doesn't come here any more. He goes to The Cottage now. He'll be down at the weekend, I expect.'

'I love Orlando,' said Rose.

'We all love Orlando.'

'Is it weird that I love him, Mrs Hissey? Mum says it is. She says I should find someone else.'

Victoria wondered what she should say. Did Rose really think Orlando was hers? Didn't she notice the girls he brought down for the weekend?'

'It's all right, I know about the others,' Rose said suddenly. 'He has to have others before he settles down.'

'Rose, you're still a child.'

'Oh, I know. I'll wait. That's why I understand he has to have others.'

Peg has to sort this out, it's not my problem, Victoria told herself. But somehow she knew she was about to make it worse.

'Peg tells me you've been learning to cook and you're really very good, a natural, just like her.'

'I love it. I just do the plain things, the suet puddings, the steak and kidney pies, shepherd's pies, apple pies. I can bake bread, I can make an omelette, do the veg. That's about it so far. I learn a new thing every week.'

'Tell me something, Rose. Are you wedded to this job at the launderette? Is it really how you want to spend your Saturdays? Could you be tempted by some other kind of weekend work?'

Rose looked suspicious.

'At The Cottage,' Victoria went on quickly, dangling what she knew would be an irresistible carrot, 'for Orlando. Your mother's getting too tired to cope with me and him. How would you like to take over?'

Victoria had heard about Rose's fear of The Cottage but she had never witnessed it. Looking now at the expression of terror on Rose's face, she moved around the table and gripped Rose by the arms. 'Rose, you're shaking. What is it about The Cottage that frightens you so much?'

'Her.'

Victoria was aware that Rose didn't normally offer any information when questioned. Should she press further now that she'd had one answer or leave it alone?

'Who, Rose? Who's her?'

'His mother. Orlando's mother.'

'Daisy?'

The girl was still shaking.

'Tell me,' said Victoria, when she had calmed down.

'I can't.'

'All right,' she said gently, 'but, Rose, The Cottage has changed. Orlando's there now. You're not frightened of Orlando, surely?'

Rose smiled.

'It's Orlando I'm asking you to work for,' Victoria continued, 'not his mother. He's the present not the past. I thought you'd like to work for Orlando. I thought you'd be pleased. Think how grateful he'll be.'

Rose looked up. 'Will he?'

'Of course he will. He adores you. He always has. There's no one better to look after him and we all know he needs looking after, don't we?'

'He's pretty hopeless around the house, isn't he?' Rose grinned.

'The thing is, Rose, as I said, Peg's getting too tired to go on cooking for both him and me and if you don't take over I'm going to have to hire someone to look after Orlando at the weekends. Or maybe he'll bring someone down from London. But whatever happens I'm not having your mother tire herself out like this. So what's it to be? If you don't want to do it, don't. But I'm giving you first refusal.'

'Thank you, Mrs Hissey,' said Rose. 'When should I start?'

9

Peg had had quite enough of Orlando's house parties. Every weekend he brought at least two friends, sometimes as many as four or five invaders who shouted at the chickens to 'shut the fuck up' as they drove past Farley Cottage. Peg seethed.

She had wound up cleaning up after his guests, doing their laundry, making their beds and acting as his housekeeper. They were a spoiled, inconsiderate bunch of young people, the kind that left their wet towels all over the bathroom floor for Peg to pick up and never so much as lifted a mug from the breakfast table to the kitchen. They treated the place like an hotel rather than somebody's home. It had become, Peg told Rose when Rose informed her mother she would be taking over at The Cottage, like it had been in Daisy Manners's day. Peg had said Daisy's name without thinking. She waited for the inevitable reaction from Rose but nothing happened.

'I'll soon sort them out,' Rose said cheerfully.

Peg was astounded. That Rose should even consider stepping inside The Cottage was something of a miracle. She wondered how Mrs Hissey had won her round. But Peg knew better than to interrogate her daughter. Rose was stubborn. If pushed she never divulged anything, as Peg had learned to her cost. So Peg went about teaching Rose what was required for a weekend house party, how each bedroom should have a bedside water jug and glass, a tin of biscuits, a vase of flowers, how the bathrooms should be kept constantly supplied with fresh soap, and clean towels left each morning on the wooden towel rails in the bedrooms. How the beds should be properly aired on the day of arrival and a fire laid in winter in those rooms that had fireplaces.

Over the next couple of years Rose watched as girlfriends came and went. Still a virgin, she dutifully brought breakfast in bed to Orlando's lovers and changed his sheets, stained with semen. Under Peg's instruction, she widened her culinary repertoire to include light, perfect pastry, cakes, roasts, casseroles, poached fish dishes, kedgeree, all Orlando's favourites, and she looked no further than the expression of rapture on his face when he ate the food she had cooked for him.

She told herself she didn't mind about the rest. Providing he was kind to her and gave her the occasional hug and kiss of gratitude, Rose would do anything for him. And, best of all, she appeared to have overcome her lifelong fear of The Cottage and what had happened there. The demons were still lurking, but now that she could share them with Mrs Hissey she could control her fear.

Then something happened that she couldn't tell Mrs Hissey, something Rose knew should be kept private between her and Orlando until they were married.

Rose was lying on her bed on a Sunday night in November, listening to the crunch of wheels on gravel as Orlando's weekend guests backed their cars into the lane ready for the return to London. Through her bedroom window she sat up and watched the flickering light of the headlamps as one by one the cars drove past Farley Cottage.

She turned up the volume on Berlin and 'Take My Breath Away' that she was listening to on the battered Walkman Orlando had been about to discard, and buried her face in her pillow. She hated Sunday nights. She hated knowing it would be a whole week before she saw him again. In the New Year she was going to have to do without him for a month. She had overheard him tell someone he was off to the Caribbean for his magazine.

Half an hour later she roused herself. She always went over to The Cottage on Sunday nights to turn out any lights left on, wash up the supper things and throw out leftover milk so it wouldn't be there stinking in the fridge when he arrived the following Friday. Her mother went in to clean at some point during the week but Rose felt it was her responsibility to tidy up after the weekend.

One car was still there. A light was on upstairs. In Orlando's room. Rose went in to turn it off and found him in bed, fast asleep. Boxes of Kleenex were strewn all over the bed. A bottle of cough mixture stood on his bedside table.

For several minutes Rose stood looking down at his face, expecting him to wake up at any second. When he didn't, she sat down on the bed and began to stroke his hair. He shifted in his sleep, mumbled something and turned away from her, drawing the covers over his head.

Rose undressed and crept in beside him. She held her breath. He didn't stir. She moved as close to him as she dared and lay, wide awake, beside him until two hours later when he rolled over and into her arms.

He was groggy. It wasn't a great success. It was her first time and he hurt her. And he was angry. By the time he realised who she was it was too late. He pulled out of her abruptly, causing her further pain. 'Rose, this is outrageous.'

She was doubled over, holding herself.

'I didn't know it was you, Rose. I was half asleep. I've got a filthy cold. I thought you were ... I responded without thinking.'

'Would you have done it any differently if you'd known it was my first time?'

'I wouldn't have done it at all, you know that perfectly well.'

'I didn't know you'd ... I thought we could just ... I wanted to be close to you.'

'Are you trying to accuse me of taking advantage of you? If anything, it's the other way round. You climb into my bed stark naked and expect me to wake up and do nothing more than tell you a bedtime story? Oh, look, don't start crying. I'm sorry, I would never have forced my way in ... You should have stopped me. Why didn't you say something?'

'I love you.'

He rolled away from her. 'Rose, this is insanity.'

'But I do love you.'

'Stop saying that. You don't understand what you're saying. You're a child. No, I don't mean that. You're not a child but you've been buried down here all your life. I'm probably the only man you know. Or have you got a boyfriend?'

'No.'

'Well, you should have. You're very pretty.'

She sat up and leant over him. 'What did you say?'

'You heard. It's true. You must know you're pretty.'

'Did you like what we did just now?'

'Well, I liked it more than you obviously did. I had a much better time. I've done it before. You have very soft skin. You'll like it better the next time.'

'With you?'

'No, not with me. This was an accident. I didn't mean to do what I did. That doesn't mean I didn't enjoy it.'

'Does it mean you care about me a bit?'

'I care about you a lot. I always have. You're part of my life in a way – but not this way. Your mother would kill me if she found out and I'm not sure Victoria would altogether approve. So we'll keep it to ourselves, OK?'

'Our secret?'

'Our secret.'

'You can't see it from here.'

'Can't see what? Pass me a tissue, Rose, for God's sake.'

'Where it happened. You can't see that part of the river. That's why you sleep in this room, isn't it? So you can't see, so you won't be reminded of it.'

'Are you talking about what I think you're talking about?'

She could feel Orlando looking at her in the darkness. 'I'm talking about when your mum and dad died, out there, in the river.'

'Don't talk about it. Don't tell me you know what I went through. I know what I went through, Rose. I don't need you to tell me. I don't need to start looking for sympathy from you. We grew up together. You're almost like family to me. I shouldn't have to explain.'

'But that's not what I'm saying.'

'Leave it, Rose. You'd better go. Get dressed, go on.'

'Can I just go to sleep now, here, with you, if I promise to go home very early in the morning?'

'And there'll be no more creeping up on me in the middle of the night – promise?'

'Promise.'

'All right. Go to sleep.'

He held her against him. Poor little Rose, she always had had a crush on him. Not so little any more, though. And very tasty. But it would be madness to encourage her any further. Pray God he hadn't made her pregnant.

Rose was suffering from severe menstrual cramps when Peg came home from cooking dinner at Laybridge one cold February night and announced: 'Orlando Manners has gone and got himself married while he was off overseas. He'll be bringing his new bride down at the end of the week.'

Later Peg turned up the old black-and-white television so Harold could hear the news, but really it was to shut out the sound of Rose sobbing in her room above.

PART TWO

10

Rose was on strike.

Peg picked her way through the rain puddles and the mud along the Bluebell Walk to Laybridge and wondered what she should do. Rose had been sitting at the kitchen table when Peg came downstairs.

'The pot's still warm,' she had muttered, without looking at her mother.

'Thanks,' said Peg. She was late. She generally had her breakfast up at Laybridge while she was preparing Mrs Hissey's but Rose clearly hadn't made tea to drink it by herself. She had the stubborn look on her face that Peg knew so well. She'd made up her mind about something and it wasn't going to be changed easily. Peg often wondered if other people realised just how determined a person Rose was. Peg knew she had – what was it they called it, these days? – her own agenda and once she decided what she wanted she dug in her heels until she got it.

'If he thinks I'm going to go on working for him he's got another think coming.'

'Who?' Peg didn't sit down. If she gave Mrs Hissey a three-minute boiled egg and some toast instead of something more substantial, she could just about do it by eight o'clock. That would give her five minutes with Rose.

'Don't be daft, Mum. You know perfectly well who. Orlando. If he's gone and got himself a wife she can bloody well cook for him. Sorry.'

Rose looked up quickly. Peg had never liked swearing and Rose had enough respect for her mother to try to refrain from using bad language.

'I expect she will on a day-to-day basis, but when they've guests down here, they'll need you over there same as usual.'

'Of course they will and I'm not going. You'll have to tell them, Mum. Speak to Mrs Hissey and she'll tell them.'

Any other mother would have told Rose to tell them herself, but Peg knew her daughter. Hot-blooded and volatile was Rose, always had been. She'd get in a terrible tizz about something, the end of the world had come, nothing would make things right – and then, a couple of hours later, she would have forgotten all about it.

'You think I'll change my mind, don't you? I won't, Mum. You tell Mrs Hissey. It's Friday. You know I go over to The Cottage every Friday at ten o'clock to start getting the bedrooms ready, discuss what he wants for the weekend meals. Well, I'm not going. I'm handing in my notice or whatever it's called. I'm doing it via you, Mum, because if I go over there myself I'll forget any manners you ever taught me.'

What should I do? Peg asked herself as she laid a fire in the library at Laybridge. Farleys didn't behave like this. She, Peg, would never have dreamed of not turning up to cook for Mrs Hissey. Someone had to uphold the family's reputation. She'd have to go herself, Peg decided. She'd have to nip back down to The Cottage and tell Orlando

Rose wouldn't be coming and offer her own services. They couldn't let him down.

'Hello, Peg my darling.' Orlando flung open the landing window as Peg came down the Bluebell Walk towards The Cottage. Before she could let herself in at the back door he was out of the house and had her in his arms. 'Bet you never thought I'd do it, bet you never thought I'd grow up and get married. I've seen you give me those disapproving looks of yours, Peg. You thought I was just a good-for-nothing layabout, oh, yes, you did.'

'I'm looking forward to meeting Mrs Manners.'

'Oh, don't be such a stiff, Peg. Call her Lindy, for God's sake. Don't go getting all formal on me. Lindy? Where are you? Come and meet Peg. I've told her all about you.'

Peg always prepared things in her mind, worked out how a first meeting with someone would be, what they would look like, how they would perceive her. She had envisaged being introduced to Orlando's new bride by Mrs Hissey, that the meeting would take place up at Laybridge and Mrs Hissey would usher Orlando's wife into the kitchen, Peg's domain, and that she, Peg, would somehow have the upper hand.

The immaculately dressed rather short woman who appeared at Orlando's side was a bit of a shock. Peg had always frowned on Rose's infatuation with Orlando, but when she looked at Lindy, all she could think was: Why? Why had Orlando married this small, rather pale creature, pretty enough but nothing special, when he could have had her Rose – tall, vibrant, brimming with colour – for the asking.

'Pleased to meet you,' said Peg, trying to sound as if she meant it.

'Oh, I'm so pleased to meet you too. You cook for us, don't you?'

'Well, I don't any more as it happens. I cook for Mrs Hissey up at Laybridge.'

'This isn't Rose, you silly goose.' Orlando put his arm round Lindy's shoulders. 'This is Rose's mother, Mrs Farley. We call her Peg. Where's Rose, Peg? Be along soon?'

'No. She's not coming this morning. I'm here instead.'

Orlando frowned slightly. 'Isn't she well?'

'You could say that.'

'Could I? I see. Like that, is it? Well, Lindy, you'd better tell Peg here what we want to eat this weekend.'

'How many are you?' asked Peg.

'Seven. Lindy, myself and five guests.'

'No, six. Four guests,' said Lindy.

'You, me, the McGills, Bobby, my photographer client I told you about. Nona, his girlfriend, she's a model. And Bruno. That makes seven.'

'What did you say? Bruno? Bruno who?'

'There's only one Bruno. Bruno Manners. My uncle. He's coming over from New York so I asked him down to meet you.'

'But why didn't you tell me?'

'I thought I had.'

'No, you didn't. You never told me.' Lindy was visibly agitated.

'OK. So I forgot. What's all the fuss about?'

'I don't know any of these people. God knows what they'll be expecting. They're all your oldest and dearest friends and I don't have a clue what to do.'

And she doesn't like having to admit it, thought Peg.

Lindy had been whispering, hissing almost, but Peg had heard every word.

'Well, that's why you've got Peg to help you. Oh, damn, there's the phone. Peg, fill her in, won't you? She'll tell you what she wants.'

'Who's she? The cat's mother?' Lindy shouted after him.

Peg stood, feeling uncomfortable. Normally she would have marched straight through the back door and into the kitchen to begin sorting things out but she didn't feel she could go in until this new mistress of the house invited her. Lindy shifted from one foot to the other in obvious discomfort until Peg took pity on her and motioned towards the house.

'First things first,' she prompted. 'When is everyone arriving? How many for Friday supper?'

'None. What a relief. They're all coming down tomorrow afternoon.'

'Well, there we are. We'd better have something for lunch tomorrow just in case they haven't eaten on the way down. Mrs McGill might be a bit peckish now she's eating for two.'

'God, so she is. I'd forgotten. Shall I – I mean, will you …?'

'I'll take care of everything. You don't have to worry. Just tell me what you'd like in the way of menus.'

'Menus?' Lindy looked completely blank.

She hasn't given it a moment's thought. Five people coming to stay and she doesn't know what they're going to eat.

'I tell you what, Mrs Manners, I'll prepare the sort of

things Orlando usually has and you see if it's what you had in mind. Now which rooms are you putting them in?'

'Oh, goodness, I hadn't really thought. I imagined everyone would just sort of pick a room. Orlando and I are in the four-poster.'

'Well, then, I expect we'll have to put Mr and Mrs McGill in Orlando's old room as it's the only other room with a double bed. Poor Mr Bruno. He'll find it a bit strange not sleeping in his old room.'

'He'll have to go in the room with the futon. We must put the other couple in the other decent spare room. She's a model.'

Do they sleep in a different position to the rest of us, Peg wondered.

Orlando came out and thrust the cordless phone into Lindy's hand. 'It's your bloody office. Some girl called Delia.'

'You know perfectly well Delia's my second-in-command. She's holding the fort while I'm away. Do try to remember.'

'What I've been trying to do is to make her understand she shouldn't bother you while you're down here.'

'We came down on Thursday. It's still part of the normal person's working week, Orlando. Delia? Hello? Sorry about that. What's up?'

Orlando stood behind Lindy and, for Peg's benefit, imitated her talking on the phone making exaggerated faces.

'Better leave her to get on with it, Peg. Are you going back up to Laybridge? Do me a favour, pass on an invitation to Victoria to come to dinner tomorrow night.

Eight for eight thirty. And you'd better tell the headmistress over there when she gets off that phone that I've invited my godmother. We don't want another tantrum. Truth is, there's another thing I forgot to mention. Bruno's coming down tonight, not tomorrow, so we'd better have something a bit more substantial than scrambled eggs for supper and Bobby and Nona specifically requested the futon, something about Bobby's back, so better put them in that room. And you can tell my wife that I've gone into Salisbury and I plan on lunching there.'

Peg almost felt sorry for Lindy as Orlando revved his engine unnecessarily loudly and drove off without even waving goodbye. She wondered whether to say something comforting like: 'He always was spoiled rotten, that boy, charming but spoiled,' but thought better of it.

'I'd best return to Laybridge for the morning but I'll be back lunchtime to sort out the beds for you, Mrs Manners, and we'll talk about menus then. I'm making a casserole for Mrs Hissey for tonight. I can easily make an extra one for you and Mr Bruno. Don't ask!' she warned, when she saw Lindy's face.

Rose, who was lying on her bed at Farley Cottage with the window open, had heard every word of the conversation between her mother and the newly-weds. She had sneaked a look every now and then and, like Peg, she had been amazed by what she saw. For some reason Rose had expected a tall glamorous blonde but from the look of her, Lindy barely seemed like someone who would cause her to get her knickers in a twist. Once Orlando's car had disappeared up the lane, Rose ran downstairs. She met Peg on her way back to Laybridge.

'Thought you'd given in your notice,' remarked Peg drily.

'Did you tell Mrs Hissey?'

'No, and I just told Orlando you were ill.'

'Well, perhaps I'm better now. Where is she?'

'Mrs Manners went indoors to arrange flowers, or whatever it is she does.'

'Not for much longer,' said Rose. 'Don't worry, Mum. I'll take over from here.' She didn't tell Peg she'd overheard everything. The less anyone realised that she could spy on The Cottage from her bedroom at Farley Cottage, the better.

'Knock before you go in,' hissed Peg, 'it's her house now. They've got five guests. Mr Bruno's coming back for the first time since I don't know when. You've to put him in the good spare room. He'll be here tonight, the others tomorrow. There's a couple who'll have the futon. Mr and Mrs McGill in Orlando's old room. He and Mrs Manners are in the four-poster. She hasn't planned what they're all going to eat. They can have some of my casserole for tonight. If you give me a list I'll go into Salisbury when I've finished up at Laybridge and get you what you need because I tell you, Rose, this new wife of his hasn't got the first idea what to do.'

Peg sniffed. She had half a mind to tell Rose to stick to her guns and stay on strike. Then Orlando would see what a mistake he'd made marrying Little Miss Useless.

Rose ran her fingers through her hair and tapped on the back door. There was no answer so she let herself in.

It took her a second or two to adjust. The kitchen was bare. Normally it was littered with a colourful array of jugs, flower vases, serving dishes waiting to be used. All the mugs that hung on hooks from the shelf had been taken down and put away. Rose looked around. Where were all her pots and pans? Where was the big casserole dish she always used? Where was the toaster? Why wasn't her apron hanging over the door?

The central part of The Cottage was nearly four hundred years old. Rose always had to remember to duck between the kitchen and the area used as part dining room part television room although occasionally she forgot and nearly knocked herself out on the beam that ran through the middle of the house. Here, again, someone had imposed a terrifying order on a room that had always had a relaxed, welcoming atmosphere. The cushions on the giant high-backed sofa that divided the room, normally scattered about, had been plumped and stacked neatly at either end. The dining-room chairs were all tucked into the table. The ornaments on the windowsill had been rearranged just so. The CDs had been put away.

Lindy was walking around the room running her finger along the surfaces of the furniture. 'Who are you?' she asked Rose.

'Rose Farley.'

'Well, Rose, I've got five guests coming to stay and the place could do with a clean. I've tidied up a bit but that's not enough.'

'Orlando doesn't usually come down till Friday night. It's bound to get a bit dusty with no one here during the week. You came down early.' Rose stood her ground.

'Fair enough,' said Lindy. 'You'll get to grips with it now, will you? Your mother will fill you in on what we've discussed about food.'

'What time will you be eating tonight?'

'You'll have to ask my husband when he gets back. I have no idea what time our guest is arriving.'

Rose didn't like the way she said 'my husband'. She was talking about someone Rose had known almost all her life. Why couldn't she just say Orlando?

'I'll leave you to it. If my husband returns, please tell him I've gone up to see Mrs Hissey to invite her to dinner tomorrow night.'

'I think he's already invited her.' Rose couldn't resist it. What had Orlando said? Something like 'tell the headmistress ...' Well, Peg had obviously forgotten. Lindy's face was a picture. A real picture!

Did I handle that right? Lindy asked herself, as she walked up to Laybridge. She'd get Victoria to fill her in a bit more on the Farley family since they were obviously going to play a large part in her life down here. Why had nobody mentioned that Rose Farley was such a stunner?

At Laybridge she hesitated in the forecourt. What was the protocol here? She was family now, wasn't she? So did she march straight in and shout, 'Victoria?' Or did she ring the bell? In the end she lost her nerve and wandered round the side of the house where she ran into Victoria transporting some logs in a wheelbarrow to the kitchen door.

'I'm sorry, I should have telephoned.'

'Whatever for? Feel free to wander up here whenever you like. I realise I should have asked you to stay for lunch. Will you join me? I'm sure Peg can rustle up something.'

'No, please don't worry. I just came to ask you to

dinner tomorrow night. I should have mentioned it when I was here.'

'Oh, I've already been asked by Orlando. He sent a message via Peg. I'd love to come.'

'Thanks for telling me, Orlando.'

'Oh, God. He's a bit like that. He'll invite the world, never say a word and expect Rose to read his mind and produce enough food. Or you, now, I suppose.'

'Tell me about it. I've handed over to Rose already. I swear he never mentioned Bruno.'

'Bruno.' Victoria let go of the wheelbarrow, which fell to the ground with a crash.

'Bruno Manners. Your brother-in-law. No, wait a minute, no relation to you, sorry. Orlando's uncle. He's the writer, isn't he? You must know each other.'

'Yes, we do.'

Lindy tried not to stare. Victoria was visibly shaken by the news that Bruno was coming. Why? Should she ask her? No, thought Lindy, I'd better get out of here. Whatever I've said, it's upset her. And I'll have to pump her for information about the Farleys another time too.

'So we'll see you tomorrow, then, Victoria. About eight thirty? Victoria?'

'Fine. Yes, that'll be fine.'

As she arrived back at The Cottage she saw that Orlando had returned, lunch in Salisbury clearly abandoned. In the kitchen Rose was busying herself preparing an omelette. She barely registered Lindy's return. Lindy couldn't help noticing that she had eyes only for Orlando.

She worships him, Lindy realised as Orlando embraced her and kissed her ear and she saw Rose's miserable expression as she tried not to look at them. She's got an almighty crush on my husband and now she's got to work for me. What in the world have I walked into?

I I

Bruno Manners saw himself as a tender-hearted man. But this was not an image he presented to the world. He came across as charismatic, successful, urbane, cultured, extraordinarily charming (when he cared to be), and an irresistible magnet for women.

He had never allowed anyone anywhere near his heart, yet if he had they would have found it tender.

Another thing he took care to hide from the world was his vanity, although he sometimes wondered if it was quite the secret he hoped. Although he was fifty-four there was not a speck of grey in his black hair. Not that he dyed it: he merely had his barber spend an inordinate amount of time clipping it out. In his apartment he kept an exercise bicycle in the dressing room and a trainer came three times a week. He made sure no one knew about this because in public he smoked and drank and ate as if he didn't care a fig for fitness. He liked the idea of people saying, 'Look at Bruno. How does he do it? He looks thirty-five.' He spent as much time with his tailor as he did with his close friends, which was quite something given that Bruno lived in New York and his tailor was in London – but the cut of an expensive, well-made suit could do more than anything to hide the expansion of his upper body.

Besides his obsession with his appearance, he cared desperately about his public profile. He had been a journalist, after all, and he knew how destructive the press could be if they had the opportunity. He worked hard to cultivate his image. Not only was he a bestselling author, he was also a personality, invited to parties and fund-raisers, to speak on television, to write columns. As a result, maître d's in restaurants always had a table for him. A good table.

So why, he asked himself, with all the importance he attached to a high-profile life, had he fallen in love with Victoria Hissey, a woman who took precious little care with her appearance. It never ceased to amaze him that a woman who could look so stunning if she tried – and Victoria did try on the odd occasion, with fantastic results, but more often when it suited her rather than the occasion – chose to spend most of her time buried in the country where no one could hear of her, dressed in faded jeans and one of her husband's cashmere cardigans from Marks & Spencer.

'I know it's not exactly the height of fashion any more but it's warm, it's comfortable, it's cashmere, there are no moth holes in it as far as I can see. Why on earth shouldn't I wear it?' she had remonstrated when he complained about it.

'But it has to be at least ten years old.'

'Precisely. Terrific value. Hasn't it worn well?'

And Bruno had wondered sadly about the Go-Silk thigh-length polo neck from Henry Lehr on Madison he had bought her for Christmas. Probably languishing in a drawer somewhere till it was old enough to be given an outing.

There was one other thing that he kept to himself, and that was that he harboured a secret desire to be married. As far as New York was concerned, he had acquired the label 'eternal bachelor'. He was still a catch. Divorced women of a certain age, and even young unmarrieds in their thirties, lived in hope. It wasn't just that he failed to propose, he had never even moved a woman in to live with him. He supposed he was something of an enigma. He had been in New York for seven years and no one really knew any more about him than they had when he had arrived. He had even heard it said, when after a year, no one had become a recognised 'item' with him, that he must be burning a torch for someone back home but no amount of detective work in London could unearth a name. No one, he assumed, thought he was gay. He'd been to bed with too many women – if only for a week or two before he moved on – to suggest that.

He had told no one about Victoria. About how unbelievably sexy he found her. Take that first time they'd gone to bed. She'd walked in on him when he was almost naked and he'd tried to make light of it by saying something flip and, within seconds, she'd been pressed up against him. From that point on he would have had to board up the house and put up the barricades if he had wanted to keep her out. But he hadn't wanted to keep her out. He had grown used to those great long legs wrapped around his back and the way she stroked his hair and moaned while he sucked her nipples. She was always ready for him, soaking wet between the legs the minute he let her in at the door of The Cottage.

Bruno grinned at the memory. She was all woman, Victoria, not like some of the scrawny, angular New York clothes horses he sat next to at dinner and who always looked as if they'd just escaped from the track at Saratoga.

Bruno might work hard at keeping himself in shape but he didn't like the idea of women sweating and straining on machines at the gym to keep their figures. He liked to think of them as having naturally well-toned bodies, however old they were. He didn't mind older women: he was attracted to faces that were a touch lived-in. He was easily bored so a good mind was more or less essential, and if a woman was sexually experienced so much the better. But he didn't care for women who were too thin.

Manhattan was full of them, prancing from one 12-step programme to another, reproving him for drinking and smoking and eating red meat, and twittering endlessly about their narrow, self-obsessed world. It was hard to get any kind of decent dialogue going with them. If he was in any danger of becoming something of a social disaster, it was because he poured scorn on any form of political correctness. He thought it was a pretty safe bet that Victoria didn't know what the initials PC stood for.

How he missed her directness. How he missed her total lack of pretension. How he railed at her in his mind, still, after seven years, for not allowing him to make their relationship public after Hugh Hissey's death. She had been riddled with guilt. And she'd been an idiot. How could their lovemaking at The Cottage have had anything to do with Hugh's death? And then he would calm down and console himself with the fact that she would have been a complete disaster as his social partner in New York. The thing about Victoria was that she never 'played the game', as he put it. She always had to be real. She refused to go to any social function if she didn't think it would amuse her. It never occurred to her that sometimes one went to these things to be seen rather than to see others, to further one's career, to heighten one's profile. But, then, the word 'profile' in Victoria's vocabulary had a different meaning from what it had in his. No, she would have been hopeless in New York. Much better that he'd come on his own.

He never allowed himself to admit that he had come to New York in the first place only because she had booted him out of The Cottage and dismissed him from her life. He liked to tell himself that it was part of his overall career plan. Whether or not Hugh Hissey had died the time would have come for him to move on.

Orlando had called him and invited him to The Cottage to meet Lindy when he was next over and he was using the invitation as an excuse to go to London to meet his new English editor. He had become intrigued by the sound of Caroline Calder. He had never met her. So far theirs was a fax relationship. She was the editor at the London publishing house who had just given him a two-book contract for half a million pounds. He had responded to her standard letter welcoming him to her list with an equally perfunctory fax in which, without really thinking what he was doing, he has asked her if she had any editorial comments to make before he proceeded with the next draft.

Caroline Calder's incisive dissection of his book had made him realise that over the years he had become complacent. He was no longer a good writer and his sycophantic New York editor had clearly been too terrified to tell him in case he took umbrage and went to another publisher. It was time, he decided, to come home and re-establish himself on his home turf. He was going to make Caroline Calder his prime editor and the Americans could go fuck themselves. He was looking forward to meeting her. It was amazing how intimate you could become with someone over the international fax line. Because Caroline Calder was not actually referring to him – or, indeed, to herself – when she sent him her long detailed insights into his characters, she could be considerably uninhibited while at the same time revealing a good deal about herself. From her suggestions as to how he might rework his novel, Bruno learnt that she was something of an expert – at least on paper – on oral sex, was able to correct him on several points relating to the crisis in the Balkans, the subject of his latest thriller, and clearly knew the difference between Croatia, Slovenia and Bosnia-Hercegovina, which was more than his New York editor did, and that she could more than hold her own when it came to enhancing a description of American football. Bruno had an editorial lunch scheduled with her for the following week. He could hardly wait.

He had been dying to ask Orlando if Victoria knew he was coming. He had reached for the phone half a dozen times to call her. Would she be there? Or if she'd been meaning to go away, would she change her plans if she knew he was coming?

Meanwhile there was Lindy. Silly name. To Bruno, it conjured up a pretty little blonde, all giggles and no brains. It was odd to think of Orlando as married. When Bruno had last seen him he'd been a young man of twenty, a touch gauche with no idea of the devastating effect he had on women. This was hardly surprising since he'd been raised by dozy old Hugh Hissey and Victoria, buried in the country, miles away from any action. Since Bruno had left he had heard that Orlando had taken over The Cottage and managed to carve out a life for himself in London. Now he was married to a woman whose image Bruno had pictured as fluffy and blonde. As he walked down the platform at Salisbury station he realised he was looking for just such a person.

A young woman put out a hand to stop him. She wasn't especially pretty and certainly not blonde or fluffy. She had typical English mouse-coloured hair and intelligent hazel eyes. Bruno liked her immediately. She had a refreshing no-nonsense air about her, refreshing because while she looked as though she meant business she didn't appear hard. This is an Englishwoman who could cope in New York, thought Bruno, still obsessed with New York women, but she would still retain her femininity. If he had analysed what he was thinking he would have realised that it was Lindy's soft plumpness to which he was responding after a diet of flat-chested Manhattan skeletons wrapped in DKNY.

'You seem to know who I am.'

She smiled, exposing beautiful tiny white teeth like a baby's. 'You're famous, at least to me. I love your books. Besides, you look just like your nephew. Or rather he looks just like you.'

'Lindy?'

'Yes. Bruno Manners? How do you do? Orlando was supposed to come but he started doing this jigsaw puzzle and I couldn't get him away from it. I don't know where we're going to eat our meals. He's got it spread out all over the dining-room table. I've got the car outside. You must be exhausted. When did you fly in?'

She has to be more than twenty years younger than me, thought Bruno, as he followed her out to the car, but she seems perfectly in control of the situation and for once I rather like it.

'You and Orlando haven't been married long, I gather. Do you spend much time down at The Cottage? I used to live there, you know.'

'I do indeed. I hope you're not going to find it too much of a pigsty. I've tried to restore some semblance of order to the place. I'm afraid Orlando had rather let it go. We're in London during the week and we plan to come down at weekends.'

'And, during the week, what do you do?'

'I'm a publishing scout.'

'You're a publishing scout. Are you really? For which foreign publishers?'

Lindy told him, knowing none of them published him.

'And what do you think of Harding's?'

'Harding's? Here in England?'

'Yes. They've just paid a pretty good advance for my new book. I've decided to come back and be edited in England. Do you know Caroline Calder?'

'I've met her. I go and see her to hear about her books. To tell you the truth I'm rather in awe of her. I sort of feel she doesn't really want to be bothered with someone as young as me.'

'She can't be that much older than you, surely?'

'Caroline Calder's been around for ever. She's one of those legendary backroom editors the whizzkids hand their manuscripts over to. She must be sixty if she's a day. Grey hair, totally, couple of grey whiskers growing out of her chin too, if I remember rightly.' Lindy sneaked a mischievous look at him.

'Well, I suppose that explains why she had no compunction about putting a red line through the word "fellatio" in my manuscript and writing, "why not just put sucked his dick?" in the margin?'

'Seems like very sound editorial advice to me,' said Lindy, and Bruno knew he had well and truly escaped from Manhattan and was back home in England where I stood not for Interior Decorator but for Irony.

12

The place is a complete dump. Guy drives me insane, he's so pathetic. Why doesn't he ever complain? Making me come down to The Cottage every weekend is the only time he ever puts his foot down. Why does he let me be so vile to him? Why is he always so understanding when I push him away each time he touches me? Why doesn't he force himself on me, demand his conjugal rights or whatever they're called? Why can't he show me how badly he wants me? Why is he always so tentative? Today is Saturday and I persuaded him to take Orlando to the movies in Salisbury so I could spend the afternoon squashed into the single bed in the little spare room with Angus Markham. Peg Farley came in and shouted upstairs at some point. I didn't answer and she went away. If only it had been Victoria and she had come upstairs and caught us then it would all be over, my farce of a marriage. If those chickens down the lane don't shut up I'm going to go mad …

Lindy pushed Daisy's Visitors' Book to one side. They were all the same, Daisy's entries, a never-ending stream of frustration and invective, often ending in mid-sentence as if she had been interrupted.

Lindy had been reading for nearly an hour. She had awakened on Saturday morning at an ungodly six forty-five and realised she had had hardly any sleep. Outside, it was barely light and there was evidence of a hard frost on the window-panes. On the drive down mid-week

Orlando had speculated that the river might freeze but when she had suggested maybe they could go skating he had winced and looked away. How could she have been so stupid? The ice could break and someone could be drowned. It wasn't hard to follow his line of thought and he was the last person who needed to be reminded of the possibility of a drowning.

She looked down at him lying beside her – fast asleep, face relaxed, making almost baby-like whimpers as he slept, eyelashes fluttering half-way down his cheeks, the closest Orlando ever came to snoring – and felt enormous tenderness for him. Who was this man she had married? This man who could behave in such an irresponsible and inconsiderate way and then lie like a child in her arms on the brink of tears and elicit her sympathy. Last night she had been ready to kill him. How dare he humiliate her like that? When Bruno and she had arrived back they found Orlando had gone out. His blessed jigsaw was still scattered all over the dining table. To make matters worse, all thoughts she might have had of playing the gracious hostess and showing her first guest to his room, offering him a bath, suggesting he might like to rest and come down for a drink before dinner at eight were blown straight out of the window by Rose Farley opening the front door and acting as if she was the one welcoming him to The Cottage.

'Oh, Mr Bruno, I couldn't believe it when I heard you were coming back. You must go round in the morning to see Mum. Let me take your bag. I've put you in the grey room. Orlando's photographer has asked for the futon. I've given you two sets of towels and there's plenty of hot water. I put the immersion on hours ago. Can I make you a cup of tea or something?'

And Bruno had followed her upstairs like a lamb. What irritated Lindy most, and she was furious to have to admit it, was the way he ogled her as he did so and said something utterly crass like, 'I always knew you'd turn out to be a raving beauty, Rose.'

'Where's my husband?' Lindy asked Rose, when she came downstairs.

'Orlando? He went out about twenty minutes ago. Didn't say where he was going. Maybe he's popped up to see Mrs Hissey. I've put Mum's casserole in the oven. I'll come over and prepare the rice about eight, shall I?'

But Lindy sent her packing. She wanted to establish some kind of control over the proceedings, tenuous though it might be. She called Victoria to see if Orlando was there but he wasn't. Victoria behaved most oddly. She asked, 'Bruno's arrived, has he?' and when Lindy said yes, she put down the phone almost immediately before Lindy could ask her for a drink.

By nine thirty there was no sign of Orlando and the casserole was nearly ruined. As she poured Bruno what must have been at least his fifth whisky, she was so flustered her hands were shaking. She suggested they should eat.

'Is your room all right?' she asked Bruno repeatedly. 'I'm so sorry. This used to be your home and you come back to utter chaos. I just don't know what Orlando's thinking of. He asks you down here and promptly disappears. It's extraordinary. Most unlike him.'

'Of course, you would know.'

Lindy looked at him. He was smiling.

'Stupid cliché. I've only known him a second, haven't I? It's just I can't understand it.'

'I think I know what's happened. Am I right in thinking you phoned Victoria not long ago?'

'Yes, he wasn't there.'

'Oh, I think he probably was but they were just keeping quiet about it.'

'Do you know something I don't?'

'Millions of things, I should imagine, but in this particular instance I happen to know, as I suspect you don't, that Victoria was my lover. Right here in this house.'

'You mean, when she was still married to ...'

'Exactly. And she hasn't seen me for seven years.'

'But why didn't Orlando tell me?'

'More to the point, it looks as if he's only just got round to telling Victoria I'm here. Probably breaking the news gently over several bottles of whatever up at Laybridge. What's he like now, Orlando?'

'He's my husband. And I told Victoria you were coming.' Now Lindy understood why Victoria had been so thrown by the news.

'OK, OK. So he's your husband. You've obviously got your head screwed on straight.' Lindy had done a hard sell on her own scouting operation earlier in the evening, ever mindful that the bestselling Bruno Manners was once again about to become a British-based author and therefore someone whose books she would hear about. She had already made a note to call Caroline Calder first thing on Monday morning and request an early look at his new book. If she worked on him hard enough maybe Bruno would even give her a sneak at the book himself. Then she'd really have the drop on all the other scouts. 'You wouldn't marry a flake.' Bruno went on. 'What exactly does he do all day?'

'Haven't you been keeping in touch with each other? Or hasn't Victoria kept you up to date?'

'It's too long a story to go into right now but you have to understand I was booted out of this place seven years ago, left under a cloud, not a particularly dark one but I got the message. Maybe I'm at fault, maybe I should have made more of an effort to keep in touch somehow, however much I was discouraged, but all I'm saying is that until Orlando contacted me through my agent in New York last week, I haven't heard a dickey from anyone around here.'

'Well, why would Orlando suddenly get in touch?'

'I expect his marriage to you has given him a boost of confidence. Wonderful Lindy enters his life and bingo! Everything changes. Except that when he has to face reality, he panics and runs a mile. He wouldn't be the first. What about his work, whatever it is? Takes it seriously, does he?'

'He bought this photographers' agency. I'm afraid I don't know much about it yet.'

'So he goes off to the office every day.'

'Sometimes. Sometimes he works from home.'

'I can tell you don't approve of that. Think someone who works from home must be a bit of a layabout, do you?'

'I didn't say that.'

'You didn't have to. It's written all over your face. So where are you from, Lindy?'

'West ...' Lindy stopped. 'South London.'

'South of the river? Oh dear.' Bruno laughed. 'What's the matter? Ashamed of your background? Only married Orlando for social reasons? Well, you've landed yourself in a real bed of nettles. I assume you've met Victoria? Well, I'm not going to give you the dope on her. You can work that out for yourself. All I will say is that she and Hugh and my sainted brother are – were – the real thing. Gents through and through. But Orlando hasn't only got their genes, you know. He's got bad blood running through his veins. Genes will out and you've only got to look at who his mother was.'

'Daisy Manners. What was she like?'

'I loathed her. She was a type. She was skinny. I never thought I'd say this but I'm quite drunk so I shall: having his mother die on him like that was the best thing that ever happened to Orlando. The only sadness is that Guy died with her. If he hadn't, he could have married again and given Orlando a proper mother.'

Lindy didn't want to break the spell. Bruno was being indiscreet because he was drunk and, while she felt like an eavesdropper, she wanted him to spill out as many revelations as possible. If she asked him a question he might come to and realise what he was telling her. But she had to know: 'How did it happen? How did they drown? What was going on that night?'

'I've never been able to find out but there's one person I'm pretty sure knows what happened and that's Rose Farley. She would never step inside this house when I lived here. It terrified the life out of her, for some reason, but there was one time I got her talking – she couldn't have been more than about eight – and she told me … Hello, Orlando, nice of you to join us. Wait, stop!'

Orlando, lurching out of the kitchen, forgot to duck and propelled his head straight into the low beam.

'Serves you right,' said Lindy. 'Do you know it's nearly midnight? You've obviously been having a high old time somewhere. Would you like to share it with us?'

'What's that disgusting mess?' Orlando looked down at the congealed casserole sitting in the middle of the table. 'You've even managed to fuck up Peg's cooking, Lindy. Congratulations.'

'You're pissed as a parrot, Orlando. Sit down and leave your wife alone. We've been getting to know each other. Probably did a lot better than we would have done if you'd been here. As a matter of fact you could do worse than to open another bottle of whisky if you've got one hanging about the place. I wanted to have a chat with you while I was down here, tell you something you ought to know. Rather a good thing if you're drunk.'

'But where have you been?' Lindy was furious. Was this going to be a feature of their marriage, Orlando going off to get drunk somewhere while she entertained his guests?

'Victoria, the pub, met a farmer I know from the next valley. He invited me back. His wife had dinner all ready. He opened a decent bottle of claret. I don't know, Lindy, I just forgot about the time.'

'But you knew Bruno was coming down this evening.'

'Of course I did but this isn't an army barracks. People can come and go when they like and that includes me. It's my house, for God's sake. It's not as if there was no one here to let him in. Peg had left a meal. What's the problem?'

Lindy felt Bruno's hand on her arm. Did he realise she was about to hit Orlando?

'Lindy, you must be wiped out. Don't worry about me any more. You've been the perfect hostess. Go on up to bed. Orlando and I can stack the dishwasher, have a nightcap. Go on. Bed!'

At half past four, Lindy heard them come upstairs to bed telling each other to 'Shhhh!' like two drunken schoolboys, Bruno crashing into the guest bathroom and peeing noisily while Orlando tiptoed into their bedroom and promptly fell over the clothes horse. Lindy slipped out of bed and closed the door before drawing back the covers and heaving him into bed.

'What did he want to talk to you about?' she asked.

'Nothing. Everything. Life.'

Lindy gave up. She wasn't going to get anything more out of him. She felt his head become heavy on her chest. Then, just as he was about to fall asleep, he opened his eyes wide and told her: 'But he thinks you're wonderful. Completely wonderful.'

Half an hour later, when she was still wide awake, she slipped out from under him and reached under the bed. She had hidden The Visitors' Book there when Victoria had first given it to her. Right now all she wanted to do was to open the brand new volume and write feverishly in it for the first time:

My first weekend at The Cottage is not exactly going according to plan. The place is a mess and I've already had a row with Orlando. He's behaving very strangely. He never told me Bruno Manners was coming. He's being no help whatsoever. I have no idea what's going on half the time. Peg Farley clearly thinks I'm not fit to be in charge. The only person who seems to take me seriously is Bruno. He's an Orlando look alike only twenty years older, for that read seriously sexy. He's taken me into his confidence as if I were one of his closest friends. Seems he had something going with Victoria. Apparently he thinks I'm wonderful and of course I'm very pleased to hear that. Very pleased indeed.

13

Rose went round to The Cottage to prepare lunch and was met at the door by Lindy, who firmly took the spinach and ham quiche Rose had made that morning and ushered her out.

'It's all right, Rose. I do know how to make a salad, you know. And we'll just have fruit and cheese afterwards. Couldn't be easier.'

'But you'd like me to come back and clear up, load the dishwasher like I usually do?'

'That'd be wonderful. When everyone's finished. We'll eat at half past one. Say three?'

When Rose went back at three everyone – Bruno and Orlando – was still in bed nursing their hangovers, the quiche was sitting in splendour all by itself in the middle of a table, laid, Rose was amused to see, with very fancy china for Saturday lunch. A Sainsbury's herb salad in a packet – a salad in packet in the middle of the country! – was lying unopened by the sink beside a bottle of shop-bought vinagrette. Rose was outraged.

Lindy was sitting at the bottom of the stairs clutching a half-empty bottle of white wine.

'Mr and Mrs McGill haven't arrived yet. My husband and his uncle are indisposed and are not yet down.' Rose thought she sounded worse than a constipated butler. 'Lunch will be late.'

'You mean Orlando's got a hangover. Mr and Mrs McGill aren't going to want lunch as late as half past three. Come into the kitchen and I'll make you a cup of coffee. Here, we'll take this quiche off the table and you can have a slice.'

Rose was beginning to feel sorry for Lindy who followed her meekly into the kitchen. Orlando obviously hadn't warned her about weekends at The Cottage. People often stayed up all night and slept all day. Rose was used to it: she went with the flow, provided meals that could enjoy a second outing if they weren't consumed first time round.

'What's all this?' she picked up the salad in a bag, 'Thought you said you knew how to make a salad. Didn't your mother teach you to cook?'

'No, of course not.'

'Why of course not?'

'Well, I was never going to be a cook like you. Besides, she couldn't cook. She couldn't do anything, really. Or, rather, she chose not to. Just sat there all day long being stupid. Oh, God, I shouldn't be talking to you like this.'

Yes, you should, thought Rose, You need a friend. 'Excuse me for saying so but it sounds as if you don't really like your mum very much and that's a terrible shame.'

'Do you like yours?'

'I love her! As a mum and as a friend. She's taught me everything I know. Of course there's a lot I've got to learn that she can't teach me but that's up to me from now on.'

'What has she taught you? She's just a cook, although I suppose that's better than my mother who never worked a day in her life. But from what I understand — and correct me if I'm wrong — it's not as if your mother's ever been anywhere other than Salisbury. Isn't it a bit of an antiquated way of life, being a cook to a widow in the depths of the country?'

Rose tightened her grip on the bottle of ready-made vinaigrette she had been about to put away in the fridge. She was half inclined to smash it in Lindy's face. Who did this woman think she was? OK, so she was Rose's new boss, in a manner of speaking, but Rose decided to go for broke. If it was going to work between them, Lindy had to understand what kind of person she was dealing with. If Rose was up front with her then she would either be fired within thirty seconds or their relationship would move on to a new footing. It was worth the risk.

'The thing is, Lindy – you don't mind if I call you Lindy, do you? Go on, sit down there and tell me what kind of coffee you want? Do you like decaff? We have heard of decaff down here, you know. We're not completely behind the times. Real? OK. Now the thing is, you ask me if my mother's way of life, and indeed mine, is a bit antiquated. Well, we don't think so. You see, we know who we are. My family has lived down here for centuries, just like Orlando's has. Their house is a bit bigger, true, but see, I love the country and my mum loves growing her vegetables and cooking them. My grandfather loves the garden up at Laybridge and he loves his horrible chickens. Life goes on here, day after day, season after season. It doesn't change and you may think that's boring. But if we love it as much as we do why would we want it to change? I know if I go to London or somewhere like that I won't be me any more and I won't know how to behave. Like you down here. You're all at sea. You don't fit in and that's because you're trying to change things, tidy everything up, instead of waiting and watching how *we* do things.'

'Now just a minute. I'm running this house now and –'

'If you've got any sense you'll see you need me to keep it running the way Orlando likes it. You think I'm interfering, don't you? Well, maybe I am but only in the kitchen.'

Lindy watched her as she moved about. Bruno thought Rose knew what had happened the night Guy and Daisy Manners drowned. If Lindy became friends with her, maybe she could get her to open up. And, as for running the house, Rose was right: it looked as if Lindy was going to need as much support as she could get.

'Well, Rose, you know I envy you your relationship with your mother. You respect Peg and I can see why you do. I'm sorry if I accused you both of being country bumpkins. It's just that I don't respect my mother. I don't have a role model like you do. I always have to work it out for myself. I want to be a good wife for Orlando, and here I am, already being as useless around the house as my mother was.'

'Because it's not what interests you. You've got your work in London. And then you'll have a baby.'

'I'll do what?'

'Have a baby.'

'Have a baby,' parroted Lindy. 'Oh, Rose, it doesn't always work like that. I have my work. I don't want my life cluttered up too soon with children. In fact, I'm not even sure I want them *ever*. Don't look at me like that. I'm not one of your grandfather's hens, reared to lay eggs to order. The thought of waddling around nine months pregnant, knocking over the furniture and knowing my body is never going to be the same again makes me want to throw up.'

'You and me both,' said a woman with a washed-out face and a vastly extended stomach as she came into the kitchen and dumped a holdall on the floor, 'You poor thing, you look exhausted. Are you Lindy? You must be. I'm Lily McGill. Didn't you hear the car? The front door was open so I just came on in. Here, I'll put the kettle on. I've been dreaming about a cup of tea ever since the motorway but Peter wouldn't stop. Where's Orlando?'

I'm Wiltshire's Golden Hostess, thought Lindy, and began to compose what she would write in The Visitors' Book by way of cathartic therapy:

My first weekend and I haven't been able to give anyone a proper meal yet. I've barely seen my husband. The cook has made it quite clear I'm not fit to run my own house and when an exhausted pregnant guest arrives she finds me half cut and offers to make me a cup of tea in my own kitchen. How could it possibly get worse?

She found out when Orlando came stumbling down the stairs and banged his head again on the low beam.

'Oh, shit a brick! Hello, Lily, come here, big kiss. Where's my jigsaw?'

'It's nearly four o'clock in the afternoon,' Lindy told him. 'I needed to lay the table for lunch. I cleared it away.'

'But there was no one here for bloody lunch. How dare you!'

'How was I to know you wouldn't be down? There's no need to behave like a two-year-old just because I put away your toys.'

'Look, don't give me any grief about this, Lindy, or

you'll be sorry. I've got a splitting headache. Peter and I always do the jigsaw together over tea when he comes down for the weekend. It stays on the dining-room table until we've finished and if that means we have to eat Sunday lunch on trays in the garden shed then so be it.'

'I don't believe it!' Lindy screamed, 'I don't fucking believe it, I –'

And then she saw Bruno watching her, an amused look on his face. He had come downstairs behind Orlando.

'I've kept it safe,' Rose told Orlando quietly. 'It's on a tray on top of the piano in the other room.'

'Good girl,' said Bruno and, to Lindy's horror, he gave Rose a pat on the bum while looking straight at Lindy to check her reaction.

Peter McGill was already going bald. He carefully took off his Barbour and hung it up in the small room to the left of the hall that housed the washing machine and the wellington boots. He dusted off a few imaginary flecks from the sleeves of his maroon V-necked Marks & Spencer sweater and adjusted the polo neck underneath so that it folded over just so. He looked in the small mirror above the wash-basin, jutted out his chin and turned his head from right to left. He did it automatically every time he saw a mirror. He had no idea why.

'See you've got a nice new washing machine in there since I was last here. Bosch. Must have set you back more than five hundred quid. Present for the little woman, Orlando? Kettle on, Lily? Soo-perb. Let's get down to the jigsaw. Haven't been cheating, have you, Orlando? Starting it early? Ah, now, you must be Lindy. Any good at jigsaws, are you? Something I said?' he asked, bewildered, as Lindy walked past him without a word and began to pour the tea.

When the phone rang in the library, Victoria pounced on it.

'Hello?'

'Vicky? You sound very strange. It's Jessica.'

'Oh. Hello, Jess.'

Victoria rarely sought advice and if she did it was generally on practical matters such as when she had had to decide what to do about opening the plant centre at Laybridge following Hugh's death. On matters pertaining to her personal life she preferred to keep her own counsel. She was astonished at the way people carelessly displayed their dirty laundry to their friends, poured out all their problems, disclosed their husbands' sexual shortcomings with no apparent concern for the gossiping about their life that was bound to follow. She knew that she was paranoid about keeping her life completely private. She had a horror of being the subject of gossip. She trusted no one.

Except Jessica Nesbit. The attraction of Jess Nesbit as a confidante was that she lived in New York. Ten years younger than Victoria, she was English and she had known Victoria since before her marriage to Hugh, but Jess had married late, an American financier with the rather pompous-sounding name of Nelson Nesbit, and had lived in a four-bedroomed duplex overlooking Gramercy Park for the last ten years. Victoria stayed there on the rare occasions when she visited New York. Jess wrote children's books, which sold in large quantities all over the world. She based the recurring characters in them on her children, who were still fairly young, disguising them as rabbits, teddy bears, Pekineses, whatever. She was probably the only person in the world who understood just how vulnerable Victoria was behind her strong no-nonsense exterior. She was also the only person Victoria allowed to call her Vicky.

'Vicky? You left a message on the machine last night. I've been at the paediatrician's all weekend. Josh keeps throwing up and no one can understand why. Anyway, he's much better now. I'm sorry I didn't call you back sooner and now you sound rather disappointed to hear from me.'

'I thought you might be Bruno.'

'Bruno? Why on earth should he be calling you after all these years? Sorry, I didn't mean it like that but I thought you were over him.'

'He's here at Laybridge. Not with me. He's down at The Cottage for the weekend. He arrived last night and hasn't contacted me, hasn't walked up the lane to see me, hasn't even phoned.'

'How do you know he's there? Why *is* he there?'

'Orlando's gone and got himself married to this girl he met in the Caribbean. A Plain Jane if ever there was one but perfectly pleasant. Obviously very bright and deter-mined, an over-achiever brimming with ambition. Any-way, it all appears to have had some kind of bizarre effect on Orlando because he's gone and asked Bruno to stay for the weekend. The thing is, Jess, I've been asked to dinner tonight and I'm not sure I can cope.'

'Anyone else there?'

'Well, Peter and Lily McGill. They're harmless enough.

But Orlando's asked one of his photographer clients and he's bringing a model.'

'Why should that worry you?'

'Well, she's probably about twenty-five and stunning.'

'So?'

'Well, I'm nearly fifty.'

'What's that got to do with the price of beans? The last time I saw you you looked extraordinary and you haven't even been lifted like your counterparts here in Manhattan.'

'Yes, but Bruno won't see it that way, will he?'

'Why should you care which way Bruno sees it? You and he are history.'

'Are we?'

'Ah. Bit of hope lurking, is there?'

'I think there always has been. I suppose I always assumed he'd come back. That's why I've never been interested in anyone else.'

'So you should be over the moon with excitement.'

'I don't know what he's been up to in New York. But even if we do start something up again, there are always going to be younger women around. I may look good when I've spent half an hour on my make-up and I'm bathed in candlelight and he's drunk enough for me to be constantly in soft focus, but in the cold clear light of day I don't stand a prayer against a woman over twenty years my junior and a recognised beauty to boot.'

'Vicky, I can't believe I'm hearing this. You've never seemed to care tuppence for your appearance. I don't mean you look bad but it just never seemed important to you. If you want Bruno back, you have to ask yourself how you landed him in the first place.'

'Sex. We were good in bed together.'

'Well, turn the lights out and get him back into bed.'

'But what about the fact that my skin isn't as soft as it was and my thighs are spreading and my hair is going dry and stringy. Maybe he won't want to touch it like he used to –'

'Enough of this crap, Vicky. How do you know he's not worrying about exactly the same things? Men are incredibly vain, far worse than us. Anyway, how long has it been? Seven, eight years? It's a long time. You may not fancy him any more.'

'I know I will. It's just that I don't have the same kind of confidence that I used to have. When I had my affair with Bruno I had my safety net in dear old Hugh. What I'm trying to tell you, Jess, is that this is the first time I've ever really been in this predicament. I've clung on to this romantic notion that Bruno is the only man for me, even though I haven't seen him in seven years. I'm like a war bride waiting for her man to come back from the front not knowing what he's going to be like and knowing also that she won't still be the fresh young face in the photograph he took away with him. You see, Jess, you and Bruno are the only people in the world who really know me. I'm not as tough as I pretend to be but if I do have any confidence in myself, Bruno gave it to me. He encouraged me in my writing. Never read a word of it, of course, but he kept asking me how it was going. I could always turn to him for advice, about clothes, money, how to deal with my publisher, where to go on holiday. He knew everything. Hugh was always so hopeless. I suppose initially my relationship with Bruno was a bit of a didactic one. I was a bit of an innocent when I married Hugh. You remember how I was. I hadn't really grown up. Bruno made me feel like a grown-up woman, and then again we'd have fun like kids, playing rock 'n' roll records till the small hours of the morning and getting drunk. I'm not really like that but Bruno knew how to bring out a part of me that liked to have fun. I want him to do that again, but I'm scared.'

'Poor Vicky. You really are a funny old stick. All you have to do is – what's that awful expression? Go for it! If you're still attracted to him, show him. There's nothing a man likes better than knowing a woman fancies him. Of course you're apprehensive. You haven't seen him in a while. You're going to be surrounded by a younger crowd but don't worry about them. The one they're going to be focusing on is Orlando's new bride. I wouldn't be in her shoes. Go and doll yourself up to the nines and vamp Bruno to death. Show these kids how it's done. But be yourself. If he loves you it's because you're a good person.'

'A good person! That's real New York talk. Jess, I don't know how you do it but every time I talk to you I feel reborn.'

'And it costs! I don't think we'd better run up Nelson's transatlantic telephone bill a second longer. Call me and give me an update and we'll dish the dirt at your expense. I haven't told you about my fantasies about Josh's paediatrician.'

'Are they likely to become reality?'

'In my dreams. See? You're the only one who gets to take lovers. Keep me posted. 'Bye, darling.'

Jessica put down the phone and congratulated herself on her diplomacy. She had never told Victoria, but she'd kept tabs on Bruno Manners's behaviour ever since he'd arrived in New York. It was extraordinary how two women who were as close as she and Victoria could see men in such a different light. Whatever else she felt about Bruno Manners, Victoria had always maintained he was worthy of her trust and respect but as far as Jessica could tell the man was clearly an egotistical user of women on a grand scale. The best thing that could happen to Victoria was for Bruno to take one look at her and dive straight into the young model's arms, although what Victoria had conveniently overlooked was that the model was coming with her boyfriend, the photographer, younger and more virile than Bruno. But as Jessica had learned to her cost, on more than one occasion, sometimes her women friends should only be told what they really wanted to hear, especially when it came to men.

14

Lindy thought Lily McGill was a nightmare.

'You mustn't worry about that wretched jigsaw, really you mustn't. Orlando and Peter were at school together and whenever they see each other they revert straight back to their schooldays. I expect we'll all be roped in for a game of Murder in the Dark later or Sardines.'

'How on earth do you play Sardines?' Upstairs in her bathroom eager for a few moments' privacy after the scene about the jigsaw Lindy had been interrupted by Lily. Lily had marched her firmly downstairs again to face the music. Now she was lying stretched out in front of a fire she knew had been laid and started by Lily. Bruno, Orlando and Peter, or The Boys as Lily would insist on calling them, were ensconced in the sitting room with the door shut. Bruno was on the phone, calling long distance judging by the sound of his voice, shouting instructions to someone. Lily had emerged from the kitchen carrying a heavily laden tea tray almost at arm's length in front of her bulge. She shouted, 'Tea, boys!' and kicked the sitting-room door until they opened it. She reported that, judging by the whiff she had received while delivering the tray, they were already drinking something a good deal stronger than tea.

'Heavens, haven't you ever played Sardines? Where have you been hiding? Ha ha!'

Lindy stared at her. Was this woman quite mad? 'No, I never have. Is it a board game?'

'No, no, no. It's a hide-and-seek game. Someone goes off and hides and we all have to look for him. Or her. And as each person discovers the hiding place they have to hide there too. It's best if the one who hides chooses somewhere small, like the linen cupboard, then everyone's crammed in like sardines. Now, what are we having for dinner? What can I do? You take a rest and I'll go and peel the sprouts or something. I'm very good at sprouts – I always make that little cross on the top, you know.'

Lindy hadn't a clue. Why didn't this bloody woman shut up and go and have a rest herself? She was the one having the baby, wasn't she?

'I think Rose has it all under control.'

'Oh, of course, where would we be without Rose? Ouch! Now, Baby's kicking. Would you like to feel it?' Lily began to heave her stomach towards Lindy.

'No, thank you.' Lindy sat up quickly.

'Oh.' Lily looked disappointed. 'When are you and Orlando going to try for one? Or perhaps you already are?'

'No, we're not. We won't … I mean, not for some time.'

'Oh, won't you? What a shame. I'd have had Baby as soon as possible after we were married if only dear old Peter hadn't had such a lot of useless sperm. That's what the doctor told him, the wretch. "You've got useless sperm," he told poor Peter. Or was it lazy sperm? It wasn't my eggs, it was Peter's fault all the time. Imagine how he'd been feeling although I must confess I was relieved I was all right. Anyway, it's all in the past now. We were thrilled when we heard Orlando had got married, we really were. Orlando's such an old friend of Peter's We couldn't wait to come down and meet you. We don't see him in town, I've never quite understood why, but we always have such a jolly time down here and ...'

Later Lindy had no idea at what point during Lily's interminable monologue she had fallen asleep. She opened her eyes to find Bruno sitting on the sofa beside her gently shaking her awake. He's caught me out again, she thought.

'Time the perfect hostess prepared herself for dinner. We've left you an inch of hot water for your bath. I'd nip upstairs before you run into Lily, if I were you. She was rather miffed that you failed to find her conversation utterly scintillating.'

'Oh, my God, what's the time?' Lindy sat up and saw that the curtains were drawn, the table was laid for dinner and Bruno, Peter and Orlando had all bathed and changed.

'It's nearly half past seven,' said Lily, coming downstairs in a peach-coloured velvet tent that reached down to her ankles. 'Rose wants to know what time to serve dinner.'

'Who's here? Has Orlando's photographer arrived yet?' Lindy was aware of the slight edge of panic in her voice. 'And Victoria?'

'Oh, shit, you were asleep when he rang,' said Orlando. 'He's stuck on a shoot in Germany. I thought he'd be back today but it was the old problem with the light. He's got to stay another day. Shame, you'd have liked Bobby. Anyway he asked if Nona could come on her own.'

'On her own?' Lindy was horrified. A spare woman and a model at that! 'Do you know her?'

'Oh, God, I don't know. I've probably met her to say

121

hello to at the agency. And Victoria's coming at eight. She'll be pretty pronto, knowing her. I'll open a bottle of champagne and we'll go in the other room to drink it. You have your bath and join us when you're ready.'

By eight thirty there was still no sign of either Nona or Victoria. To Lindy's amazement no one seemed remotely put out and she began to understand the value of Rose Farley's presence. If Lindy had been in charge of serving dinner she would have been catapulted into a flat panic by this stage but Rose was calmness itself.

'I never put the vegetables on till everyone's sitting down. The starter's cold – I thought we'd have the quiche no one ate at lunch. No point in letting it go to waste. There's one of my rabbit casseroles in the oven, Orlando's favourite. It's turned way down low, and it doesn't matter how long it stays there. The longer it stews away the better. Hold on, who's this then?'

She peered through the kitchen window and Lindy, who was behind her, saw a car draw up on the gravel outside. A door opened and one of the longest legs Lindy had ever seen appeared.

'She's here, whoever she is,' said Rose, with a grin. 'Aren't you going to go and greet her at the front door? You know what they say about models. She's probably got fewer brains than all Grandad's chickens put together.'

Nona was wearing a floor-length fake leopardskin coat. She barely looked at Lindy as she came into the house. She rushed straight up to Orlando and kissed him on the mouth in a surprisingly intimate fashion. At least Orlando had the grace to look a little thrown, Lindy noted.

'Darling, I really appreciate this. I couldn't stand the thought of being cooped up in London all on my own.

Isn't this a cute little place you've got but, Jesus, it's cold in here. Can I eat dinner on a tray by the fire and who do I have to fuck to get a drink around here?'

A stunned silence was broken by Orlando. 'No one. At least not before dinner. Glass of champagne all right? Now let me introduce you to everyone or do you want go upstairs, bathroom, powder your nose, stuff like that?'

'No thanks, I'm all ready.'

'Well, can I take your coat?' asked Lindy. *And would you mind at least acknowledging my presence, you rude bitch*, she seethed inwardly.

'In a place where there's no central heating? I'll probably wear it to bed.'

'I put central heating in at least four years ago, Nona.' Lindy could tell that Orlando was insulted. He was terribly proud of his central heating and the fact that the boiler had never broken down. Touch wood!

'My bag's in the car,' Nona said to her.

Oh, great, thought Lindy. I wear my best Nicole Farhi and she thinks I'm the maid.

'I'll get it later,' said Orlando quickly. 'This is my wife, Lindy, and this is Lily and Peter McGill. And my uncle Bruno, who's just arrived from New York.'

'It's a most unusual name, Nona,' said Lily. 'I've never come across it before. Nina, yes. But Nona, never.'

'My parents called me Nona because I was born on the ninth of September.'

Lily looked blank. Lindy felt sorry for her even though she had already decided Lily was a crashing bore.

'The ninth day of the ninth month, Lily. Ninth. Nona.' prompted Bruno.

'Which means I'm a Virgo, of course,' Nona told them. 'What are you, Bruno?'

'Maybe we should all sit down,' said Lindy, when she saw Bruno's face. It gave her a chance to exercise some kind of control over the gathering. 'All right, everyone, placement,' she said brightly. 'If Orlando and I go at either end, then, Bruno, I thought I'd put you here on my right and Peter on my other side. Victoria can go next to you, Bruno, if she ever turns up, and then Lily can be on her right next to Orlando. Nona, perhaps you'd like to fill up the gap on the other side next to Peter?'

Nobody moved. Lindy made shepherding movements towards the table but everyone seemed to be ignoring her. Finally Lily came to her rescue. 'I'm afraid it's another tradition down here at The Cottage. For dinner all the boys sit down one side of the table and all the girls down the other.'

'That's a bit sexist, isn't it?'

'Traditionalist, you mean,' said Bruno. 'Come along, Lindy. We newcomers had better fall in with what's gone before.'

'Well, it's simple, I'll sit here in the middle and you can sit opposite me, Bruno, and then we can play footsy-footsy all through dinner.' Nona was standing next to Lily when she took off her coat. Her skimpy dress would barely have made a sleeve of Lily's spreading tent. It was skin tight, with a halter neck that revealed to their best advantage Nona's coat hanger shoulders. Her nipples protruded like the tops of biros waiting to be clicked shut. She was so skinny that her pelvis was outlined through the fabric. Seeing Nona standing beside Lily, with her child-bearing hips ready to go into action, Lindy found herself wondering what kind of a grotesque picture Nona would present if she was pregnant.

'I'm in pretty good shape, huh?' Nona was irrepressible, 'I've got abs of steel. Here, Peter, want to cop a feel?'

Lily opened her mouth and Lindy guessed she was about to ask Nona if she wanted to feel *Baby*.

'Mrs Hissey's here,' said Rose, coming in with the quiche.

And when Victoria made her entrance, Lindy nearly applauded. Nona and her abs of steel were history. Lindy looked at Victoria and suddenly saw the advantage an older woman could have over a younger one if she put her mind to it. Victoria had probably never been pretty in the classical sense but tonight she looked beautiful. She was as tall as Nona and she held herself just as erect. But whereas a minute ago Nona had looked unbelievably glamorous, now, beside Victoria, she looked just a touch tacky. If Nona's body was exposed for all to admire, Victoria's was hidden in a flattering trouser suit for all to wonder about. Victoria had Hissey diamonds in her ears, Hissey pearls at her throat. She looked rich and experienced and, because they were used to seeing her wandering round the grounds in gumboots or working in her study in jeans and sweaters, mysterious. Nona looked stunning – and suddenly rather cheap.

Victoria's a triumph, thought Lindy. I could learn a lot from her.

By the time they had finished the quiche, Lindy was beginning to relax. It was all going rather well and as if she had suddenly appeared, all the attention was focused on her.

'So tell us, Lindy, how exactly did you find Orlando? We heard it was on a beach. Was it on one of those package holidays? I hear you can spend two weeks in the Caribbean for under two grand. What kind of a deal did you get?' God, he was like an automaton.

'Lindy, what sign are you?' Nona wasn't much better. Lindy saw Orlando's look of despair.

'Have you done anything to Orlando's house in London? Because he won't let you change anything down here, that's for sure. I know a builder who's extraordinarily reasonable. You want to watch out for these cowboys.' Peter again.

'And, Lindy, I simply must tell you,' Lindy shuddered inside, wondering what inanity Lily would come up with now, 'I simply love that little basket of goodies you've put in our bathroom. Free samples, are they? It's like staying in a hotel. Will we go upstairs and find a little choccie on our pillow when we go to bed?'

There was an abrupt silence round the table. Lindy looked puzzled.

Oh, Lord, thought Victoria, Lily's such an idiot. She means well but she always puts her foot in it. Does Lindy know she's just been put down in the nicest possible way? Are there really hotel samples upstairs in the bathrooms? Well, what of it?

She caught Bruno's eye and looked away. He'd aged. Not much. He looked great but there was a puffiness under his eyes and a slight thickening around his jaw. He wouldn't be pleased about that, she thought, with a smile.

He was probably a closet exercise fanatic in New York. She'd heard they all were. But that kind of exercise didn't do much for middle-aged double chins.

As if on cue Peter began babbling away to Lindy. 'Lily's got it all planned. Tomorrow we're going to take you on a big hike up to the chine and then you can look down and see Hissey land spread out before you, land that will one day be yours when Orlando inherits. He will inherit, won't he, Victoria? Lily will lead the way. She's not due for another week. It's The Cottage tradition. Every Sunday after lunch, up to the chine. I've even bought new walking boots. Bit of a bargain, actually, only thirty-five pounds and they're the real thing.'

Why is it that I'm fond of Lily but I find Peter dreary beyond belief, wondered Victoria. If he wasn't so loyal and supportive to Orlando I know I wouldn't tolerate him at all.

He was turning his attention on the model. This will be a disaster, thought Victoria. He'll be out of his depth in no time with this little minx. What on earth was she doing here?

'So you're a model, Nona?'

'Absolutely.'

'What was your last job? Do tell us all about it.'

'I bet you've been swanning around all the sunspots,' said Orlando. 'That's what models and photographers do in the freezing depths of winter, rush off to Florida and Africa and do swimwear shoots. All my photographers are the colour of mahogany. Make us all madly jealous, Nona, tell us where you've been.'

'I did a fashion spread for one of the Sunday magazines

over here before Christmas. I was on the cover, actually. Maybe it's not one of the ones you take, Peter.'

'Oh, we get them all,' said Lily. 'What else is there to do on Sunday mornings? Did you see that marvellous guide to men's health in one of them last weekend? Fascinating. I never knew that a forty-five-year-old man had greater control over ejaculation than a twenty-year-old one, did you, Victoria?'

'Actually, yes,' said Victoria. She resisted the temptation to wink at Bruno.

'And sixty per cent have all their own teeth. Do you have all your own teeth, Bruno?'

'Actually, no,' said Bruno. This was a first. The Bruno Victoria knew hated admitting that anything about him was not as nature had intended.

'Well, twenty per cent snore enough to disturb their own sleep. That's true of you, Peter, and you're only twenty-eight. It said intelligence in men is moving towards its peak at twenty-six. Moving a bit slower for you, dear, isn't it, if at all? Testicular cancer is the commonest malignancy in the twenty to forty age group. Isn't that awful?'

'Lily, darling, I think we've had enough of this, my love.' Victoria was immensely relieved when Orlando reached out and patted Lily's shoulder. He was always sweet with her but only, Victoria suspected, because she was Peter's wife. She held out her glass to Orlando for more wine as he asked Peter, 'Have you seen *The Grifters*?'

'Have I seen *The Grifters*? I bet I saw it before you did. I couldn't wait.'

'I was invited to a screening, actually.' Victoria sensed

Orlando sounded rather smug. These two had always been competitive in a healthy way.

'I even preferred it to the book. I lusted after Anjelica like you wouldn't believe.'

'The book?'

'You've never read Jim Thompson? Christ, Orlando, where've you been? Forget Chandler, forget Hammett. Though I suppose Thompson is a bit of a cult author really, only a few of us connoisseurs know about him. His work is tailor-made for adaptation to the *film noir*, of course.'

'I've never understood what you mean by *film noir*,' said Lily, 'and who's Anjelica, Peter? Do I know her?'

'No, my sweet, I don't think you do. And never mind about *noir*. It isn't for you.'

'Isn't it? Well, if you say so ... probably not.'

Victoria saw that Lindy was horrified. Probably found it amazing that Lily had never heard of *film noir* or, more likely, she was appalled that the woman let her husband patronise her to such an extent. She wouldn't let you get away with something like that, Orlando, thought Victoria. You've taken on a handful, I hope you realise that.

'I can't believe you guys have only just seen *The Grifters*,' said Nona. 'It came out in the States years ago. I saw it when I was over there for a commercial. You're all so behind over here, I don't know how you stand it. Wouldn't it drive you crazy, Bruno?'

'Actually I'm thinking of spending more time in England. I've had enough of New York for the time being.'

Had they heard her? Victoria tried to concentrate on a minute piece of quiche that she was trying to manoeuvre on to her fork but she knew she had let out a gasp of excitement at Bruno's remark. Where did she figure in this equation?

If anyone else had heard her, Nona certainly hadn't. Victoria had come across people like her all too often. They asked a question of other people only because they wanted a chance to answer it themselves.

'So how did you like *Godfather III*, Bruno? I thought it was dreadful. Francis has lost it – what do you think? Although Andy Garcia was kind of cute.'

'I suppose it had its moments,' Bruno conceded. 'The way he intercut all those brutal killings with *Cavalleria Rusticana* at the end was quite something.'

'I don't suppose you and Lily have been able to get to the opera much lately, Peter, what with the baby coming and everything?' Victoria asked.

'The opera? Us? At fifty quid a ticket? You must be joking. I went to La Scala once when I was staying with this Italian family. Must admit it was rather jolly. But they were paying, of course.'

'Actually, Peter, I think it would be rather a good idea if you took me to the opera,' said Lily. 'I've been reading this book. It says that Baby can recognise music from the fourth month in the mother's womb. They like music with lots of instruments, particularly the flute. There we are: what about *The Magic Flute*? I'm just a bit worried. Virginia Palmer-Ross who lives up the road, her baby gets frightfully excited when she hears the *Eastenders* theme tune and I know for a fact Virginia never misses an episode. We wouldn't want Baby to ...'

Only Lily would refer to her unborn child as 'Baby', thought Victoria. Somebody's going to have to do something or else, from the look on Lindy's face, Lily's going to be the victim of some grievous bodily harm.

Lindy stood up and began to collect the plates. Lily leaped up to help her and had to be forced down again by Peter and Orlando.

'Lindy, Rose will do that,' Orlando told her with, she thought, a degree of menace.

'And so will I,' she said, and departed for the kitchen.

'Excuse me for just a second.' Orlando followed her. 'Rose, could you collect the rest of the plates? Thank you.'

'Those are two of the stupidest women on this planet. Nona is just plain thick and the worst of it is she doesn't know it. Plus I cannot stand the way she says everyone's name when she's talking to them, like she's been on some kind of management training course. It's worse than Frank Bruno talking to Harry Carpenter after a fight. "Right, Harry, good to talk to you, Harry, I gave him a good left-right-left when I hit him upstairs, Harry." And as for Lily. If I hear one more word about Baby I'm going to throw up. They're seriously dumb, Orlando, you've got to admit it.'

'And I suppose you're the Brain of Britain?'

'I never said that. I just want to know what you see in these people. Peter McGill keeps going on about how much things cost. You must have noticed. It's so boring. I thought he and Lily were supposed to be your closest friends.'

Orlando moved to stand very close to Lindy. 'Read my lips, Lindy. You're right. They are among my closest friends. I was at school with Peter. We go back a long way. So what if he goes on about the price of things. They're a bit strapped for cash at the moment. Just because he hasn't as much money as I've got doesn't mean I should drop him as a friend. Yes, he is a bit boring but he's a loyal decent friend, and that's important to me. OK, so Lily is a bit of a twitterer but she's one of the kindest people I know. She really pulls her weight whenever she comes down here. There have been times when I couldn't have coped without her. I deliberately didn't ask them round in London because they're broke and they'd feel they'd have to have us back and I don't want to get on to that kind of merry-go-round with them. Peter's quite proud about money. The way Lily rushes round helping out down here is their way of paying me back for my hospitality and what's wrong with that?'

Lindy was quite shaken. 'Well, how are you going to defend that stupid model?'

'Lindy, don't be so judgemental. You think just because she's a model you can write her off as a silly piece of fashion fluff. Give her a chance. At worst she's harmless and she's pretty with it. She's probably insecure, they usually are, and you're making it worse.'

'Now who's being judgemental?'

'Well, why shouldn't I defend my guests and my friends? You'd defend yours if I were rude about them which I can't be because you're too ashamed of them even to introduce me to them.'

'What did you just say?'

'Well, it's true. You've never suggested inviting any of your friends round. I've never even met any of your family except for that time I came home unexpectedly and found you having tea with your aunt Mary. And then you couldn't wait to get her out of the house. From what little I saw of her she seemed like a perfect sweetheart. Your father's dead and I've never even met your mother.'

'I told you, I never speak to her. We don't get on. She lives up in the north of England with a widow friend.'

'But she's your own mother. Are you ashamed of her too?'

'What's all this ashamed nonsense? Maybe it's you I'm ashamed of.'

'Well, is it?'

'No. I just know you wouldn't get on with my friends. They're not even my friends any more. I mean, I didn't really have many friends. I was hoping to meet lots of new people through you, if you really want to know. People our age. But I seem to have more in common with Bruno and Victoria and they've got twenty years on us.' And with Rose Farley, she thought, as Rose came back into the kitchen to collect the rabbit casserole. After all my dreams of being the glamorous country hostess, I find I wish I was sitting down to dinner with the cook rather than the guests. 'Anyway, Bruno and Victoria are being a bit low key. They're obviously as bored with Nona and the McGills as I am.'

'You're the one who's thick, Lindy. I told you about Bruno and Victoria's affair. I'm not supposed to know about it. This is the first time they've seen each other in seven years, as far as I know.'

'And Nona's flaunting herself in front of Bruno. Oh, poor Victoria, she probably feels about a hundred and ten.'

'Well, get back out there and start being a grown-up. Try to bring her into the conversation like a proper hostess. Try to be my wife, if it's not too much to ask.'

*

Rose had heard every word.

As she loaded the dishwasher with the plates from the first course, she tried to decide whether or not she felt sorry for Lindy. Peg had always said that Orlando was spoiled rotten but Rose had a feeling that Peg didn't really know Orlando. Peg just wrote him off as Daisy Manners's son and that was that. Rose knew that, underneath his rather flippant exterior, Orlando was a kind man and, like her, he wasn't happy when things changed. Rose had known that he would want things to continue at The Cottage exactly as they always had. She also understood that, however much Lindy might try to change things, she would never get the better of Orlando. Orlando and me, Rose thought, we're country people. We want to keep things the way they are down here. Women like that model Nona, or Lindy, they're not right for him. They don't understand him like I do. As she removed the cling-film from the lemon mousse she told herself that no one would ever be able to cook for him like she could.

The second half of dinner was almost worse than the first. With Orlando's words almost choking her, Lindy asked Victoria, 'Have you heard of a novel called *Damage*? By someone called Josephine Hart, married to one of the Saatchis.'

'Funny you should ask, someone's just sent it to me for review. I do the odd bit of reviewing now and again.'

'And I had an advance proof for my foreign publishers. Isn't it wonderful? So tightly structured. I love that opening line, "There is an internal landscape, a geography of the soul." She's Irish, isn't she? Who are you reviewing it for?'

'One of the more downmarket women's magazines. And I'm afraid I don't agree with you about it, not at all.' Victoria shook her head vigorously and the Hissey diamonds sparkled. 'I think it's utter pretentious crap. It's a good yarn, I'll go along with that, but it's masquerading as literature and that really annoys me. "Geography of the soul." I ask you! I'd like to see someone take her to task about that line, it's so over the top.'

'Oh, they did,' said Lindy. 'I heard someone question her at this party the other night and she really acquitted herself very well. She said that the geographies that we are first introduced to as children sometimes never enter our souls but that once you do suddenly understand the dimensions of your own inner being then you'll know in a split second when you meet the only person on this earth who is on the same planet as you are psychologically.'

'What a load of baloney! Or is that what happened when you and Orlando bumped into each other on a Caribbean beach? You found the geography of your souls!'

'I didn't like the characters,' said Nona suddenly. 'If you ask me they were a bunch of spoiled, cold fish. I like my characters to be warm and likeable in a book.'

'You've read *Damage*?' Lindy was amazed.

'Of course I have. How could I talk about it if I hadn't read it? I've got a friend who's a film producer. He got his hands on it, thinks it'd make a fantastic movie.'

'I didn't realise you liked books.'

'Lindy ...' Orlando's tone was a warning.

'Because I'm a model? Is that it? I'm too stupid to read?

Oh, God, it's always the same. It's late. I'm quite drunk. I hardly know you, Lindy, but I'm too far gone to watch what I say. I hate being a model. You dismiss me and all models as being stupid but probably deep down you hate us, you women anyway, because you can't forgive us for being conscious of our beauty and using it to get rich, for forcing you to look at us in magazines. I bet you think all I have to do is arrive late at a studio and complain for the rest of the day – and, by the way, if I do arrive late in New York I have to pay for everyone I've kept waiting. Bet you didn't know that, did you? What's the point of trying to explain to you that I lucked into this modelling game because I photograph well and now I earn so much it's just plain hard to turn round and walk away? Can't you see I'm unfulfilled? All I ever get is "You're so cute, you're so great, you look terrific, let's go dancing." Life is one long party but don't ever tell me it's simple for me. I want an ordinary life. I want a husband and babies. I want to be like her.'

She nodded at Lily who, to everyone's relief, had fallen asleep at the table and was snoring quietly. After a while Orlando and Peter struggled upstairs with her and put her to bed. When they came down they had begun a long, rambling journey down Memory Lane back to their schooldays, which no one could understand. Lindy continued to extol the literary merits of various novels to Victoria who firmly debunked every one. Nona, finding herself excluded from both conversations, had turned her attentions to Bruno and slipped round the table to sit beside him. Her arm was round the back of his chair.

Victoria stood up abruptly.

'Orlando, Lindy, I'm sorry but it's time I went home.

It's way past my bedtime and I try to do a little work even on Sunday as you know. Will you forgive me if I run away?'

By now Nona was leaning heavily against Bruno. 'Bruno, you understand, don't you? You don't think I'm stupid?'

What happened next astounded everyone. In one swift movement, Bruno shunted Nona aside and on to the next chair. 'Victoria, I haven't had much of a chance to talk to you all evening. If I walk you back up to the house, would you give me a nightcap?'

They were out of the house in less than five minutes. Lindy saw them to the front door. As she was about to shut it she saw them stop and begin to devour each other with desperate, hungry kisses. For an instant Lindy wondered if they would fuck right there in the middle of the Bluebell Walk, and she shut the door quickly before she was caught spying on them.

The evening was over. Peter was on his way up to join Lily. Nona was stretched out on the sofa.

'Here, Nona,' Orlando threw her a blanket, 'wrap this around you. You might as well sleep down here. You go on up,' he told Lindy. 'I'll clear the table and tidy up in the kitchen. Go on now, I always do this, it's tradition here at The Cottage.'

'You and your bloody traditions,' murmured Lindy, still thinking about Bruno and Victoria. She glanced out of the landing window and saw no sign of them. Why had the sight of them kissing disturbed her so? Was it because they were so much older? Or was it the thought of Bruno about to make love to someone that excited her?

She could hear Orlando clattering around downstairs.

There was no sound from Peter and Lily's room. It was unlikely that Bruno would sleep in his tonight. Lindy undressed and removed her makeup. She slipped into bed and retrieved The Visitors' Book from its hiding place to record the evening's events before Orlando came upstairs and saw it.

Five minutes later she was asleep with the book still lying open on the bed beside her.

'Weird evening, wasn't it?'

How typical Bruno, thought Victoria. We step outside the door, he can't wait to give me a passionate kiss but as soon as he's done that he embarks on a perfectly normal conversation as if he were just a friend giving me a lift home. No 'Oh, God, Victoria, I've missed you so much', no walking up the Bluebell Walk in the moonlight kissing as they went, just business as usual.

It was almost as if he had never been away. When they had been conducting their affair at The Cottage he would be intense and desperate for her in the privacy of his bedroom but elsewhere he behaved so distantly that sometimes she had to stop and remind herself that they actually had been to bed together. Fuck like crazy but don't talk about it, that was Bruno's code of behaviour. If they talked about it that would make it real and then he might be forced to take it seriously and have to think about commitment to her. Out of the question.

'In what way was it a weird evening?'

'Well, she doesn't fit in, does she?'

'You mean Lindy? Don't you like her?'

'I do, actually. She interests me. At least she's different. What about you?'

'She came up to the house yesterday. She's not stupid, I'll give her that. I found her a bit pushy.'

'Pushy? Jesus, Victoria, you should see girls her age in New York. She's just driven and there's nothing wrong with that.'

'Yes, but is she smart? Her taste in books is a little pretentious. I notice you didn't give me any lift when we were talking about Josephine Hart.'

'I like Josephine. Why would I want to dump on her book? To be perfectly honest I haven't read it.'

I like Josephine. Victoria had forgotten this side of him. The grand, social, gregarious Bruno Manners, who knew everybody and thrived on it. It had always irritated her, this almost social-climbing aspect of him, name-dropping whenever the opportunity presented itself. The trouble was, he really did know everyone whose name he dropped and they clamoured for his company. What she had never been able to understand was why he had ever singled her out in the first place, she who had to be dragged to parties grumbling all the way.

'Whatever do she and Orlando have in common? They didn't seem to be getting on very well.'

'Sex, I should imagine. Usual thing. She kept looking at him to see if he was watching her, if he was impressed by what she was saying. She wants his approval.'

'But I don't think she has it. Didn't you hear them arguing in the kitchen and then she came out and made much more effort. I think you're wrong, Bruno. I don't think she cares enough about pleasing him.'

'Then it has to be sex – because there is something between them. He fancies her, he looks at her a lot. It's a sexual thing. They're not all lovey-dovey and silly but I bet they go at it like rabbits when they're alone.'

Like we used to do, thought Victoria. It takes one to know one. Is Orlando like Bruno? Betrays nothing in public but goes mad in private? But at least Orlando has committed himself to marriage even if he has done it a bit hastily.

'She doesn't look very sexy to me.'

'Oh, she is,' said Bruno quickly. 'You can tell.'

No, *you* can tell, thought Victoria, a tiny dart of jealousy stabbing her. 'But whatever she is I don't think she's right for Orlando. She strikes me as being quite hard and he's a softie underneath, he's terribly sensitive. He craves affection. I'm not sure she'll give it to him. Sex, maybe, but affection's something else.'

'Indulging in a bit of projection here, aren't we?' said Bruno, squeezing her arm above the elbow. 'You're the softie, as I recall. You're the one who needs affection.'

This was the moment, this was the opening he was giving her to turn towards him, lean into his embrace.

But she didn't. Why am I like this, wondered Victoria. I have some innate fear of rejection which stops me from making the first move. Even though he kissed me back there outside The Cottage I'm terrified to throw myself at him in case he didn't mean it, in case it was just for old times' sake. It's not my style to make the running. I want him to spell it out to me in black and white: 'Victoria, I've been waiting for the right time to come back to you and this is it. Let's go and talk about where we go from here.'

But that was crap. Bruno would never come out with anything like that and nor did she want him to. It was because he was master of the understatement that she had always admired him. His approach was subtle, gentle, non-threatening. Until it came to the crunch. Then he moved in quickly for the kill. Decisive. Controlling. Passionate. Just as he had been that first time at The Cottage. The trouble was that she had never known where she stood with him. He had declared love several times but had never followed it through. And he was not a man to be pushed. What would happen now?

Oh, well, nothing ventured ...

'Did I hear you say you were thinking of spending more time in England?'

'Did I say that?'

'I think so. Are you?'

'Why do you want to know?'

Now she remembered why she never made the first move, never said anything to imply they had an ongoing relationship. Typical Bruno. Immediately suspicious. Always answered her questions with one of his own.

'Are you going to be working over here? You've got a new book contract with a British publisher, haven't you?'

'Who told you that?'

There he went again. Hated it when she knew something about him that he hadn't told her himself.

'I think it was Lindy.'

'Have you two been talking about me?'

'Not really. It just came up.'

'What else did she tell you?'

'Bruno, calm down. Why are you always so paranoid about anybody knowing anything about you? Why do you always have to be so secretive?'

But she didn't have to ask. She knew why. Bruno had always been a control freak. Knowledge meant power so the less anybody knew about him the less power they had over him.

He gave her a shifty look. She knew he didn't like it when she challenged him but it was because she had had the spirit to do it that he'd been attracted to her in the first place. She wasn't a pushover. She was direct. She said exactly what she thought. She wasn't frightened of him. She knew all these things but they were getting her nowhere.

'OK, here we are, end of the Bluebell Walk. There's Laybridge. Thanks for walking me home. I expect I'll see you tomorrow. I've got a lot of work to do but maybe I'll pop down for tea or something during the afternoon.'

She waited. She had always known how to programme Bruno if she had to. He would have wanted to be the one to say something like 'Well, I'll leave you now. There's Laybridge. I don't need to see you to the door, do I?' thus leaving her disappointed and frustrated that he wasn't taking things any further. Well, she had beaten him to it.

And it worked.

'Trying to brush me off, are you? Don't you want to ask me in?' Victoria knew exactly what was running through his mind. He was worried. Why was she stopping here? Had he done something to upset her? Bruno couldn't bear anyone to be angry with him.

They'd never made love at Laybridge before. It had been Hugh's domain when he'd been alive. Victoria poured Bruno a large Armagnac. He would be twitchy. Her house. Not his territory. He wouldn't like it. But he wouldn't want to leave her. She didn't turn on the lights in her bedroom, just led him by the hand until they reached her bed. She undressed completely and slipped between the sheets. He took off his sweater and trousers and joined her, still in his underpants. He drew her into his arms and held her so tight, it was painful. She could feel his erection straining against her thigh.

'I've missed you so much,' he said, through gritted teeth into her hair so that she barely heard it.

'You could have phoned or written. You knew where to find me.' She spoke into the darkness.

'You were the one who sent me away.'

Bruno hadn't changed. He had always turned things round so that whatever happened it had been her responsibility. He hadn't ended it. She had sent him away. If she wanted it to start up again in earnest she was going to have to be the one to engineer it.

As he shifted himself to enter her for the first time in seven years, she was delighted to find herself accepting him into her body as if it had been seven days since they had last made love. He remembered everything about her, how she liked to be brought almost to a climax, then to slow down for a second to share a moment with him before she finally came. He didn't speak. He never had. His love-making was so affectionate and patient that words weren't necessary. In sex Bruno had always dropped his suspicious nature, his posturing. In sex Victoria had always known she had the real Bruno and here at least nothing had changed.

But afterwards, while he slept beside her, she found herself asking, Why me? Why do I have to be the one to make all the running? I'm too old for all these games. I'm not going to beg. If Bruno wants me, he's going to have to show me. He's going to have to come right out and ask me to be with him.

Lindy sat up in alarm as someone came crashing into the room in the middle of the night. The Visitors' Book fell off the bed when she glanced at the luminous clock and saw the time was five thirty. Peter McGill stood there in his pyjamas.

'Lindy, the phone. Where is it? Where's Orlando? What's the number of the local hospital? Lily's having the baby. Her waters have broken. I'll drive her in. Can you call and tell them we're coming?'

Lindy saw that Orlando wasn't in bed with her. She dialled 999 and asked for an ambulance, then changed her mind and asked for directions to Salisbury Hospital. She dressed quickly and went to help Peter shepherd Lily downstairs.

Lily was terrified. 'I haven't packed. My overnight case is in London. It's all ready and now I won't be able to use it. Peter, will you go to London to get it?'

'Not tonight, Lily.'

'I'm frightened. I want Baby to come peacefully. Peter, it's not how we planned. What if something goes wrong?'

'Nothing's going to go wrong. I'm going to be with you.'

'And Lindy?'

'And Lindy too. Lindy, you'll come with us, won't you?'

'Yes, of course, if you want me to,' said Lindy, trying not to sound thrown. 'You go out to the car. I'll just grab my coat.'

As she was getting it out of the hall cupboard she heard

sounds coming from the sitting room. Then she peered through the darkness. First she saw clothes strewn all over the floor and then, as she struggled sleepily to get her arms into the sleeves of her coat, she saw Orlando and Nona lying together on the sofa.

'Lily's having her baby,' was all she could think to say before she rushed out of the house.

PART THREE

15

Victoria had always been crabby and prone to flashes of exasperation when forced to deal with a prosaic mind. She was well aware of the devastating effect her bite could have on perfectly harmless people who were often trying their best to help her. As she grew older she tried to be more tolerant, to soften her tone. Only when she had not had enough sleep the night before did she resort to snarling down the telephone.

'Beeson's,' drawled Pat, the receptionist who had been on the switchboard at Victoria's publishers for over thirty years and always sounded as if she were furious with you for disturbing her. This rather amused Victoria, who was aware that Pat knew absolutely everything there was to know about anyone connected with Beeson's.

'Morning, Pat. How are you? Is Toby in yet?'

'My daughter's getting a divorce. He wants the stereo and the caravan but she's standing her ground. I'll try for you, Mrs Hissey.'

Pat's life put *Coronation Street* in the shade and she could always be relied on to supply some tantalizing snippet about it before putting a caller through. Victoria smiled. She had not even had to say who she was. But it was from here on that she would have to watch herself.

'Hello. Toby Marriott's office. Judy speaking. How may I help you?'

Yet another new voice in Toby's office. A bad sign. What had happened to 'Toby Marriott's office. Sally speaking. How may I help you?'

'I suppose he's not in yet?'

'I'm sorry? Toby Marriott's office. Judy speaking. How may I help you?'

Victoria's blood began to simmer. People in offices didn't sound like human beings any more. They sounded like machines. They were all brainwashed into speaking half a dozen sentences over and over again and if they had to deviate in any way they lost the plot.

'Is he there? Can I speak to Toby?'

'Who may I say is calling?'

It was the 'May I say' that enraged Victoria. Why couldn't the girl just ask 'Who's calling?' Victoria was tempted to say, 'No, you may not,' and see what happened.

'Victoria Hissey.'

'Victoria ... Could you repeat your last name for me please.'

I've only been a Beeson's author for eleven years, why on earth should she know who I am? Victoria was beginning to lose it.

'Victoria. Like the Queen.'

'Yes, I know, the pub in *EastEnders*. Do you watch it, Victoria?'

Victoria knew she was old-fashioned but she detested unwarranted familiarity, especially in the young.

'Could you put me through to Toby if it's not too much trouble ...' Victoria searched for the name '... please, er, Judy.'

'Absolutely.'

There was a silence. Then: 'I'm afraid he's just stepped away from his desk.'

'Well, will you please ask him to step right back and when he has made that infinitesimal leap perhaps he could find it in himself to call me.'

Victoria put down the phone.

'Why don't you go the whole hog and stamp your foot? Really, Vicky, if you could only hear yourself sometimes. Oh, darling, don't cry. What's the matter? Why do you always get like this before your books are published? God knows, you've been through it enough times.'

Jessica Nesbit put her arm around Victoria and patted her back. She had returned to England for her father's funeral and now that it was all over she had come to Laybridge ostensibly for a few days' rest before going back to New York but the real reason was to check out Victoria. Victoria had not visited New York as usual that spring, nor had she written Jess anything more than a scribbled note inside a Christmas card since they had last spoken on the telephone over a year ago on the night when Victoria had been about to see Bruno again.

Jess had been at Laybridge for twenty-four hours and Victoria had not mentioned him once. Jess knew her friend of more than twenty years. Victoria looked wonderful. She was taking care with her appearance, something she normally neglected. Yet she was edgy and distracted. It didn't add up.

'I'm sorry, Jess. I know I've always been like this and I do try to be more agreeable but I just can't stand all these morons who answer the phones in offices these days. I tried to leave a message for someone at a hotel the other day and they said, "I'll pass you to her voice mail."

Whatever happened to concierges, or even Front Desks? It's the same in restaurants and on trains and planes. They will add the words "at all" to everything they say. "Coffee for you at all, Madam?" "Will you be checking any luggage at all?" Somewhere there's some dreadful phrase book being handed out on training courses with all these superfluous bits and pieces to be tagged on to anything they say. And whenever you ask them to do something they always say without fail, "No problem," and then they go and fuck it up.'

'Vicky, it's not them, it's you,' Jessica said gently. 'You're absolutely right. There are a number of standard expressions that people use over and over again. There always will be but you shouldn't let it get to you like this. You're becoming an irascible old bat, way before your time. If you're like this now, what are you going to be like in ten years' time? Why do you need to see your editor anyway? If the book's finished and in the shops what do you want with him?'

'I have to go in and discuss my idea for the next book. I want to change direction. This book about the Hisseys and Charles II is the last historical novel I shall be doing. In the old days with my old editor it would have been so simple. I would have called and spoken to his secretary Mary and discussed with her the best way to break the news to him, whether it would be better to do it over tea at the Ritz or lunch at the Tate Gallery. We would have had quite a laugh about it. Now, with Toby, all I get is "he's stepped away from his desk" as if he were prancing about with the Royal Ballet. And, of course, even though I don't give a damn about this wretched historical novel I'm nervous about its reception on publication. Supposing it does terribly well and they want me to go on with the same sort of thing? Or suppose it does terribly badly and they don't want me at all any more? Take no notice of me, Jess, I'm just worried about the book, that's all.'

She's lying, thought Jess. I wonder why.

When the phone rang Victoria disappeared into her bedroom to answer it instead of taking the call in front of Jess.

She reached for the receiver uttering a silent mantra: Please let it be Bruno, please let it be Bruno, please let it be Bruno, please let it …

'Victoria, it's Toby. I'm so sorry I wasn't available to take your call. I'd just stepped away from my desk …'

It wasn't just the Judys and Sallys of this world, thought Victoria. In the eighteen months since he had been her editor, she had watched Toby Marriott turn into a similar kind of management clone, talking less and less about books and writing, and more and more about sales figures and marketing plans. She outlined briefly her plans to abandon historical fiction and concentrate on contemporary novels from now on and then braced herself for the inevitable moment when he would tell her he had a 'window' for lunch in six weeks' time to discuss everything. Yet Victoria had decided long before Jessica's words of warning that she had to get a grip on herself. Times had changed, and they changed for the young not the old. Not that she was old, just getting on a bit and if she wanted to go on being – what was it Toby called it? a player? – then she had to make compromises and try to take seriously the people twenty years her junior who were in charge of her career. The last thing she needed was for them to brand her a dinosaur.

'You will bury yourself in the country – what do you expect?' Bruno goaded her at every opportunity. 'Get a place in London, go about a bit, be seen in all the right places, heighten your profile, that's what it's all about.'

Bruno had a point. Toby was always going on about her profile. So far, she had got away with it by setting all her books in Laybridge where she lived but if she changed direction now and wrote a contemporary novel, set God knows where, would that wreak havoc with her precious profile?

Bruno hadn't been down to Laybridge for nearly two months and he only telephoned intermittently. Victoria knew why. His book, the Balkans thriller, was due to be published a week ahead of hers. He was in the process of doing pre-publication interviews. It was make or break time. He didn't have a second for her. She knew exactly what his answer would be if she reproached him for not calling. It was always the same.

'For Christ's sake, Victoria, I love you because you're the one person I feel I don't have to call, don't you see? You make no demands on me. I've got people on my back, morning noon and night. I don't want to feel I've got to call you too. I want to know I can call you when I want to, don't you see?'

Don't you see? That was what he always said. She could hear his voice pleading, his eyes beseeching her with the silent words: Don't cause trouble for me, don't make waves, be good-natured, uncomplaining, loving, sexy Victoria and you can have me whenever I've got time for you.

Never mind about the kind and gentle vet who had recently moved into the area and taken over the Laybridge practice. His wife had died of leukaemia five years earlier, his children were at university and he was rattling around in a beautiful rectory the other side of Salisbury. He could rattle all he liked, as far as Victoria was concerned. She didn't find him remotely sexy. He was too sweet to her. Poor bloke. Too lazy to accept his invitation to dine in a restaurant, she had asked him instead to a cosy supper at Laybridge, cooked by Peg, without realising that she was giving him the wrong idea about her intentions. She had chucked him out by eleven without so much as a goodnight kiss. When he called again, she suggested he come over and watch *Inspector Morse* with another Peg-prepared meal on trays on their knees. And when he bashfully admitted to having read all her books, she demanded perversely to know what he was doing reading romantic historical novels for women.

Yet still he telephoned – and Bruno didn't.

'Darling, there's the sweetest little boy down there. He's almost still a baby and I can't see anyone with him. Ought we to go down and investigate?'

When Victoria returned from the phone Jess was looking out of the window. Victoria joined her and watched little Pepper McGill take a few faltering steps up the south lawn and knew she should be worrying about him rather than about Bruno. He sneezed and fell over, sneezed again and shook his head. He was always sneezing and there was no apparent explanation for it. It had earned him his nickname: the first time he'd done it someone had been sprinkling black pepper over their scrambled eggs and they had all assumed that that was what had made him sneeze. Victoria was glad in a way. It was a sweet name:

Pepper. He'd been christened Peter, after his father, and Lily had been threatening to call him Peter Junior, or just Junior, which would have been irritating. As it was, he was Pepper and it suited him.

The sneezing might be something of a joke but Victoria was convinced that it masked something more serious and possibly unconnected.

'Oh, that's Pepper,' she said. 'You remember me talking about Peter McGill, Orlando's best friend? Well, he and his wife Lily had a baby and there he is, little Pepper, so called because he sneezes a lot. I worship him unashamedly. I suppose I sort of think of him as my grandson even though he's no relation whatsoever and it doesn't look as if ...'

'As if what? Come on, Victoria, what were you going to say?'

'I was going to say it doesn't look as if Orlando and Lindy are going to have any children but that's being a little impatient on my part. They've only been married for just over a year.'

'Is Orlando at The Cottage this weekend?'

'Yes, Lily and Peter are staying with him. They all came down this morning. Lily's bringing Pepper to tea.'

'Oh, great! Will Lindy come too? I'm longing to meet her, after all you've said.'

'Lindy isn't there. She's staying in London for the weekend. Oh, look, there's Lily running after Pepper.'

'Naughty little monkey, isn't he?' Jess observed. 'She's shouting so loud at him even I can hear it but he isn't even turning his head.'

'I know.'

'Vicky, what is it? You look so worried.'

'You can yell his name while you're standing right beside him but he takes absolutely no notice. He only responds if you stand in front of him or touch him.'

'Is he talking?'

'No.'

'He's how old? A year? Hasn't anybody done anything about it?'

'About what?'

'Vicky, for heaven's sake, you're so clueless sometimes where children are concerned – just because you don't have any of your own. If a child doesn't start babbling, however incoherently, as it approaches its first birthday and if it doesn't jump or turn towards any kind of loud sound can't you work out for yourself what the problem might be? I'm talking about deafness.'

'Oh, no! Oh, Jess, please, no. How do you know about this?'

'I've had children of my own, remember? It's one of the things you look for if you've read all the books. And now is probably as good a time as any to tell you. I've been having an affair for the last six months with, don't laugh, a paediatrician.'

'The one you took Josh to that time I was in such a panic about Bruno.'

'I wondered when you'd get around to saying his name.'

'Not now, Jess, please. We were talking about Pepper. I can't believe what you've just said.'

'Well, it may be nothing. I'll sound out Lily this afternoon over tea.'

'Oh, no, I couldn't possibly interfere ...'

'Vicky, why don't you listen to what I say once in a

while? I said I'll sound her out. You don't have to do a thing.'

Victoria tried hard not to be too critical of other women's appearance but she could not help comparing Jess's confident elegant look unfavourably with Lily's scruffy washed-out clothes. Jess's blonde hair, expertly high-lighted, was tied back off her face, a brilliant white T-shirt could be glimpsed at the top of her navy Gap sweatshirt and her jeans were clean and crisp. Lily was wearing a grey T-shirt that had once been white and a faded floral skirt with an elasticated top. She still looked pregnant except that while her skin had glowed throughout her pregnancy now it was pale and greasy-looking, and she had dark circles under eyes.

What made it worse, Victoria was forced to admit, was that Lily was the kind of mother who was obsessed about her child. Everything focused around Pepper. Lily did not listen to anything anyone said to her unless they were talking about him. In the middle of a conversation she would say, 'Oh, do look, Pepper's doing such and such …' It was as if she no longer had a role of her own in life: she had become an extension of her son.

Which made Jess's sudden attack all the more brutal.

'Lily, I don't want to worry you but have you by any chance been having a problem with Pepper's hearing?'

Lily's reaction was instantly defensive. 'How did you know? You haven't told anyone, have you?' and she went on, without waiting for an answer, 'At first I thought it was glue ear, poor little Pepper, I thought he was too young for the doctors to do anything about it. But he makes this awful high-pitched shrieking noise. I don't know what to do. There's no history of deafness in my family or in Peter's. He *can't* be deaf. All that music I played to him when he was in my womb.'

To Victoria's horror, Lily began to weep. It was eerie watching the mother sobbing loudly while her child sat beside her oblivious of the sound. Suddenly Victoria longed for the usual litany of Pepper's bowel movements with which Lily regaled them at frequent intervals. Anything was better than this.

'Is Peter supportive?' asked Jessica.

'Peter doesn't know. Oh, he might suspect something's wrong. He's noticed the lack of response from Pepper. The irony of it. There's me going on about how wonderful, how brilliant, how marvellous, how advanced our child is – oh, yes, I know it irritates you, I'm not completely insensitive, Victoria, whatever you may think – and all the time Pepper's displaying hardly any of the normal traits in a child his age.'

'He's not retarded,' protested Victoria.

'No. He's deaf. There, I've said it.'

'You do have to tell Peter all about it. You know that, don't you? What about when you took Pepper for his standard developmental check? When was it? You told me he had to have one when he was about eight months? What happened then?'

'He passed most of the hearing tests first because he had a cold and then because he's so visual he turned to look at the doctor and she thought he'd heard her. I kept quiet and I just kept hoping.'

'You mean you've done nothing about it?'

'I've spent hours making different noises to him. I really do believe there's some response.'

'Lily, you have to take him for more tests and the sooner the better. And you must tell Peter. If you don't I will,' Victoria warned her. And I imagined I had problems, she thought, as Lily nodded miserably. What is Bruno Manners, Invisible Man, compared with having a deaf child?

16

Lindy wasn't a great one for introspection. Soul-searching and exploring the inner self didn't agree with her, because she never much cared for what she found. What made it worse was that now she was having to admit to failure, something she had vowed she would never have to do.

Not as far as her work was concerned. In fact, her business was growing all the time. Only this week an eccentric French publisher had materialised from nowhere, demanding that she become his London scout. He was sufficiently obsessed to go so far as to have her handwriting analysed in the hope that it would reveal something about her that would enable him to snare her. He had even sent her the graphological report, which had arrived in the mail that morning as Orlando was leaving for The Cottage.

'The handwriting shows energy and will-power. She is a busy person, optimistic, enthusiastic, restless and ambitious with something of a fighting spirit.'

'You can say that again,' Lindy muttered. Talk about fighting spirit, it seemed to be the only thing left between her and Orlando.

'She is a leader and enjoys organizing and supervising, sometimes in a manner that doesn't always meet with popularity.'

Spot on! Over the past year she had organised every-thing for their weekends at The Cottage, had supervised the smooth running of the place so that their guests were comfortable and the meals were available whenever anyone wanted them, she had pandered to Orlando's every need yet now, when she felt she had earned the right to devote more time to her business, he had thrown a fit. As a result of their latest quarrel, she had dug in her heels and refused to go down to The Cottage. Let him try organising everything for himself for a change, she had plenty of work to catch up on here in London. Of course she knew exactly what would happen. Peter and Lily were going down and Lily would be in her element, rushing around and taking charge. And there was always Rose, hovering in the background, ministering to everyone's needs. Poor Rose. Lindy felt bad about the way she had snapped at her down the telephone.

'I'm just not coming down this weekend, Rose. That's all there is to it. I've got work to do here in London and I'll welcome the peace and quiet to get on with it while Orlando's out of the house. Give them whatever they want to eat but leave me out of it. Take your instructions from Orlando.'

'Will you be down next weekend?' Rose sounded bewildered.

'I haven't the faintest idea.'

It was the truth. Lindy had no idea what would happen.

She would soon be thirty and what did she have to show for it? Plenty on the career side. A less satisfactory picture, if she were honest, on the personal side. Her domestic life was not as she had envisaged it. She thought she loved Orlando but she wasn't entirely sure she loved herself. Eighteen months ago she had not had a clue who the real Lindy was. She had had this picture in her head of an imaginary woman, someone who thought she could bury her background like an ostrich and step calmly into a new life where all her problems would be over. Yet what she had not bargained for was that while Orlando might be sexy and affectionate and fun to fool around with, he was also one of life's romantics, a dreamer, a procrastinator – at times he was even somewhat other-worldly. Whereas she, Lindy, was relentlessly driven. The charming laid-back Orlando she had encountered on a Caribbean beach was just as laid back at home in London, and his easy-going inertia clashed daily with Lindy's frayed, nervous energy. She didn't know the meaning of relaxation but Orlando was a master of the art and it drove her mad.

Then there was the question of Orlando's friends. Lindy had envisaged hostessing the kind of chic media dinner parties she had read about in glossy magazines. The people Orlando seemed to want to invite to their house were non-threatening, bordering on the cosy. If she were pinned to the wall she'd have to say they were a bunch of losers. OK, they were nice, they were witty, they were charming, and they were unfailingly polite to her. But they had no edge. More to the point, they didn't add up to a list of useful contacts: they weren't going to get her anywhere. So when Orlando mentioned that the McGills were coming down to The Cottage yet again, Lindy had announced she would be staying in London.

'I haven't asked any models,' said Orlando. It was an old joke and a dangerous one. He had had a hard time explaining what he had been doing on the night that Lily had had her baby.

'She was kissing me. I wasn't kissing her,' he had protested, when Lindy had challenged him the next morning. Lindy had waited at the hospital in Salisbury long after Peter had told her to go home. As she had sat with him she imagined Orlando and Nona back at The Cottage, going upstairs hand in hand, creeping into Nona's room, closing the door, locking it and ...

Of course when she had arrived back at The Cottage Orlando was dead to the world, fast asleep in their bed. Lindy had propped herself up against the pillows and waited to tackle him when he woke up.

'She just wanted to confide in me about how worried she was about the way her career was going. Or rather wasn't going. She's over thirty. She's older than you are. There's not a lot of work around for girls that age. I'm in the business, I'm a photographers' agent, I have contacts. She thought I might be able to help.'

'Which involved taking off most of her clothes and sticking her tongue half-way down your throat?'

'That's exactly it. She was doing the sticking and the taking off of clothes. Didn't you notice that I was still fully clothed? She'd had a hell of a lot to drink. She didn't know what she was doing.'

'Just as I can't see a large pig flying above my head as you say that.'

'Well, I'm sorry. OK? I promise it won't happen again.'

It won't happen again. Why did he always have to put her in the position of an irascible schoolteacher ticking him off for being a naughty little boy? Why was she the one who always had to take responsibility? Because if she didn't, their life would be a shambles. Orlando was barely capable of running a bath without disaster, let alone a weekend in the country.

'I managed perfectly well before I married you,' he told her, whenever she complained of having to do everything herself.

'That's because you had Rose Farley and Lily McGill running after you all the time.'

'No, it's because I spent weekends as I wanted to spend them. They weren't the military operations you've turned them into.'

'Well, then, fine, you can go back to the old days because I'm not coming down this weekend. Let's see what a mess you get into.'

The trouble was, Lindy knew he wouldn't get into a mess. Or, rather, he wouldn't think he was a mess. He would just think he was enjoying himself. It would only be regarded as a mess if she were there. She was the one who was paranoid about everything being organised down to the last detail. She couldn't help it.

For the past few weeks she had begun to wake up early. She didn't want to. She was working flat out and she needed the sleep. But she couldn't sleep past six, sometimes waking as early as five thirty. Every morning she lay there beside Orlando and felt more lonely than she ever had before she was married, an isolation far exceeding that which she had experienced as a child. Every morning she found herself reaching for The Visitors' Book hidden under a pile of *World of Interiors* on the bottom shelf of her bedside table, and scribbling away in it. It was so cathartic. She could pour out on to the page all the questions that tumbled around in her head and gradually her mind began to empty. This was the closest she ever came to relaxing.

Why am I such an obsessive? Why do I find it so intolerable when other people leave things to run their course rather than organizing everything in advance? Why is it that the minute I achieve something I don't want it any more? What on earth do I really want? I didn't want my family, least of all my mother. Why am I so ashamed of my background? In the eyes of most people it's a perfectly respectable background yet I know it isn't what I want for myself. Why don't I love my mother? I've done all right, I've proved myself and yet over and over again I wish I'd had a mother I could have been proud of. She's a phone call away, growing old and frail. I could ring her every week to find out how she is but I don't. Why not? Because I just don't care? Does that make me a horrible person? I am not a horrible person. I know I'm not. And nor is my mother. And why do I have such a hopeless husband? Yet he isn't hopeless, not to most people. Why am I so judgemental? Why do I always feel so much stronger than these people? How am I going to learn to compromise and adapt to Orlando's devil-may-care attitude? Because if I don't our marriage will founder.

Lindy dreaded to think what anyone who read her ramblings might think of her. It wasn't as if she ever came up with any answers but somehow just writing down the questions, admitting them before the day began, gave her courage. She knew she was paranoid about her image, about making a success of herself but, then, so were loads of people, weren't they?

Funnily enough, it was her paranoia that made her so good at her job. The foreign-rights scouting world was a small one. There was only a handful of scouts in London and they were all fiercely competitive. Bootleg typescripts slipped to them under the table by editors whose friendship they had cultivated were the scouts' currency.

Lindy's first big break as a scout had come with a writer called Leah Warden. Very few people in England had ever heard of her: she wrote historical novels focusing on the medical profession and set in America. Her books had offputting titles like *The Obstetrician* or *The Mind Reader*. Leah Warden's début novel had been among the first manuscripts Lindy had recommended to her German publishers, Kieler. Her competitors all took one look at the manuscript of *The Mind Reader* and dismissed it as boring, old-fashioned and not remotely commercial. Kieler had snapped it up cheap. Now, five years later, the book was still floating about somewhere on the German bestseller lists and Kieler had sold over 600,000 hardback copies and had become the most respected German publisher with the biggest chequebook. As their scout, Lindy had a powerful calling card. But in the beginning it had been rough. Time and time again she found herself being summoned by snooty literary publishers, who insisted she came in at ten thirty on the dot then left her sitting on their overstuffed sofas for twenty minutes before they finally appeared and wittered on about some useless academic no-hoper that happened to be their great passion.

Still her perseverance had been rewarded. Now Kieler paid her £30,000 a year to tip them off and her Italians rather less. They weren't the most prestigious publishers in Italy and Lindy didn't get on with their editor-in-chief, who was fat and balding and exceptionally lazy. He reminded Lindy of a slug and he never offered enough money for the big books so no one took him seriously any more. Lindy was contemplating dropping her Italians. She had a Japanese and a Dutch publisher, who both wanted the top quality end of commercial fiction. Kieler wanted literary and commercial fiction, both of which Lindy enjoyed. Her problem, as far as they were concerned, was their passion for popular science, and anything esoteric, philosophical or even mystical for some weird New Age list they had started. Lindy hadn't a clue about this area and it was for this reason that she had recently hired Oscar.

Oscar and Delia ran her office. Orlando might think she ran it herself but she spent most of her time out of it, seeing publishers and agents, or occasionally visiting her clients abroad, and she left the day-to-day administration to Oscar and Delia, especially Delia. Lindy knew perfectly well that Delia would never make a good scout if she chose to go off on her own. Poor Delia, she just didn't get it. She didn't understand that you had to be a good judge of people and what their particular tastes were. She thought you read something, wrote down what it was and bunged it off. But when it came to keeping records, an essential element of scouting, Delia was a star.

As far as the actual scouting was concerned, Oscar showed more promise but his taste was so weird and off the wall that he was only useful when it came to books most people couldn't begin to understand. But Lindy had spotted him and used that quality to supply Kieler with the best possible product for their new list.

It was Oscar who had developed Lindy's highly sophisticated database through which she could access anything by subject, author, literary agent, editor, date of publication – whatever she wanted to know Oscar had it stored somewhere. It was Delia who collated all the information that came in each week and sent off a weekly round-robin newsletter to all their clients. It was a necessary chore and a boring one, but Lindy made sure that Delia thought she had the most important job of all.

Lindy's favourite editor at Kieler in Berlin was Luzie Springer. Luzie was in her fifties and epitomised the three Ks – *Kinder, Kirche, Küche* (children, church, kitchen) – of the old style German *hausfrau*. Yet when it came to business she was also the shrewdest publisher at Kieler. It was Luzie who had seen the potential of Leah Warden in Germany, and now Lindy had been able to persuade her to try to repeat this success story with another writer of historical novels: Victoria Hissey. Victoria's first novel, which had been out of print for years in England, had been on sale in Germany for nearly two weeks. Lindy was anxious to know how it was selling so she phoned the office.

'Oscar's called in sick. Again. He's pretty pathetic, Lindy. He's only got a sniffle. Why do men always make such a fuss?'

She's right, men are terrible hypochondriacs, thought Lindy, but you're the expert when it comes to making a fuss, Delia dear.

'Delia, have we heard anything from Luzie in Berlin? About Victoria Hissey?'

'Yes, a fax came through this morning. She will write in German, silly cow, so I can't understand a word. But it's very short. I think I can read it to you if you'll forgive my pronunciation. It says: "Victoria, *Nummer 5 diese Woche*." What's that mean?'

'It means Victoria is number five on the bestseller list in Germany. It means she's going to be a huge, huge hit. In fact, it's completely unbelievably wonderful.'

'Oh, that's nice,' said Delia, unmoved. 'Can I have an extra hour at lunch-time to go shopping?'

That was typical Delia. She always slipped in some outrageous request when Lindy was on a high after she'd received good news. But what the hell? The sooner she got Delia off the phone the sooner she could call Victoria and tell her she was about to become a star in Germany.

She stopped in the middle of dialling Victoria's number. She would have to explain to Victoria why she wasn't down there for the weekend. Victoria was no fool. She would become suspicious about Lindy's marriage, if she wasn't already. Lindy dialled another number instead.

'Can I speak to Hilary Coleridge, please?'

Lindy didn't especially like Hilary Coleridge, who was a rather self-important executive editor at one of the big publishing corporations. Ever since she had risen to grand heights and been given that title she had not touched a manuscript but she was privy to a lot of publishing gossip and, since a crucial part of Lindy's job was to keep her ear to the ground, a weekly call to Hilary was part of her routine.

'What's going on? It's very quiet at the moment, isn't it?' Lindy asked hopefully. She hadn't heard of any exciting books being commissioned in the last week but there was always the chance that her rival scouts were at that very moment busy xeroxing manuscripts of hot properties she knew nothing about. It was the eternal scout's nightmare: had she missed out on something?

'Oh, it's a terrible time at the moment,' confirmed Hilary, to Lindy's relief. 'Simply nothing worth reading is coming in. But have you heard the news about Bruno Manners's new book?'

'The one that's just come out? It's had some rather bad reviews so far.'

'The reviews over here are nothing compared to the stinkers he's been getting in the States,' crowed Hilary. Her conglomerate didn't publish Bruno. 'I heard last night that his American publishers have dropped him. They've refused to sign a new contract with him. His agent over there is trying to hawk him around town to get a new contract in New York but his sales have gone right down and no one wants to know. He's dead in the water. I wonder what Caroline Calder will do over here.'

'Doesn't she have a two-book contract?' Lindy pointed out.

'Bet she's regretting it.' Lindy could almost hear Hilary rubbing her hands in glee. 'Maybe they'll get rid of the old bag. They need some new blood at that place. Maybe I'd better investigate ... Oh, and there's trouble brewing at Beeson's with Victoria Hissey.'

Does she know there's any connection between Bruno and Victoria, Lindy wondered. Is she sounding me out, trying to coax a bit of scandal out of me?

'What's up?'

'She called Toby Marriott this morning – you know what a motormouth he is, can't resist telling the world everything everyone's said to him. Well, apparently she wants to change direction, write a contemporary novel. Poor old Beeson's wouldn't know what to do with her if she suddenly turned into Jilly Cooper or Penny Vincenzi. They think they're in line with the rest of us when it comes to marketing but, really, they haven't got a clue. I'm wondering whether I should try and poach her. Who's her agent?'

Typical, thought Lindy. Just as I'm about to make Victoria a success in Germany she changes direction and Kieler probably won't want her any more. And what about Bruno? It didn't sound like anybody wanted him anywhere in the world. Lindy wondered if Victoria knew about Bruno's imminent decline.

'Anyway,' continued Hilary, 'I heard Beeson's were up for sale. Don't your German lot, Kieler, already have a thirty per cent stake in them? It's only a matter of time. Bye bye, Beeson's, by the end of the year, I'd say.'

I wonder what Hilary would say if she knew I was off to lunch today with the editor-in-chief of an American publisher who's thinking of buying Beeson's, Lindy asked herself with not a little satisfaction as she hung up. Rubinstein and Rose had contacted her because they were looking for a London scout. They had asked in the initial interviews conducted in the lobby of the Connaught Hotel what she thought about Beeson's. Did she have good contacts there? I should tell Victoria what's going on, thought Lindy, for the umpteenth time. It might all affect her future. She's Orlando's godmother. I owe it to her.

When she came back from lunch, Lindy had more good news for Victoria. On hearing that Kieler were about to make Victoria a bestseller, Charlie Rose, of Rubinstein and Rose, had begun to show interest.

'Maybe the goddamned historical novel's coming back,' he told Lindy. 'Maybe we should give it a whirl with old Vicky in the US.'

'Maybe you should,' Lindy had told him, carefully omitting to mention that Victoria might be changing direction in her writing.

I'd better tell Victoria what's going on, Lindy told

herself firmly, and dialled Laybridge. She was somewhat thrown when Peg answered. 'Mrs Hissey's gone for a walk in the gardens. She was a little upset after Mr Bruno called. What shall I tell her when she gets back?'

'Tell her I've got some good news for her, would you, Peg?'

'And will there be any message for your husband? I understand you're too busy to come down this weekend.'

'None whatsoever, thank you, Peg.' Nosy old bat. Lindy felt a momentary pang of guilt about Orlando having to face all the gossip that would be spread as a result of her non-appearance. Well, tough. And as for Peg's indiscretion about Victoria being upset by Bruno's call, that was outrageous. All the same Lindy couldn't help wondering what Bruno had said.

Tears of rage blinded Victoria as she trod carelessly over the carpet of creeping thyme in the herb garden. If she hadn't been in such a state about Bruno she would have paid more heed to Peg's precious culinary herbs, her sage, her chives and her sweet cicely, but she tramped on regardless. Her patience had finally run out and she had called Bruno all over London until she reached him. She should never have done it. He was in a foul mood. No, he didn't want to come anywhere near Laybridge. Didn't she understand what a crisis he was having with his career? The Americans were behaving like complete arseholes just because he'd had a few unfortunate reviews. The Brits were wimps: they'd got his book out in such ludicrously small quantities he couldn't find it in a single bookshop. His publicist was a scumbag who hadn't even got him on any talk shows.

'Shall I come up to London to be with you?' Victoria asked, knowing the response she would get.

'What on earth would be the bloody point of that? What help would you be? You might as well stay buried in the country.' Where you belong, were the unspoken words hanging on the end of his sentence.

It was always the same. These days he seemed to have forgotten that she, too, was a writer, and on the rare occasions when he remembered there was always an oblique reference to her paltry advance or her low profile. He refused to take her career seriously any more but she knew she would have to live through every detail of his current problems. She realised that she had begun to hope his book did well not because she loved Bruno but because it would mean their relationship would go more smoothly.

Victoria stepped on yet another plant and this time guilt provoked her to look up. Was that Peg standing at the window? No, the figure was too tall. It must be Jessica. Victoria recalled Jess's words earlier in the day, admonishing her not to overreact to the management style of the young. Here she was again, Victoria reflected, overreacting to Bruno. Why did she allow herself to play such a passive role? And why did she then feel so angry and frustrated when he walked all over her? If she could take a firm line with the Toby Marriotts of this world then there was absolutely no reason why she shouldn't make an effort to strengthen her position with Bruno.

He might not like it. He might not even notice. It wasn't as if she even saw him that much any more. But from now on Victoria resolved to get on with her own life and her career and to devote considerably less time to worrying about Bruno, though it would, she knew, be easier said than done.

She was so preoccupied that she didn't notice the body lying among the lavender bushes until she almost fell over it. She almost laughed. Here she was, feeling guilty about treading on Peg's precious herbs, when she'd caught Harold Farley indulging in a mid-afternoon kip lying on top of them.

As Victoria stepped over him she noticed that his eyes were open. It was a few seconds before it dawned on her that he was dead.

17

Peg was in a state. She had a funeral to arrange but that wasn't the only cause of her anguish although, as usual, she blamed it on Harold Farley.

She talked to Harold as if he were still alive instead of lying frozen in the morgue waiting for someone to do something about him. She had always used him as her sounding board when she wanted to let off steam, and she wasn't going to stop now. When Charlie had been alive she had yelled at him, even though he was invariably too drunk to heed her rantings. On his death she had transferred her exasperation to her father-in-law, although towards the end he was too old and deaf to hear. At home only Rose escaped Peg's caustic tongue and that was because Peg knew when she'd met her match. If she attacked Rose, Rose would turn on her and strike back.

Up at Laybridge, Peg had trained herself never to voice her worries. Instead, while she cooked she carried on long conversations inside her head. 'You pick your moments, don't you, Harold Farley? You always pick your moments. There I was in the middle of making my French puff pastry for the mushroom *feuilletés* Mrs Hissey asked me to make for her American friend on her last night here and you have to go and drop down dead. Needless to say, they were ruined. Now Mrs Hissey wants a do for your funeral. We've all to come up to Laybridge. Harold, are you listening? I don't know, the way she's carrying on anyone would think you were royalty. We'll be having meat-paste sandwiches in the library, Harold, because they were your favourite. When you remembered to put your teeth in, of course. Orlando's taken it pretty bad. Turns out he was very fond of you.'

It wasn't as if she could even sit down for a chat about Harold with her employer, get it out of her system that way. Mrs Hissey could be very sympathetic. But for some reason Harold's death had given her the idea for a new book and she had shut herself away, oblivious to the world outside. Peg went in one morning to sweep out the grate and heard her on the phone to someone in London, 'There he was, lying dead at my feet in the middle of the herb garden, and I couldn't stop thinking about all he'd done for my roses, my "William Lobb"s and my "Jacques Cartier"s, and then the book started to form right there and then as I stood looking down at poor Harold's body. It's a thriller about a woman who finds her gardener lying dead in the rose garden and knows the victim was meant to be her. It's called *Deadhead* and …'

Peg was beginning to wonder if she was cooking the right kind of food for Mrs Hissey's brain.

There was another thing: Mrs Hissey had offered Rose a job as her secretary. 'This would never have happened if you hadn't died,' Peg told Harold, 'and why did you have to go and pick my herb garden?'

Then there was Mick. She'd had to ask him to the funeral. He was Harold's son. And Rose's uncle. High time Rose saw him again. But he'd cause trouble. He always did.

As usual, Peg was worrying more about her daughter

than anything else. Rose was changing every day. For one thing, she was going into Salisbury far more than usual. She was reading women's magazines, *Options*, *She*, *Elle*. She was hoarding her money and instead of giving it to Peg for the housekeeping as she'd done in the past, even though Peg had never asked her to, she was spending it on clothes from shops called Next and Benetton. Before, she'd made do for years with the same M&S sweaters and jeans. All sorts of lotions from the Body Shop began to appear in the bathroom, peppermint foot lotion, hawthorn hand cream, orange creme bath oil, and Peg discovered in the drawer of Rose's bedside table a range of Boots No. 7 beauty products and a neat little pile of perfume samples in plastic sachets torn from magazines.

Mrs Richards from the butcher's reported seeing her going into the Odeon 'many an afternoon' but the final straw came when Rose paid a visit to 'that hairdresser', Toni & Guy, and had all her hair chopped off. 'For the funeral, I expect,' said Mrs Richards knowingly. Peg wept. All those long black Farley curls lying in a bin bag in a place called Toni & Guy.

'It'll grow, Mum,' Rose told her wearily.

'It's for that job Mrs Hissey's gone and offered you, isn't it? So's you'll look like a proper secretary.'

'No, it's not, Mum, and I'm not going to be a secretary. No one has secretaries in the age of computers. I'm going to be her assistant.'

'So have you told Orlando you won't be looking after him any more?'

'Not yet. Mrs Hissey's going to tell him.'

'It'll mean more work for me. I'll have to go back to

working at The Cottage now. Never thought of that, did you?'

'Course I did. Won't be a problem. Lindy'll get someone from London, you'll see. It's what she's always wanted to do anyway.'

'Over my dead body.'

'That's what I thought you'd say.' Rose sounded triumphant. 'You go back to The Cottage. It's time I moved on.'

Peg looked at her daughter's sleek cropped head, the boyish haircut that exposed the long neck, the foxy features, the pointed nose, the high rosy cheekbones, those flashing gypsy eyes, and knew why it disturbed her so much. Without the curtain of long black curls to hide it, Rose's face was the image of her father's and Peg hadn't allowed herself to think about Charlie for a long time.

Charlie, Mick and Rose. All Farleys. All trouble. To hell with you, Harold Farley, look what you produced.

Rose overheard the row Orlando had with Victoria on the telephone about Lindy not coming down for Harold's funeral. She couldn't help it. She was in the process of making the four-poster bed and cleaning the bedroom, probably the last time she would do so before Peg took over, and Orlando rushed in to answer the phone.

'Victoria, I don't know why you're making such a thing about this. Lindy barely knew Harold. She's got a lot on. I see no reason why she should drop everything for Harold Farley. No. You've got it all wrong. There's nothing the matter between us. She just needs to be in London at the moment. All right. *All right*, Victoria, it's no good making a fuss. It won't make a jot of difference. Lindy's not coming and that's fine by me.'

'That's not what you said yesterday,' Rose pointed out, as Orlando slumped on the bed, crumpling the hand-embroidered duvet cover that Rose had just straightened.

'What do you mean?'

'You know. Now, please could you get off this bed so I can change your pillowcases.'

'Been listening at keyholes, have you? Better watch out I don't tell Victoria. Secretaries are supposed to be discreet.'

'I'm not going to be her secretary. I'm going to be her assistant.'

'Oh, for God's sake, Rose, you're getting as bad as Lindy. Everything's got to revolve around your brilliant career.'

'Well, perhaps you should pay a little more attention to yours,' retorted Rose, and noted with satisfaction his look of astonishment.

'What's got into you? Tough little fighter standing up for herself all of a sudden. Are you angry with me? I'm sorry about your grandfather, you know. I probably made it sound as if he wasn't worth Lindy driving down for but I didn't mean that. I really admired him. We used to spend hours together when I was a boy. He loved showing me things in the garden. He taught me an awful lot.'

'I know,' Rose said softly. She knew because she'd heard the row he'd had with Lindy on the phone the night before: 'Please come down for the funeral, Linds, *please*! Do it for me. I loved that old man. I really think you should. The Farleys are like family to me. You know that. It's always your bloody work with you. Work first, me second. Make an effort for me, for a change. Please come down, just for the day. It'd mean so much to me. Will you?'

Then Rose had heard him slam down the phone.

Never mind. She'd be at the funeral for him if Lindy wasn't coming; and he'd be there for her.

It seemed to have completely escaped Mick Farley's notice that it was Harold Farley, his father, who had died. From the minute he arrived it was clear that he had come to mourn his brother Charlie.

'Your uncle Mick's his usual self, I see,' observed Peg, as Mick walked out of the church, bypassed Harold's open grave with the casket waiting beside it, and set off for the Laybridge Arms. 'It's like having Charlie back from the dead.'

There was enough of a resemblance for people to see that they had been brothers but whereas Charlie had been handsome with his mop of jet-black hair, his sharp foxy nose, his eyes that had always flashed with amusement until the light went out of them, and the high colour in his cheeks initially from his work outdoors in all weathers and latterly from the drink, Mick had a mean ferret face, sharp, with eyes too close together, and a thin strip of a mouth that showed teeth stained by nicotine and compared poorly with Charlie's generous flash of white when he smiled.

Mick Farley was the epitome of a caricaturist's shifty travelling salesman, which was exactly what he was. Peg was furious with him for ducking out of Victoria's reception at Laybridge, but in the end she was relieved. It was a sticky affair. Those villagers who had not accompanied Mick to the Laybridge Arms stood around awkwardly, unsure how to behave. Peg bustled about dispensing cups of tea and sandwiches, and beer for those who wanted it. Victoria made a speech about Harold's invaluable contribution to the gardens at Laybridge but Peg knew it was falling on deaf ears when Victoria's familiar opening line, 'I'm not a plantswoman but ...' failed to raise even a smile.

And then, of course, there was Rose. Her strange new haircut and her smart little black jacket and short skirt – too short in Peg's view – served only to set her apart from the rest of the village. And the way she clung to Orlando's side as if they were a couple. In the church she'd had to sit with Peg and Mick in the front as a chief mourner. She couldn't cross the aisle to the Hissey pew to sit with Victoria and Orlando – but if she could have, thought Peg, she would. The minute the service was over Peg watched her daughter slip her arm through Orlando's and walk with him down the aisle leaving Peg with Mick.

Now, at Laybridge, Rose wasn't helping her mother. She was acting as hostess alongside Victoria and Orlando, thanking people for coming, playing the gracious lady. They didn't like it, Peg noticed. It wasn't right. It was only when old Tom Heale began to reminisce about Harold's bee-keeping days that everyone began to relax a little. Later, some of them begin drifting in pairs down the dark, panelled passage to the kitchen to be served yet another cup of tea by Peg and to tell her privately how they would miss her father-in-law. It was odd. Harold had not even been her blood relative yet they were consoling her, not Rose or Mick. Finally they straggled off down the drive to pay their last respects to Harold in the manner they found most comfortable, over a pint in the Laybridge Arms, and here they found Mick.

'What were you all doing? Charlie wouldn't have liked you being up there.'

'Not Charlie. Charlie's long gone. We were there for Harold,' they told him warily. They didn't know Mick well. When Charlie had been alive, Mick had come down from wherever it was he lived to see his brother maybe two or three times a year, and the pair had sat talking for hours on end in the pub. It was noted that Charlie, a secretive man, had been close to his brother, had confided in him, but because Harold had had little time for his eldest son and Peg even less, Mick had sought Charlie's company away from Farley Cottage where he was not welcome.

'OK, OK, me dad's gone and about time. But I'm here for Charlie. Nobody invited me to his funeral. Bit hush-hush, was it? What did you do with him? Throw him in the river?'

The bar was very quiet. Then Peg spoke up. 'We told you when Charlie's funeral was going to be and you never showed up. His grave's where it's always been if you ever bothered to look, Mick. Up there in the graveyard right next to your father.'

'So why didn't you have a do for Charlie when he died, Peg?'

'He'd had enough dos to last him a lifetime – in here every night as he was. There was no need to carry on after he'd gone.'

'That's a bit mean, Peg. What I want to know, what

I've always wanted to know, is why did he drink so much?'

'Same reason you do, I should think. Why do you drink, Mick?'

'Normally because I enjoy it. Same as the next bloke. Right now because I miss Charlie. And Charlie drank because he was bloody miserable.'

Peg didn't know when she'd last been this miserable herself. At Mrs Hissey's do they'd all been so choked and constipated and here they were all agog, privy to Farley family secrets. Everything was being stirred up when all she'd wanted was to lay poor Harold to rest.

'I'm sorry to hear that,' said Peg, without any feeling.

'Yeah, well Charlie didn't deserve it.'

'Didn't deserve what?'

'To be miserable. He never used to be. He was always the cheerful one, was Charlie. He was a happy-go-lucky bugger. Lived for his fish, daft little things. Lived for you and all, Peg. Worshipped you. And Rose. She was his little sweetheart.'

Peg didn't know what to say.

'Then what happened, Peg? Do you know? Why did he start drinking so much? What made him so bloody miserable all of a sudden? A man doesn't go and ruin his liver like that for no reason. Do you know, Peg? Do you? Because I do.'

Peg didn't know what he was on about, but whatever it was it sounded ominous. Charlie had always told Mick everything, silly old fool that he was. Something was about to come out and the entire village, gathered now in the pub, was going to hear it.

Rose came into the bar, radiant as a bride when she

should have been the dejected mourning granddaughter. Peg soon saw why. Orlando followed her in. Immediately the atmosphere changed. Everyone shuffled into some kind of order, glasses were raised, rounds were fetched. Relief swept over Peg. The moment had passed.

But not for Mick.

He clambered off his bar stool and lurched towards Orlando, a few steps back, and a few steps forward again.

'It's your lot. Charlie told me all about it. All your lot's fault. If it hadn't been for your lot he'd still be alive.'

Rose cooked Orlando lunch the next day before he left for London. Fish pie. Green beans. Peas. And a sticky toffee pudding to follow. She felt so relaxed with him that she sat down to join him at the table.

He kissed the top of her head in thanks when he left and she put her arms around his waist under his jacket and clung to him.

'I'm sorry about your grandfather, Rose. He was a good soul. If my godmother wasn't so immersed in her new book I know she'd want you to go up and mourn him with her. We'll all miss him but you'll get over it.'

But Rose wasn't hugging him to be comforted for her loss and they both knew it.

Still, after Orlando had gone she felt she deserved some kind of consolation and before she cleaned The Cottage for the last time, she went upstairs to indulge in her new favourite pastime: trying on Lindy's clothes.

Lindy didn't keep much at The Cottage but Rose knew that she liked to change for Saturday-night dinner when she came down. Rose was taller and slimmer than Lindy and she knew that Lindy's chic little dresses looked infinitely better on her slim figure than they did on Lindy's. Rose loved throwing them all over the four-poster bed and selecting them one by one, parading in front of the full-length mirror, admiring herself. It gave her a confidence she had never before experienced. She waved to the sheep outside and imagined they were all lined up along the riverbank watching her in admiration.

She was in a little black wool number from Joseph when she heard the crunch of wheels on the gravel outside. Before she could begin to gather up the clothes on the bed, Orlando's footsteps were coming up the stairs. Rose knew it was no use. She could see the Filofax he'd left behind on his bedside table. Why hadn't she noticed it?

He was coming down the passage shouting, 'Rose, where are you? I've left ...'

He stood in the doorway. Rose was still over by the window. Lindy's clothes lay between them.

But Orlando didn't seem to see them. All he said was, 'I've never seen you look so beautiful, Rose.' Then he snatched up his Filofax and left.

18

Peter McGill knew he would feel eternally guilty that his first thought on being told by Lily that their son was deaf had been: Will it cost more to have a deaf child? He adored this funny little boy, who had Lily's fine unmanageable fair hair and his own brown eyes and ruddy cheeks. Peter loved his son's hair, loved to bend down and stroke it like a dog's, as if he could somehow communicate in this way to Pepper that he loved him.

Peter felt an affinity with the child. He believed he got through to him. When they were alone he talked to him all the time. He was talking to him now as they picked their way through the puddles along the Bluebell Walk. Pepper was wearing his new red wellies for the first time. His denim dungarees from Gap Kids were soaking and covered in mud. After he had helped Peter wash the car, a regular weekend ritual, Pepper had proceeded to upend the bucket of water and make himself a mud bath in the middle of the lane in which he jumped and splashed about until he was truly filthy. Peter had grabbed him and marched him off for a walk before Lily saw him and had a fit.

'She wouldn't like it, you know, Pepper. She'd be furious. All that washing she'd have to do. We don't want her moaning, do we? Rain's stopped now. Sun's out. No doubt you'll have dried out a bit by the time we get back.'

He was talking rubbish. He knew perfectly well that Lily would never ever be furious with Pepper. He had become her life's work. When she had first accepted that Pepper was deaf she had gone into overdrive and contacted all the organisations while Peter had done nothing. But that was Lily's way and this was his. At first Peter had felt uncomfortable having a deaf child. He had found it hard to accept that he didn't have a perfect child. Now he was just upset that Pepper wasn't the same as him. In the beginning he had accompanied Lily to all the places she went to seek help, and he had found that as far as the outside world was concerned all deaf children were lumped together. Their individuality, their intelligence, even their background were not taken into account. They were handicapped children, full stop. This outraged him and he dealt with it by quietly spending as much time as he could on his own with Pepper.

'You like your new wellies, don't you? Means you can splash about in all the puddles. We got them in the sale. Always got to look out for a bargain, you know, Pepper. Money's the thing. Bit of a problem in life but you'll learn to cope. Always be on the lookout for a bargain and you'll be all right. Shall we go and take a look at the fish?'

Half-way along the Bluebell Walk on the way to Laybridge the river Lay divided into several channels, fanning out to pass through a sluice. In among them were the trout stews, laid out like long stone swimming-pools covered with netting to keep out the birds. Perched above the churning waters of a weir stood the old moss-covered turbine house with its water wheel that used to generate the power for Laybridge.

'Now you take my hand and we'll go across this bridge

and look at the fish. You must be very careful, Pepper. One slip and you might fall in that water down there. Off we go.'

'I'll come behind you just in case,' said Rose who was on her way from Laybridge. Peter jumped. He hadn't been aware of her coming along the lane. He felt embarrassed. He only talked to Pepper when he was alone with him. He didn't like people to hear him.

'Thank you, Rose. Look, Pepper, here's Rose.'

Rose knelt down beside the little boy.

'Talk to him, would you, Rose? Please. I believe we must talk to him.'

'No problem,' said Rose. 'So how are you doing, Pepper? Shall we go and see the fish? My dad used to be the person who looked after them. I always came with him when he fed them. We can do that now, if you want. I know where the fish food is kept. Would you like that?'

Pepper's hand reached out to Rose's chin and she looked at Peter, wondering what was happening.

'No, let him take your face,' Peter told her. 'He wants to turn your face to his so he can see it. It's his way of listening.'

Once they were across the bridge – no more than a plank secured from bank to bank – Rose went round to the back of the turbine house. It was a low building, barely higher than Rose herself, with the roof coming down almost to the ground on one side. Rose felt along the wall until she found a key hanging on a hook. She unlocked the door and took Pepper in. 'My father used to come here all the time. Now, here's the fish food in these buckets.'

'He's made it quite cosy in here, hasn't he?' Peter followed them in and saw the table and folding chairs.

'Oh, my father, Charlie, he's been dead for years. This isn't his stuff. A young man on the estate looks after the fish now. But if you think this is cosy you should have seen it when Dad was alive. He even had a bed so he could come up here and have a quick kip when he'd had a few too many down the pub and he didn't want to face Mum.'

'Yes, I've heard about his reputation in the Laybridge Arms. No offence, Rose.'

'None taken. Now, Pepper, you take a handful of this fish food, here you are, they're like little pebbles – they smell a bit funny so don't go taking them home – and what you do is you throw them in the stews like this.'

She hurled a spray of fish food into the water and immediately the fish began to twist and turn, rising out of the water to grab it.

Pepper clapped his hands in delight and dropped everything. Rose gave him some more and again showed him what to do. When he saw the fish leaping up to grab his food he smiled and began to make a monotonous noise.

'What does that mean?' asked Rose.

'How can we know? He makes that kind of sound all the time, but I imagine – given the smile on his face – that it means he's happy. How long do they keep the fish in these stews?'

'They let them into the river when they're about three pounds. They're not allowed to grow too big before they're let in otherwise there isn't enough food in the river to feed them and they either deteriorate or become carnivores. That's enough, Pepper. We mustn't give them too much. Don't want them to get too big.'

'Time we took you home for tea.' Peter guided him back across the bridge. Half-way across Pepper stopped. He was staring at something, his little face crumpled, close to tears.

'What is it? What's the matter?'

'It's a dead fish,' said Rose flatly. 'We've had a lot of rain lately and the river rose up quite high. Sometimes in the flooding the fish are thrown out of the stews. Mostly they go into the river but this one must have landed on the bank, poor thing. I'm sorry, Peter, but I must get on home. I'll see you later. Mrs McGill's going to try me out as a babysitter when you all go up to Laybridge for dinner tonight.'

Rose knew she was being rude leaving them so abruptly but she couldn't help it. It was always the same when she saw a dead fish. It made her think of what had happened to Orlando's parents. That's how she always saw them in her nightmares: dumped lifeless on the riverbank just like dead fish.

Lindy threw the manuscript on the floor in a fit of pre-menstrual blues. Why did she have to feel so useless before her period? The loose pages scattered and, too late, she remembered that the editor who had given her the script had said that the middle section wasn't numbered. It was a piece of shit anyway: a feeble story of a loveless marriage set in the northern town of Huddersfield. How on earth was she supposed to interest the Japanese or the Germans in translating something like that? Although if anyone were capable of delivering a sensational pitch about a marriage in trouble, she was.

What had induced her to return to The Cottage? It had been well over six months since she'd been down. Orlando still came every weekend, sometimes on his own, sometimes with the ubiquitous McGills who, hell and damnation, were here now. How was she supposed to get any work done with Lily rushing around all the time? It had been bad enough when she was just rushing around. Now she rushed after Pepper, which was fifty times worse because she expected everybody else to join in.

Then there was Peg. Now that Rose had gone to work for Victoria up at Laybridge as some kind of assistant – what was that all about? – Peg was back working for them at The Cottage. But as Lindy hadn't been down for so long and Lily had, Peg had transferred her allegiance to Lily. Talk about attitude! Peg had all but ignored Lindy and awaited instructions from Lily. It was outrageous: Lily giving out shopping lists and discussing menus; Lily announcing they'd be going up to Laybridge to have dinner with Victoria on Saturday night. Nobody told me, thought Lindy. Then there had been the little matter of the chocolates and the notepads.

'Peg,' Orlando had shouted the minute he came down on Saturday morning, 'what on earth induced you to put silly chocolates on our pillows and leave little notepads and pencils on the bedside tables? Are we supposed to be recording our dreams for posterity?'

'Mrs Manners called and asked me to organise that. I was only doing what I was told.' Peg's tone implied that she had been deeply insulted by the request.

'Lindy, did you seriously ask Peg to put chocolates on everyone's pillows?'

'Yes. What's wrong with that?'

'Because this is my home not a bloody hotel. It was bad enough having all those frightful miniature shampoo and conditioner and bath oil samples and what have you in the guest bathroom. I'm surprised you didn't have them put in little baskets tied with a big bow.'

'Oh, go ahead, sneer all you want but everybody used them or they stole them. There was never anything left on a Sunday night.'

'So what are the notepads for?'

'Telephone messages, of course.'

'In the bedrooms? Have you completely lost your mind? There are no telephones in the bedrooms.'

'Not yet. I'm having them installed next week.'

'Over my dead body. What on earth do we want telephones in the bedrooms for?'

'Because we're going to start having some of my friends down, people whose work is important to them, people who need to be at the end of a telephone at all times. If someone calls from the States or Australia they might be in their bedroom.'

'Oh, fantastic! Then we'll all be woken up. Can't wait. Lindy, this is a country cottage where people come to relax for the weekend, to get away from the phone. It is not an office. It is not a place to work. Amazing as it may seem to you, some of us have a life outside work.'

'Well, if you want me to keep coming down with you then you're going to have to adapt a bit. I've got a fax machine being delivered today too.'

'Well, perhaps you'd like to go and negotiate with the

sheep about a helicopter pad in the field across the river while you're at it. Lindy, read my lips. No phones in the bedrooms. No chocolates on pillows. And absolutely no fax. I'll just have a couple of slices of toast, please, Peg, I seem to have lost my appetite.'

'I suppose that means I can't have any friends either,' Lindy spat at him, and caught Peg's smirk.

She gathered together the pages of the hapless manuscript and put it to one side. She had another one to read. Something so hot she could hardly wait to start it. After the humiliation he had suffered following the out-and-out failure on both sides of the Atlantic of his last book, Bruno Manners had gone back to the drawing board. Lucky for him he had a two-book contract in the UK. From the transatlantic grapevine Lindy had learned that his American publishers, Rubinstein and Rose, had dumped him. But she had secured the contract to be their London scout. Maybe she could convince them to take him back. Harding's, his UK publisher, were over the moon about the new book. The buzz was already beginning about it and Caroline Calder had slipped her an advance copy of the manuscript. But how could she settle down and concentrate with all that yakkety-yak going on in the kitchen? Peg must have finished unloading the dishwasher after lunch by now and she had no dinner to prepare for that night. Why was she still here yattering on to Lily? Or, rather, listening to Lily's never-ending monologue about Pepper.

'There's this virus called CMV which might cause a baby to lose its hearing. Apparently I contracted it during pregnancy and poor little Pepper was born deaf. At first I thought it was glue-ear – that high-pitched shriek, you know? – and I thought it couldn't be treated when a child is tiny so I put it off just hoping and hoping I'd got it all wrong. I was so frightened.'

'What about Mr McGill? How's he taking it?'

'Peter's devastated. I know he is. I found him crying the other day. Peter, of all people! We're so different, Peter and I. I know I'm an old fusspot but Peter's so – what do you call it? Buttoned-up. He never lets his emotions show and there he was crying in our bedroom. He said he'd just realised he'd never be able to read little Pepper a bedtime story.'

I wish she wouldn't always refer to him as "little Pepper" or "poor little Pepper", thought Lindy, listening in spite of herself. Why was she so irritated by Lily and Pepper? Was it because she was jealous of Lily's happy marriage and that she had a child, the missing piece of Lindy's jigsaw? Or was it just PMT? She didn't want to be like Lily, she didn't want Lily's lifestyle, but there were times when Peter put his arms around Lily's shoulders, hugged her with real affection, asked. 'All right, old girl?' and Lindy felt seriously lonely. How long had it been since Orlando had behaved like that towards her, as though he really cared?

'Of course he's going to be just like any other child, Peg.'

Like hell, thought Lindy. Who does she think she's kidding?

'Everything is going to be just as if he was a hearing child. We're going to treat him just the same. Won't make any difference to us.'

'That's very brave of you, Mrs McGill. Does he have, you know, one of those ...'

'Oh, he has hearing aids. I'll never forget when he first got them. He went so quiet and I was worried sick but, if you think about it, it's obvious. Suddenly he had all that sound he'd never had before. He must have been in shock. But he's naughty about it. When he gets tired he tears them out because he wants to switch off. Now he's beginning to understand that if I try to make him do something he doesn't want to do, he can take his hearing aids out. It's pretty maddening but I forgive him because it's a form of communication.'

'Does he have other deaf friends?'

'Oh, Peg, you know he doesn't. Peter doesn't believe we should ghettoise him like that so I invite all my friends to come over with their hearing children. But it's horrible. They never invite him back. I know the parents feel funny about having a deaf kid. They don't want the responsibility. I was talking to a mother at the clinic the other day. She said her only friends are people with deaf children now because no one else understands. Isn't that awful?'

Lindy gave up. By the sound of things they were going to go on all morning. She might as well go and join in the conversation and show Lily what a concerned and caring person she really was.

'Does little Pepper know he's deaf and dumb?' she asked, going into the kitchen. 'Is this coffee fresh?'

There was a silence. Lindy had poured herself a cup and taken the milk out of the fridge before she realised Lily hadn't answered her. Then there was an outburst which nearly caused her to drop the milk.

'He's *not* deaf and dumb. He's just deaf. Why do people always say deaf and dumb? It's so cruel. He's not a bit dumb. He's not stupid and he chatters away whether we understand him or not. And in answer to your question, he won't understand that till he's at least seven or eight. He just knows he's different.'

'OK, OK, keep your hair on. I didn't mean it that way. So are you all learning sign language or whatever it is?'

'No, we've opted for Oral-Aural.'

'I beg your pardon?'

'One tends to opt for this approach or the signing approach. Signing's much quicker. They understand and communicate.'

'Well, then, why on earth don't you go for that?'

'Because we want to give Pepper the chance to be as much like us as possible. Don't look like that, Lindy.'

'Like what?'

'So disbelieving. 'I really believe in Oral-Aural.'

'What is it? Tell me. I'm bound to be sceptical if I don't know what it is.'

'It's lip reading, reacting to expressions, oral-signing. It takes longer but they end up with a better way of communicating and understanding life generally. We'll be more like a hearing family. Also it's much easier for other people if you leave your child with them, like babysitters. Last week we ...'

Lindy was bored. To her intense irritation she found she rather admired Lily for her courage and perseverance in the face of what to Lindy seemed the worst possible adversity. Being tied to a child was bad enough but being lumbered with a special-needs toddler must be absolute hell. And it appeared to have brought out a new fighting spirit in Lily, which Lindy hadn't seen before.

She drifted off and went to the sitting room to make phone calls. Why hadn't they delivered the bloody fax machine? Maybe Oscar had read that incomprehensible New Age manuscript that everyone was so hyped up about and could explain it to her over the phone so that she could start planning what to with it first thing on Monday morning. If only she'd brought her laptop she could be getting on with something instead of wasting time. At least Orlando was out of the way. He'd been gone for hours. She wondered fleetingly where he was as she punched out Oscar's number.

'You're my godmother, Victoria.'

'I know I am.'

'Some say your godmotherly duties cease when your godchild comes of age. Where do you stand on that?'

'I'm your godmother, Orlando. You've got me for life, I'm afraid. Have another cup of tea. What a treat seeing you twice in one day. You're all coming for dinner tonight. You haven't forgotten, I hope. And I gather Lindy's come down again at last. How is she?'

'You'll see.'

'Sounds ominous. Does this have anything to do with me being your godmother?'

'Spot on. You're so perceptive, Victoria. I wanted some advice. I didn't know who to talk to. I felt I should talk to a woman.'

'An older woman?'

'My godmother,' said Orlando tactfully. 'I imagine you know we lead pretty separate lives. You see quite a bit of her, don't you, when you come up to London?'

'Yes, but we don't talk about your marriage. Ever. Whatever else she might be, Lindy's not a gossip.'

'What do you mean by "whatever else she might be"?'

'Oh, that's just me being a bit menopausal and resentful. You must see that Lindy is a phenomenally ambitious young woman. Her work is everything to her.'

'Tell me about it. I hit the roof this morning because she's talking about putting phones in all the bedrooms and getting a fax and God knows what else. She never stops, Victoria. She's thinking about her work all the time. I have nothing to say to her any more. She goes to drinks parties every night. She gets back about nine. Then she expects to be taken out to dinner because while she might be roaring away on the fast track as far as her career's concerned – or so she keeps telling me, but to be honest, Victoria, I don't really understand what it is she actually does – she's pretty useless in the kitchen. Then all through dinner she'll go on and on about the kind of day she's had, who she saw and whether or not she got the better of them. That seems to be very important to her. It doesn't even stop once we're back home in bed because she's always got some manuscript that has to be read overnight so she can get her report on it ahead of her competitors. What is this scouting lark? When people ask me what Lindy does and I tell them she's a publishing scout, they've no idea what I'm talking about.'

'Scouting isn't a particularly high-profile part of publishing, I admit, but it's pretty important. By getting that amazing German sale for me, Lindy almost single-handedly lifted me into bestseller status. The Americans sat up and took notice and then the dozy old Brits followed suit. I owe her everything. *Deadhead* got to number four on the bestseller list. The paperback's out any minute and they've printed over a hundred thousand copies. Suddenly I'm right up there with Ruth Rendell and Barbara Vine. OK, maybe I'm getting a little carried away, and anyway they're the same person, but if Lindy were an agent I'd switch to her immediately. Yet I agree with you. I'm not sure I entirely approve of how obsessive she is about her work. I benefit from it yet it scares me. I feel she's sort of wasting her youth. She ought to be, I don't know, out having –'

'Babies.'

'Actually I was going to say out having fun. Can I ask you when you're going to think about having a baby?'

'It's a question of "if" rather than when.'

'Well, it's fine to wait a while.'

'I don't want to wait at all. It's Lindy who doesn't want one.'

'Never?'

'So she says. Why do you think I come down here so much with Peter and Lily? Pepper's my godchild. I adore him – he's such a game little chap, I love it when he comes down to The Cottage. Plus it looks as if it's as near as I'm going to get to having my own child.'

'That's awful. I had no idea. But you never know. Things may change. She's a success now. She may calm down. And just because having a baby's not on her agenda right now, you might well find that when she sees everyone around her starting families she might well want to start one too. Lindy's pretty conventional – and you know what they say about ambitious women, they're determined to have it all.'

'You make it sound as if she might decide to add a baby to her list of requirements rather like a fashion accessory. Got the job, got the husband, got the house in London and the cottage in the country, got the fax, got the modem, all I need now is a baby.'

'The thing is, Orlando, there are always going to be people whose work is more important to them than anything else. Than their wife or husband or the person they're involved with, than their children, than their health, you name it. Lindy's like that. Bruno's like that, if you really want to know. I know I come second to his work, to his ambition. I've always known that. And you're going to have to face up to that about Lindy. You married her very fast, Orlando. You obviously didn't have a chance to see her in work mode in the Caribbean.'

'You don't approve. Come on, Victoria, out with it. Please tell me the truth. You don't like her, do you?'

'Hold on. Not so fast. It's not that I don't like her. I do. I confess I never expected to but there's something rather honest about her. I'm pretty direct myself and what I like about Lindy is that she's so straightforward. She knows what she wants and she gets on with it and there's something about that that I respect. The trouble is, she doesn't have much regard for what other people want. She's insensitive. Obsessively driven people like her often are. But I don't think she has much idea how to change herself. I suppose what I'm building up to saying is that I don't think she's right for you. You're sensitive, Orlando, but you always were impulsive. You obviously plunged into this marriage without giving it much thought.'

'OK. All right. You're absolutely right. I made a mistake. Don't rub my nose in it. I'm not a puppy.'

'Aren't you?' Victoria smiled fondly.

'Do you think we can make it work?'

'That's hardly up to me. What do you think?'

'I've wanted to get married ever since I was twelve years old, ever since my mother died. I wanted someone to love me and flatter me and encourage me like she did. She was my best friend. When I met Lindy in the Caribbean she seemed so strong. I thought I would always feel safe with her.'

Oh, God, thought Victoria, you've done exactly what your father did before you. You've gone and married totally the wrong woman. Lindy isn't a promiscuous bitch like your mother was – at least, not as far as I'm aware – but she's not the kind of caring, understanding soul you really need.

'I realise that in many ways I'm desperate for her approval. It's pathetic. And yet I hate the way she dismisses my friends. She's so contemptuous of poor Peter and Lily. She thinks they're dull sticks-in-the-mud. Boring. She's always saying everyone's boring and ignoring them. I mean, boring people exasperate you, Victoria, we've always known that about you, but at least you're nice to everyone.'

'I wasn't always. You get more tolerant as you grow older. Besides, Orlando, you've sought everyone's approval since you were tiny. Your mother smothered you in approval. As far as she was concerned you could do no wrong. You were her darling little boy. She absolutely adored you.' Because you were so adorable to look at, added Victoria silently. You were a fashion accessory for her if ever there was one. I doubt if she ever had anything other than an adult conversation with you. You were her little puppet. And if you're not careful you'll become Lindy's but it'll be your own fault. Daisy and Lindy are manipulators. Real operators, as Toby Marriott would say.

But there is a difference between them. Daisy was totally selfish. Lindy just wants things to go her way and if you let her get away with that, Orlando, you're done for. But if you stand up to her, she'll respect you. She needs a man who's even more of an operator than she is.

But you're not that man, Orlando, she thought sadly.

'Marriage is about compromise, Orlando. Surely somebody must have told you that before now. Maybe you and Lindy are poles apart but if you make an effort to compromise a few of the things you both want, you'll meet in the middle. Tell her you'll come to her work parties during the week and take an interest in her world in London, and in return she has to put work aside when she's down at The Cottage at the weekend.'

'Fat chance.' Orlando looked extremely gloomy at the prospect. 'Not exactly my ideal bride, is she?'

'Who is?' said Victoria.

But after he had left Victoria thought about it for a minute and found she knew exactly who would be.

Orlando walked into bedlam at The Cottage. Lily was demonstrating to Peg how she taught Pepper the concept of 'same' in oral-signing. She placed him on the floor and put two identical yoghurt pots in front of him. She pointed to one yoghurt pot with one index finger, and to the other pot with the other. Then she brought her two index fingers together while she mouthed the words 'the same' at Pepper over and over again.

'You see, Peg. You're using your lips to say 'the same' which is the same as the thing you're doing. Later, he'll grasp the words, he'll know what they mean so he'll drop the sign. If you were just opting for the signing route, the child would be taught this using my voice. This way by the time he's older he won't be saying clear words but I'll be able to understand what he means, or at least I hope I will.'

But Pepper got bored, opened the yoghurt pot and spilled the contents all over Bruno Manners's manuscript, which Lindy had left lying on the floor.

Lindy went ballistic. 'How in hell am I supposed to get any work done around here with Pepper doing something like this? Last night he emptied all my shampoo into the bath. This morning he upset my coffee. Now this.'

'You're not expected to work, that's the whole bloody point! And if you feel you have to then perhaps you'd better not bother coming down again.' So much for Victoria's words of wisdom about compromise.

'Pepper, darling, don't pull your hearing aid out. Auntie Lindy isn't really angry with you.'

'Lily, for God's sake, I am not nor will I ever be Auntie Lindy. And I bloody well am angry. Furthermore, if you feel like that, Orlando, perhaps I'd better leave right now. I'll take the car and go back to London tonight. Lily and Peter can give you a lift back tomorrow. You can sit in the back with darling Pepper here. Make my apologies to Victoria. Tell her I'll speak to her during the week. Now I'm going to pack.'

'Lindy, I'm so sorry. He didn't mean it. He's only a child,' said Lily.

'Who are you talking about? Orlando or Pepper?' shouted Lindy, from the top of the stairs.

She didn't say goodbye. In fact nobody heard her leave and nobody heard her sobs of frustration as she drove up the lane. Why did she always have to go and spoil everything?

Orlando asked if he could give Pepper his bath. Godfather's rights, he called it. In the end Rose helped him and it made him feel even worse about Lindy to see how gentle and maternal Rose was with Pepper.

'How do you feel about babysitting for him?'

'Do you mean am I worried because he's deaf? Not at all. I've been watching Lily – sorry, Mrs McGill – these last few weekends when she's been down. If anyone needs a break, she does. She's on the go with him from the minute he wakes until he goes to bed. He won't play on his own, you know. Deaf children have so much adult stimulation they find it hard to entertain themselves. I'm only too happy to help. I think Mrs McGill's wonderful. Besides Pepper's an adorable little boy.'

'And you're adorable with him,' Orlando told her.

He changed for dinner, went downstairs and realised he'd left his watch upstairs.

'Is Pepper asleep?' he asked Rose, who was coming down.

'I've just got him off.'

'Don't worry, I'll tiptoe past his room. I won't make a sound.'

'Orlando, you can make all the noise you want. He's hardly likely to hear you, is he?'

19

'Mr Marriott? Hello, it's Rose Farley here. We're very sorry but Mrs Hissey won't be able to make it to the sales-conference dinner next week. She really is deep into the new book and it just wouldn't be a good moment to take her mind off it. We do hope you understand.'

Victoria suppressed an explosion of laughter. She hadn't had so much fun in years. Now every time her editor Toby Marriott called with yet another irritating demand there was Rose poised to head him off at the pass. It must be driving him mad. Rose was so good at it. Victoria was amazed. Eighteen months ago, when Rose had first started working for her, Victoria had envisaged her running minor errands: going to the post office, taking pages to be photocopied, being sent off to do some undemanding research. But those plans had been nothing short of patronising, as she had soon discovered. One of the first things Rose did was to suggest she enrol herself on a computer course.

'Why would you want to do something like that?' Victoria was mystified. 'I don't use a computer. I'm wedded to my portable Adler. I've had it for over thirty years.'

Rose's look of near disgust indicated how she felt about the Adler. 'It's just that I was talking to the production department at Beeson's. They were asking if they could have the new book on disc.'

'You're not serious?'

'Well, I think they're still assuming they'll have the manuscript delivered as hard copy for Mr Marriott to read but I don't think they realise you haven't even got a computer. The thing is, wouldn't that be one of the things I could do for you? Why don't we get you a computer? I'll go on the course, you always said I could one day, and then I can transfer everything you write on to it for you. We could put all your research into it and I can teach you how to call it up whenever you want it.'

So Rose was ensconced in a small panelled room off the library where she clicked and whirred away while she watched the swans drift by along the river Lay outside the window. Victoria refused to have the Apple Mac in the room in which she wrote. She was secretly bemused by the incongruity of having modern technology in a Jacobean house but the library was sacrosanct.

She couldn't get over the new Rose. For about two months, before the computer had arrived, Rose had sat in with Victoria, listening to her conversations on the phone. Before Victoria even knew what was happening, Rose was reaching for the phone when it rang and answering it for her. 'Victoria Hissey's office.'

She appeared to have learned considerably more on her course than how to access a computer. She did not find it necessary to ask, 'Who may I say is calling?' Neither did she ever suggest that Victoria might have 'stepped away from her desk'. Somehow she had managed to infiltrate every area of Victoria's working life and protect her from all the unwelcome distractions that had hitherto interrupted her writing. After the success of *Deadhead*, Victoria knew it was vital that she follow it up with another winner.

'Darling, you sound like a new person. Are you on HRT at last?' asked Jessica, from New York.

'No, I'm on Rose,' said Victoria, and proceeded to outline the way Rose had changed her life for the better. 'She screens all my calls, she pays all my bills, she puts my book on the computer, she answers my readers' letters – I sign them, of course. I don't know what I'd do without her now.'

'Vicky, you'd better make sure she doesn't get fed up and leave. What kind of perks do you give her?'

'Perks?'

'Well, it sounds to me like a pretty dreary job for a young girl, buried down there in the country. How old is she?'

'Oh, Rose must be about twenty-one by now.'

'Quite. Well, you need to bear that in mind. Take her out and about a bit. Take her to London when you next have to go, buy her some new clothes, take her to restaurants. Make her see how lucky she is to be working for you. When are you next going up to see Bruno, or does he come down to Laybridge? You haven't mentioned him in quite a while.'

'That's because I haven't heard from him in quite a while. Not since before *Deadhead* was published, now I come to think of it.'

'Didn't you celebrate with him?'

'He was terribly busy that week.'

'Doing what?'

'Oh, I don't know. He couldn't come to my publication party. I've called a few times, left messages.'

'Did he send you flowers?'

'No.'

'Vicky, doesn't that tell you something?'

'You think he's found someone else?'

'Actually, no, that's not what I was thinking. I suspect he's jealous.'

'Of whom? Me? Why?'

'Suddenly you're a writer, just like him.'

'But I've always been a writer.'

'But now you're a bestselling writer.'

'Well, he should be pleased for me.'

'Darling, he's a man. And you're moving in on his territory. Plus you're successful and, if I remember rightly, his last book was a dud.'

'Oh, Bruno's not like that.'

'Vicky,' said Jessica, exasperated, 'get real.'

Victoria was mildly miffed. For all Jessica's talk of 'perks', Rose appeared to be taking her trip to London very much in her stride.

She stated her demands immediately, without any apparent show of excitement. 'I'd like time to go to Kensington High Street, if possible,' she told Victoria politely. 'I've studied the stockists' pages in my magazines. I could go to Oxford Street but – and this is a just a guess – it sounds pretty tacky. Sloane Street and Bond Street would be way out of my price range but if we went to Ken High Street we could go to Jigsaw and Gap and Benetton.'

'We?'

'Sorry, I mean I could. I thought about Covent Garden but that's a bit out of our way if we're going to Beeson's and I think it'd be a bit pricy for me anyway. I don't think I earn quite enough for Agnès B or Nicole Farhi. Where do you shop? Harvey Nicks?'

She's been watching too much *Absolutely Fabulous*, thought Victoria, and what's all this 'I don't think I earn quite enough'? Is she negotiating for a pay rise? What have I let myself in for? I only offered her the job in the first place to give her a bit of encouragement.

Yet, once again, Victoria found herself wondering, Where would I be without Rose? She had become almost totally dependent on her. It was an odd feeling, not entirely unpleasant.

'Yes, Rose, I do go to Harvey Nichols but for one reason only. I hate shopping and I can generally get everything I might need there without having to go traipsing round the city lugging loads of parcels.'

'One-stop shopping.' Rose nodded knowingly. 'That's what it's called. So where are we going to have lunch?'

'Kensington Place. Very convenient for your shopping.'

She glanced at Rose and found she was not entirely surprised that the irony was lost on her.

'And what time is our meeting at Beeson's?'

'I'm seeing Toby Marriott at eleven thirty. He wants to show me the visual for the jacket of my new book. It's six months before I'm even supposed to deliver it. I asked him to mail it to me at Laybridge and I can only imagine, since he's insisting on showing it to me in person, that he knows I'll hate it and he wants to charm me into going with it. Probably over a glass of champagne in that ghastly boardroom with the salmon pink wallpaper and the gruesome portraits of all the old Beeson ancestors. And he wants me to meet some new whizz kid marketing director they've hired.'

'Oh, yes, he said something about the new marketing director. I think his name's Kevin. He's come from Harding's. They're Mr Bruno's publishers, aren't they? Toby said he'd welcome my views on the new jacket.'

'He did, did he?'

There appeared to have been quite a bit of – what did Jessica call it? – bonding going on during those telephone calls between Rose and Toby Marriott. He evidently thought that if he sweet-talked Rose into being on his side he could get anything past Victoria. Fat chance, thought Victoria, and started up the car before Rose had even come out of the house.

Half-way up the motorway she began to feel a twinge of remorse. 'Rose, you know I'm terribly grateful for the way you've become such a support to me while I'm working. I can't tell you what a difference it makes having all those people kept away from me and you do it so politely. It's quite an art.'

'Well, I know how important it is to you. And I love talking to everyone, I really do. I've got the best of both worlds working for you. I'm still living here in the country. I love it down at Laybridge. I'd hate to work in a city. Yet I'm in touch with what goes on up there whenever I talk to your publishers and everyone. They tell me what movies to go and see and we discuss what we've watched on television. Mr Bruno's even begun to tell me about New York.'

'When did he call?'

'Oh, he calls occasionally. He's so nice to me. He

always says he'll ring back later on. He must have missed you. You leave the answering machine on sometimes, don't you? Doesn't he leave a message?'

'No. Rose, you really ought to let me know when people call even if they don't leave a message. It's what you're there for.'

'Oh, well I'm sorry.' Rose sounded a bit put-out. 'You don't really want to see him, do you, not while you're so busy with the book?'

She's still a child in so many ways. Does she know about my affair with Bruno or is she being deliberately naïve?

The façade of Beeson's building was impressive – a Georgian mansion nestling behind the hustle and bustle of Kensington High Street – but once she went inside, Victoria's heart always sank. The features of the original hall were now obscured by a long bar-like construction that formed the receptionist's desk and housed the switchboard. A tall vase of silk flowers stood on a coffee table, around which were grouped three sofas covered in a rather garish chintz. The old fireplace had been replaced with a hideous modern one made of pine.

'This is Victoria Hissey and I'm Rose Farley,' said Rose, marching firmly up to the receptionist. 'We're here to see Toby Marriott.'

That's absolutely the way to do it, thought Victoria, filled with admiration. I wait till they say 'How may I help you' and then become enraged.

They were ushered into the lift by Toby's latest assistant, Justine. Victoria watched in amusement as Rose studied Justine from top to toe, taking in the haircut, the severe little grey jacket, the white blouse with the Peter

Pan collar, the matching grey skirt, the black shoes with the chunky heels.

'I like your shoes. Where did you get them?'

'Hobbs.'

'In Kensington High Street?'

Justine nodded. 'Forty-five fifty.'

Rose's face fell. Victoria made a mental note.

'How have you been keeping, Victoria?'

Victoria bristled. She'd never clapped eyes on this girl before and as far as she knew, had never even spoken to her on the phone yet here she was being incredibly familiar.

'Mrs Hissey's been extremely busy with the new book,' Rose pointed out quickly, putting emphasis on the Mrs Hissey.

'Here we are.' Justine's look implied that it had been a rhetorical question anyway.

Victoria prepared herself for the onset of yet more depression. These rooms on the first floor, with their high ceilings and magnificent proportions, must have been stunning once but when Beeson's had bought the building they had gone partition crazy and the once gracious rooms were now a mass of paper-thin dividing walls through which everything could be heard and nothing seen, including light. The furniture was of the order-in-bulk-for-a-modern-office variety, and as Toby Marriott leapt out of his revolving fake black-leather squidgy chair it made a revolting farting sound.

Victoria wished she could have had a camera to record the look on Toby's face when he saw Rose for the first time. She didn't know what he had been expecting, and he probably hadn't known himself, but the sight of Rose, tall and willowy like a black swan, with her cropped raven curls and her long neck, stopped him dead in his tracks.

'This is Rose, my personal assistant. You two have got to know each other quite well over the telephone, I understand,' she said.

'Absolutely!' said Toby, an expression Victoria particularly loathed. 'Coffee, Victoria? Rose? Justine, three coffees, please.'

'Everything's right on target,' Toby told them.

'What is? I'm only half-way through the book.'

'Victoria, I've told you, we have to start really early now. We have to have the cover, the copy, the promotion, everything in place at least five months before publication. Now here's the jacket. Isn't it just brilliant? The figure in the middle will be spot laminated and the type will be embossed, of course.'

'It's dreadful! Why is it in a graveyard? It's supposed to be set in a rose garden like *Deadhead*. There are no graveyards in the book. Why have you got roses in a graveyard?'

'Victoria, you mustn't be so literal. You have to admit it's a good jacket and that's what counts.'

'For a penny dreadful, maybe, but not for the book I'm writing. I suppose it's not really your fault. You haven't read the book so you're just guessing. You'll change it when you've read the book.'

'It'll be too late then, Victoria. You must try and understand our time frame. Ah, here's Kevin. He'll tell you all about his wonderful plans. Kevin, meet Victoria Hissey. Victoria, meet Kevin Duggan.'

'Pleased to meet you,' said Kevin. 'I'm one of your biggest fans around here.'

'To be translated: you haven't actually read *Deadhead* but you can't wait to read it on holiday.' Victoria was feeling mischievous and knew she'd struck home when Kevin looked embarrassed. He couldn't be more than twenty-seven, twenty-eight. Why did they never give her someone her own age to deal with? Then she remembered Jessica's constant pleading with her to be more tolerant. 'Don't worry, Kevin, I won't hold it against you.' She smiled at him and wondered why he was wearing makeup. Perhaps Rose would know.

'Victoria, I wanted to tell you about the big event we've planned for the paperback launch of *Deadhead*. At Harding's, I was the one who masterminded the campaign behind Bruno Manners's new book. Too bad I had to leave before it reaches number one. I want to try an event with your book similar to the success we had with Bruno's. We're going to call it the Victoria Away-Day. We want to hire a pleasure boat and invite all the key accounts to cruise down the river Lay to Laybridge. We'll fill them to the gills with champagne and then you'll greet them for a picnic in the rose garden.'

'Key accounts,' said Victoria vaguely, still trying to work out why her book should be mentioned in the same breath as Bruno's.

'Booksellers,' explained Toby.

'Ah,' said Victoria. What on earth could she say? It was a truly terrible idea. Nobody cruised down the river Lay, and the thought of hordes of booksellers rampaging all over her rose garden made her feel faint.

But before she could speak, Rose held up her hand. 'Could I say something, please?'

'Of course you can,' said Toby, relieved that he did not

have to find a way to defuse the impending explosion from Victoria.

'I don't know if any of you know Mrs Manners – Lindy Manners? I think she works in publishing too.'

'Well, I do,' said Toby. 'She's a scout. She comes to see me sometimes. Why? Do you know her?'

'She's related to Bruno Manners and she's married to my godson,' explained Victoria. 'They have a weekend cottage at Laybridge.'

'I overheard Lindy Manners describing *Deadhead* as being much more upmarket than Victoria's earlier books,' Rose said. This was the first time she'd called Victoria by her first name and she glanced nervously at her employer. Victoria smiled. It was OK. Go ahead.

'This thing about upmarket and downmarket: it's a polite way of saying upper-class readers, isn't it? *Deadhead* appeals to a better class of person, only nobody really wants to come right out and say it. So instead of taking them to the river, much better to invite a select few to a slap-up dinner in the old hall at Laybridge. Make them wear black tie, bring their wives. Get the candelabra out, make it all look a bit spooky, shadows on the walls and all that. It is a thriller, after all. That would make it special. More, what's the word? aspirational. Victoria's cook would do us proud, wouldn't she, Victoria?'

Poor old Peg. Where on earth did Rose learn a word like aspirational, wondered Victoria. 'I'm sure she would, Rose, if she had the right help.' .

'Not far from Swindon, are you?' asked Kevin. 'We could get people over from W. H. Smith. An At Home in a stately home. An invitation to dinner from the mistress of the house. I like it.'

*

'It's always like that,' Victoria told Rose, as they walked up Kensington Church Street to the restaurant. 'They drag me up to London and go on and on about some ludicrous idea and I'm supposed to jump up and down for joy. All I want to do is go home and get on with my book. I don't want to go anywhere or see anyone ever again. We'll have a nice lunch, you can go off and look in the shops while I pop over and have tea with Lindy. Bless you for getting me out of that awful cruise idea. I imagine I can survive a dinner. Maybe I can make it a theme party and arrange huge bowls of roses everywhere and we'll drug Orlando and leave his body lying on the floor.'

'Now you're getting the idea,' said Rose. Then, after a beat, she added, 'Victoria.'

I'm not the only one, thought Victoria.

Rose loved Kensington Place. Victoria could see she was particularly fascinated by the food.

'I'm getting all sort of ideas to tell Mum about. Do you think they'd let me have a copy of the menu to take away? All these peppers. Where can we get peppers in Salisbury? Probably at Sainsbury's. I never thought to bake them in the oven in olive oil. It's delicious.'

As Victoria was paying the bill Rose suddenly shouted, 'Oh, look who's over there!'

It was Bruno. Victoria continued signing her credit-card slip. She needed a moment to regain her composure. Her heart was rounding. She could feel herself going red. Any moment now should have to look up at him.

'Hello, Rose, what a surprise. I thought Victoria was too busy for trips to town. I've been meaning to call you,

Victoria. My new book's going to go through the roof. Forty thousand copies subscribed and we're more than a month from publication.'

'We're going to have a dinner at Laybridge for *Deadhead*,' Rose told him proudly.

'What's that?'

'It's my book,' Victoria said, without smiling. 'The one where you missed the hardback launch. Too busy.'

'Sorry, sweetheart. Don't get in a grump. I know you're really trying with these new kinds of books. You'll make it, don't worry.'

'She *has* made it,' insisted Rose. '*Deadhead* was a bestseller.'

'Course it was, darling. Now, I want to buy you both a drink. What'll you have? Come on, it's Friday. I always come in here on Fridays. Usually I go and booze with a bunch of guys from the *Standard* but I'll make an exception today.'

'Don't strain yourself,' said Victoria. Why did he have to look so gorgeous? Why, when she'd had it all worked out – she'd come up to London with Rose as protection, that way she wouldn't be tempted to call Bruno – did she have to run into him like this? Of course, it was her own fault. She knew he was almost always in Kensington Place on a Friday. What was she doing behaving like a lovestruck teenager? She hadn't slept with Bruno for over six months. She had even entertained the notion that it might be over, that she could survive without him, bury herself in the country, immerse herself in her work.

But one glance as he sat down to join them and took her hand told her she was leading herself right up the proverbial garden path.

'I've missed you,' he said. That was always a killer and he knew it. He only ever came out with something like that as a last resort.

Victoria was thrown. She was no longer a young woman. She had to behave in a dignified manner but it was hard when she wanted to fling her arms around him in a way that would have been over the top even for Rose. She found herself staring at his lips, always rather pink and rosebud-like. Sensual lips. A full lower lip. Feminine lips. She knew what it was like to kiss them. So did hundreds of other women, she wouldn't be at all surprised. Oh, damn Bruno.

'I've been trying to reach you, as I said. I've got a plan, Victoria, and you're part of it.'

For one glorious second she thought he was going to propose right in the middle of Kensington Place.

'I want to go on a sensational holiday – the Caribbean, the Far East, Africa, somewhere amazing, somewhere to really celebrate the success of my new book. And I want you to come with me.'

'When?' asked Victoria, very quietly.

'Soon. Once my book's published.'

'For how long?'

'Month. Maybe six weeks. Be heaven, won't it?'

Rose chipped in. 'What a shame. Victoria's at a crucial point in her new book. She couldn't possibly go anywhere till she finishes it.'

'Why can't you just put it aside and come with me? Come on, you know you can.'

Rose was looking at her. So was Bruno. It was utterly outrageous of him. He ought to be able to understand how it would be madness for her to go anywhere at this stage. He ought to support her in her writing. He ought to have been there for her publication. Instead he didn't give a toss about anyone but himself. She had to face up to what a shit he really was and turn him down flat. Now was the perfect opportunity to do just that.

'Bruno,' she heard herself say, 'that sounds completely wonderful. Where shall we go? I can't wait.'

And she knew that throughout the holiday, wherever it turned out to be, she would be haunted by Rose's look of complete and utter disillusionment.

When she rang Lindy's doorbell, Victoria felt depressed. She wanted to be with Bruno. She resented playing the dutiful godmother, keeping her promise to Orlando that she would go and have a talk with Lindy. She had felt enormously envious of Rose, being swept away down Kensington Church Street by Bruno who had said that, if Victoria didn't have time for him, he'd take Rose shopping.

Typical Bruno! Always turning everything round so that it was her fault. If he'd wanted to spend the afternoon with her – oh, God, they could have been in bed by now – then he could have telephoned in advance and suggested it instead of assuming she would drop everything for him.

But then, of course, he had telephoned, and Rose had elected not to put him through. What a mess.

Victoria disliked what Lindy had done to Orlando's house in Elgin Crescent. She hated the way Lindy had thrown out Orlando's old furniture – faded, filched from Laybridge and, no doubt, extremely shabby – and replaced it with stark, unfriendly new stuff. At least the old furniture had been comfortable. Victoria could never relax with modern furniture, always found herself perching on the edge of it. And why was there so little? She admired the beautiful hardwood floors Lindy had put in but because the room was half empty it looked more like an art gallery than a sitting room.

She remembered when Orlando had first bought the house, how he had taken her outside and shown her the communal grounds stretching like a private park beyond the gardens attached to the houses. They were big family houses. Orlando had bought his with a view to the family he would start one day. As Lindy let her in Victoria realised that the arrival of a child in this house would change its very nature. Yet, by her own admission, the closest Lindy ever came to thoughts of children was when she enquired after the offspring of a foreign publisher, a reflex question and she never listened to the answer.

Lindy took her to the small room half-way up the stairs that had been converted into an office for the odd days she worked at home. I'm an author so she can treat me like work, thought Victoria. Not that there was any sign of it. The black table was almost bare, save for a laptop, a Rolodex and a telephone. The walls were lined with grey doors, hiding cupboards that Victoria suspected housed all the kind of paraphernalia she had littered over her desk in the library at Laybridge. Trust Lindy to hide it all away. Lindy was wearing grey. To match, Victoria wondered? She gestured to Victoria to sit across the table from her.

'It's so good to see you,' began Lindy, sounding rather false, Victoria felt. 'I haven't seen you for ages. Orlando brings me news of you when he's been down to The Cottage with all his mates, entertaining them all the time. That's so Orlando. He just has to be everybody's friend.'

'But do you let him be yours?'

'Oh Victoria!' Lindy's spirit when faced with a challenger was rising to the surface as usual. She knew she was being rude but she couldn't help it. 'You're always so direct. Shouldn't we make a little small-talk before you plunge in with whatever it is you've come to see me about? Oh, no! You have to get straight in there, so in answer to your question, Orlando's my best friend. I'm married to him.' Victoria just looked at her. She knew Lindy was right about her directness and she was a trifle ashamed. 'Oh, come on, Victoria, why are you behaving like some shrink waiting for me to come out of denial?'

'How much do you see of Orlando?'

'As much as I can. What is this all about? Why did you really want to see me? Does this have anything to do with the fact that I haven't been down to The Cottage much lately? I have stuff to read every weekend, Victoria. Everybody in publishing does. You must know that. And I can't work down there unless we make a few changes. And he doesn't want to make them. Up here he's running around with his photographers and I'm scouting and reading and, yes, I suppose you're right, we don't see much of each other.'

'Do you make time for him?'

'Do I make time for him? What about does he make time for me? All right, Victoria, I can talk to you about Orlando. You know him. You'll understand. Orlando loves to be needed. As I said he wants to be everybody's friend, right? Everybody's adviser, everybody's confidant. Yours, Rose's, Peter and Lily's. If Pepper could hear him, he'd be Pepper's. Sorry, that's a bit below the belt but you know what I mean. The thing is, what no one realises is

222

that Orlando is the neediest of all of us. He's a big baby. I fell for him because of his helplessness. He gave me a sense of control. Only now I call it his hopelessness. I have to run everything, Victoria. I had to completely redo this house, it was in such a shabby state. Why are you smiling? I haven't started on The Cottage properly yet because I haven't had time to get round to it. I've been too busy making my scouting business work. And it does, Victoria. I'm about the most successful scout in London now.'

'I know you are,' Victoria reassured her, feeling rather bludgeoned by this seemingly tireless creature seated across the table from her. 'I don't know where you get the energy. But, Lindy, can I just let you into a secret? Something that must never go any further — at least certainly not as far as Orlando. Has it ever occurred to you why he's so needy?'

'Oh, you mean because he lost his parents?'

'It's a bit more than that. You know how he worships the memory of his mother?'

'He never stops going on about her. It's a bit of strain, living up to her.'

'Don't even think about trying. She was a cow, Lindy. She was a truly horrible woman. I don't know why. Maybe something tragic happened in her childhood to make her like that. I never wanted to get close enough to her to find out. Orlando thinks she was a goddess but she treated him appallingly. She made him her little slave. 'Orlando darling, bring me this, Orlando darling, fetch me that. Sit at my feet and worship me, be my adoring little angel and I'll love you for ever.' Then she went and drowned. But the point is, Orlando has to be weaned off her. If all you want to do is to control him, then the kindest thing you could do would be to leave him. He's a sweet, nice man, Lindy. There aren't many like him around. Think about it. I know you imagine he can't do anything for himself but how can he until you let him try? Forgive me, but you've got it all wrong. As women, of course we have to take the initiative. If we left it all to them nothing would ever happen. I had to do it with dear old Hugh – now there was someone who was truly hopeless – and in a way I'm having to do it with Bruno.'

'Bruno's not hopeless. He's a highly successful writer. In fact he's –'

'Yes, yes, I know, he's the saviour of the book trade. I'm not saying he's hopeless at all. What I'm trying to make you understand is this: no matter how useless your man is or no matter how successful he is, you must never let him think for one second that you are the one in control. I know you're stronger than Orlando, I know you hold it all together. I did exactly the same with Hugh. You have to humour them. Even when they know exactly what you're doing their pride never allows them to accuse you of being patronising. They lap up all the praise you give them even when they know you're only flattering them to get them to do what you want. I promise you, I've learned over the years, humouring them is the only way.'

Listen to me going on, thought Victoria. All I'm doing is recycling what Jessica's been trying to get through to me for ages. Why is it that we never see it for ourselves yet we can always dish out advice to other people? If I want to hang on to Bruno, tentative though our relationship is at the best of times, I know I'm going to have to let him think I'm a less successful writer than he is, whatever happens.

'But why do we always have to play games with men? I accused you of being direct just now, Victoria. I want to be direct with Orlando. Times have changed. Women have more of a say. A woman is a fool if she's a doormat in this day and age.'

She's right, thought Victoria. She has a point but, then, so do I and I have the experience of age. And yet I'm floundering with Bruno. Oh, what a mess. Still, she does have one card left to play.

'Of course, there is one area where you could still be top banana, Lindy.'

'Really? How?'

'Motherhood. I can't speak from experience, never having had a child myself. Orlando's desperate for a family, as I'm sure you know, but at the end of the day, you're the only one who'd actually be able to give birth.'

'Why didn't you ever have children, Victoria? Didn't you want any?'

'I always thought there would be plenty of time. Then Hugh and I stopped sleeping together. You never met Hugh otherwise I wouldn't have to explain. When it came to sex he just wasn't interested, weird though it may seem. That's why when Bruno came along I took my chance and ran with it. And, of course, I couldn't possibly have had a child by him. I understand why you don't want a child right this minute, Lindy. You're obsessed with your work and somehow it's become more important than your marriage, but things change. You'll calm down. Don't shut Orlando out. Don't make him think you never ever want children. Make him think he's important to you but that now isn't the right time for you to have children. Hold it all together until it's the right time for you to have a baby, but make sure he understands why you're doing it.'

I've said more than I meant to, thought Victoria, but God knows I couldn't have spelled it out more clearly. Even so, I doubt that marriage will last much longer.

That night, Lindy reached across the great divide that had been the centre of their bed for so long and fondled Orlando through his pyjamas.

'What's all this about?' he mumbled.

'Don't you want to?'

'I've been wanting to for months. I thought you didn't want me any more.'

As Lindy pressed herself against him she was transported right back to their honeymoon, the way he had kissed her in the shower. Orlando had not realised how much he fancied her. To hell with all that rubbish about him being afraid of spiders, the proximity of the shower had literally thrown him into her arms. The thing about sex with Orlando was that it was the one time when she relinquished control, whether she wanted to or not. The problem was that he was not very good at instigating love-making. Invariably he waited for her to make the first move, as if he were frightened of rejection. But when she did give him a signal, there was no stopping him. He was like an animal unleashed – ferocious, but tender with it.

'Do you love me?' he asked suddenly, his head above her in the darkness. 'Do you really love me?' He was half inside her, gently pulling in and out, and she felt as if her entire body were being stroked. He had extraordinarily soft skin for a man and she clung to him, feeling him. It was like this every time they made love, so why had she pushed him away for so long? She adored this hopeless creature who was so bewilderingly strong and powerful in intimacy. It made up for all his other shortcomings. How could she ever begin to compensate for the tragedy in his past that he barely even knew about? She would have his child. She wanted it. Of course, she did. She told him so over and over as she came.

But she never answered his question.

20

Lindy could tell that the Italian publisher found her attractive. Ordinarily she might have felt tempted to flirt with him. It was no wonder she was giving out signals after the night she had had with Orlando. It was a real drag that she had arranged to see Giuseppe, or whatever his name was, on a Saturday but when she had made the appointment, she had assumed she would be spending the weekend in London. Not for one moment had she imagined that she would be desperate to jump on a train from Waterloo to Salisbury and join Orlando at The Cottage.

To make matters worse Giuseppe had been late. They had arranged to meet at her office at eleven and then go for an early lunch nearby. He had not turned up until nearly twelve, pleading some crisis with an author back in Milan. Now here they were, still in the restaurant at two thirty, and she would miss her train and have to take the next one.

Lindy didn't like Giuseppe, not because she found him unattractive – she rather liked his deep-set brown eyes and olive skin – but she had known within minutes of meeting him that he was not particularly good at his job and thus she lost interest in him. He was a new editor at the Italian house for whom she scouted and they had poached him from somewhere else, luring him away with the promise of an astronomical salary like the transfer of a premier-league footballer. Lindy had been looking forward to meeting him and to hearing which of the British books on the list she submitted weekly to his office he was interested to see while he was in London. She had called in a few markers and persuaded several editors to part with bootleg copies of their best upcoming fiction. They were unusual books, predicting new trends. Lindy was excited. But Giuseppe didn't understand what she was talking about. He was unadventurous, hungry for more of the same, definitely not a gambler, totally without vision.

That he should be tentatively flirting with her was in itself an insult. She was not flattered, merely irritated. Couldn't he see the wedding ring on her finger? Glancing down she realised that no, he couldn't because, of course, she had taken it off some time ago. To pass the time she tried to analyse why he was coming on to her. Perhaps he thought she taunted him. Yet all Giuseppe was picking up on was the residue of her renewed desire for her husband. Tough shit, Giuseppe. Nothing doing.

As soon as she was shot of him, she took a cab to Elgin Crescent. She restored her wedding ring to its rightful place and grabbed a weekend holdall from the closet. There was something in it. She reached in and found her Visitors' Book. On the train she began to scribble copiously in a state of rising euphoria.

Thank God Victoria came to see me when she did. Thank God there's still a chance to rescue my marriage. Thank God I still have time to put everything right. If it means so much to Orlando I'll have a baby. We must raise the child in the country. Note: persuade him that I definitely need a fax down at The Cottage for when I'm off

having the baby. Delia and Oscar could come down and stay and
work with me from there. We could set up the computer down there.
There'd be room for them and a nanny. They can see the agents and
everyone in London and come down and brief me. I can read down at
The Cottage. Orlando's going to be so pleased I want to spend so
much time there. I'm going to show him I can change my life for him.

She telephoned from Salisbury station and Rose
answered. 'They've all gone out. They went to meet the
earlier train and you weren't on it. I think Orlando
thought you might not be coming after all so they've gone
off to see a movie.'

'Who's they?'

'Orlando and Mr and Mrs McGill. I've got Pepper here
with me to give Mrs McGill a bit of a break.'

During the taxi ride from Salisbury Lindy's jaw
clenched with frustration. She would not cry. Why hadn't
he told her that Peter and Lily were going down? She
wanted to run things, she wanted to show him how it was
going to be, yet how could she begin to take control with
Lily interfering at every opportunity? But she would not
cause any aggravation. She would be sweetness and light
the entire weekend. That was the way to regain her
position as mistress of the house. No sharp words to Lily,
no sign of exasperation when Peter became insufferably
boring about money, no challenging Orlando.

But the biggest effort she would make would be with
the brat. She would bend over backwards to make Pepper
adore her in preparation for her role as the best mother
Orlando's child could possibly have.

Rose and Pepper were in the garden when the taxi
deposited her in front of The Cottage. Lindy slipped

upstairs and returned The Visitors' Book to its hiding place in the linen cupboard. By the end of the weekend she would be recording her triumph in regaining control of The Cottage. And where better to start than with Pepper?

'Rose,' she called out through her bedroom window, 'I'll look after Pepper. You get on home.'

'It's all right,' said Rose, when Lindy joined her in the garden. 'I love being with him. I always look after him when they're down. If you look in the kitchen, you'll see Mum's made a cottage pie for dinner. You'll have asparagus to begin. Mrs McGill brought some down. Mum made a chocolate mousse yesterday. You'll find it in the fridge. Why don't you go and have a rest or read one of your manuscripts, put your feet up for a bit before they come back.'

This didn't fit in with Lindy's plan. And she didn't need Rose here. She needed to be found on her own with Pepper. They would be playing together, an idyllic picture of Lindy as a caring child lover.

She tried to deflect Rose. 'How's it going up at Laybridge? Victoria on course with the new book? Am I going to be able to read it soon?'

'She doesn't really like me talking about it while it's still a work in progress.'

'Work in progress? That sounds a bit pompous, Rose. Anyway, I'm family. You can tell me anything.'

Rose looked worried. 'Well, to tell you the truth she's not working on it at all at the moment. She's all excited about her holiday with Bruno Manners. They're going off next week.'

'Are they really? Where to? Oh, never mind. You don't have to give away any more state secrets. I'll ask Victoria when I see her. At least tell me what the new book's about. I mean, you owe me one, Rose. I had a call from Toby Marriott blaming me for putting ideas into your head about Victoria's books being much more upmarket than they really are. Apparently you piped up at some meeting and nearly ruined Beeson's marketing pitch.'

'But I heard you tell Victoria that *Deadhead* was more literary than her earlier books.'

'I'm sure you did because that's what she wanted to hear. Authors always need to think they write better than they actually do, no matter how many copies they sell. And *Deadhead* is an improvement but it's still stuck in a category. When will the new book be ready?'

'She'll have it finished by the summer – June, July, I expect, the way things are going. Now, if you'll excuse me, I'd better think about Pepper's tea.'

'Rose. I mean it. I really want to be with him. I hardly ever see him and he is Orlando's godson.'

Rose's look implied, 'and whose fault is that?' She said, 'Actually, he's quite tired. He might even have a sleep. I took him for a walk up to the trout stews. If you give him a handful of fish food he throws it in himself and –'

'Yes, wonderful. Now, let me have him. Come here, darling.'

Pepper stiffened visibly when she reached for him.

'He hasn't got his hearing aid in. He hates wearing it. We took it out to go and play in the garden.'

Pepper emitted a high-pitched shriek.

Lindy jumped. 'What's that mean? Is he in pain?'

'No. That's just a sound he makes. You do know all about his deafness, don't you?'

'Of course I do. I can handle him.'

'He'll need his tea if he doesn't go off for a sleep. Marmite soldiers. Spaghetti hoops if he wants them.'

'Fine, fine. Thanks, Rose. You've done quite enough. You're a star.'

'Don't forget to put his hearing aid back in when you go indoors.' Rose departed reluctantly.

Pepper didn't want Marmite sandwiches. He didn't want spaghetti hoops. He didn't want to stay indoors. If she were honest, Lindy understood he didn't want her anywhere near him. She had spread out his toys on the floor in front of the fire and tried to entice him to play with them but he just stared at her, making a monotonous humming sound that grated on her nerves. She rose from her knees and perched on one of the armchairs that stood on either side of the fire. She tried to imagine herself sitting opposite Orlando, the fire burning between them and their child playing on the floor. They wouldn't watch television. They would be good enough company for each other without it. Maybe they might even start a new trend by listening to the radio. That's what couples had done before television, how they had coped during the war. They must have been much more aware of each other then, thought Lindy, when they had to look at each other instead of the television screen.

Except Orlando wasn't there. And even if they got rid of the television there would always be weekend guests like Peter and Lily to contend with. Maybe a baby was the only thing that would keep them together. A nice healthy son who would knock Pepper out of the picture.

'Pepper, please, come and sit on my lap and have a cuddle.' She reached out to lift him up but he resisted her. 'At least let me take off those muddy wellies. You're making a mess all over the rug.' But Pepper eluded her once more. 'Stop staring at me like that. You look like the kid in *The Omen*. Oh, Christ, I give up. Play on your own if you don't want to play with me.'

She decided to phone Oscar. He was out. It was Saturday afternoon, after all. He was probably at the match. She would try Delia. She dialled again. As she waited for Delia to answer she grew excited. She could tell Delia about the dreadful Giuseppe – they could have a laugh about that, woman to woman. And she could outline her plan to have a child and how she and Oscar would be coming down maybe two days a week to work in the country. Delia would be in her element. She could set up new systems. She could lord it over Oscar. She could probably organise it so that he never actually had to go down to The Cottage. She and Lindy would work with the baby beside them. Oscar, as a man, would be very much out of it. This would be Delia's chance to move in on Lindy and bond with her, once and for all.

Lindy liked people to endorse her plans and support her ideas. She hated anyone to dampen her enthusiasm for a project or be reluctant to fall in with what she had in mind. Even Pepper's failure to respond to her attempts to win him over had frustrated her.

And once she got through, as she listened to Delia wittering on about their new life, Lindy never noticed Pepper calmly walk out of the front door and down the lane.

'*Pepper!*' Lindy screamed, running along the Bluebell Walk. 'PEPPER!'

When she reached the trout stews, she remembered.

Rose had told her to put Pepper's hearing aid back in and she had forgotten.

She saw one of his little red wellingtons lying on its side on the riverbank and she stopped dead.

She didn't go any further. Was there any point? In a calm, deliberate manner that belied the panic inside her Lindy retraced her steps to The Cottage.

'Rose, we're back.'

'Rose, where are you? Has he had his tea? We'd better start thinking about his bath.'

'They're not here. Maybe they went for a walk. Bit late.'

'No sign of Lindy either. I'll give her a ring in London. See if she's left.'

'Orlando, there's someone drawing up in a car outside. Peter, open the door, it's a police car.'

'We're looking for a Mr and Mrs McGill.'

'You've found … I'm Peter McGill.'

'You have a little boy?'

'Yes. Almost three. What's happened?'

'We had a call from a woman who wouldn't give her name. Said to come here. Said he'd fallen in the river. Sorry, miss, who are you? You can't come in just now.'

'I'm Rose Farley from next door.'

'Rose! Where have you been? Where's Pepper? It sounds as if he's fallen in the river. What could you have been thinking of? You bloody stupid –'

'Orlando, leave her alone.'

'I left him with Lindy.'

'Lindy's not here. She hasn't arrived. How could you have left him with Lindy? At least accept the responsibility for what you've done, Rose. We should never have left him with you.'

'If the young lady could tell us exactly what happened, sir. We're standing by to drag the river.'

It was Victoria who found the note.

Lindy had told her that she had taken to hiding The Visitors' Book in the linen cupboard. When they finally understood from Rose that Lindy had been there but had now left, Victoria, acting on a hunch, went to the linen cupboard. There was an envelope inside with her name on it. The note inside had obviously been scrawled in such a hurry that it was barely legible.

Victoria, please, PLEASE, tell Orlando that I've gone. I couldn't face seeing him. It was my fault. I wasn't watching him. I didn't push him in but you'll always think I killed him. I know none of you will want me here any more. Tell the police to contact me at the office. I'm not going back to Elgin Crescent. Tell Orlando I'm sorry – for Pepper, for going, for being the worst possible wife he could have married.

Victoria had to show Orlando the note but she spirited The Visitors' Book out of The Cottage without him seeing it together with the first volume she had given Lindy when they had met at Laybridge. She had found it hidden under some towels. If Orlando saw it and realised his mother had been keeping a journal, he'd be bound to start asking questions as to why it ended so abruptly. The last thing he needed to find out on the day his wife left him was that the mother he worshipped had let him down just as badly.

PART FOUR

21

Why did Harold Farley have to go and die on me? Victoria asked herself. Without him she had really let the gardens go at Laybridge. In a valley, they were vulnerable to frost and this year's had wrought havoc with her young shoots. She stared out of her bedroom window at the back of the house, which overlooked the grounds. The hedges were a disgrace. Harold had always seen that they were clipped. It was almost as if nature had pounced the minute he had died, judging by the jungle of weeds she saw spread out below her, smothering her herbaceous borders. Bloody bindweed strangling everything! What had they all been doing? Harold would never have let it get this far.

Oh, how she missed him. She recalled how they had pored over photographs of the gardens at Laybridge, taken by Hissey ancestors in Edwardian times, and then drawn up plans on paper spread over the dining-room table based on the original layout of the Edwardian period. Together they had gathered cuttings from shrubs and trees in other people's gardens. Victoria remembered whole areas being sheeted with black polythene acting as a mulch to keep the soil warm and moist. Harold had abhorred the use of chemicals. Where had she put those plans? She would dig them out and find someone to help her restore the gardens in Harold's memory. She owed him so much. If she had not found him lying dead at her feet in the rose garden, would she ever have had the idea for *Deadhead*? The idea that had made her so successful. She owed it all to Harold Farley and yet what wouldn't she give to have him back?

Down by the river she could see the jumps being put up for the event that was to take place the following day. Every year the gardens at Laybridge were opened in aid of Riding for the Disabled, although quite why they had to have it in freezing February was beyond Victoria's comprehension. In a couple of years Pepper would be old enough to be placed on a Thelwellian Shetland pony and led round the field, although whether Lily would ever be able to face bringing him to Laybridge again was another matter altogether. Thinking about Pepper brought back the nightmare conversation she had had with Bruno on the telephone the night before.

'I could understand it if the kid had actually been drowned but since he's still with us, what difference does it make?'

'Bruno, if I have to spell it out for you then that's another reason why I don't want to go on holiday with you.'

Victoria was miserable. This man was supposed to mean something to her. There had been a time when she had thought him the most important person in her life. Maybe she still did. She hated it when he disappointed her like this. When he didn't understand something so simple as her no longer wanting to go away with him after what had happened to Pepper. It was a reminder to her that while on occasion Bruno could be a kind and attentive listener if she ever went to him with a problem, he hated it when she tried to interest him in someone's else's problem, especially if it affected him. The other thing she was beginning to understand was that he wasn't remotely interested in children. Had that been what had attracted him to her? The fact that she was someone else's wife and could not have his child.

'But it's not as if you have to hang around for the funeral or anything. I'm not even asking you to go away before his wretched birthday party. We can leave the day after. I can't understand what's the matter with you. I've made all these arrangements. Why are you being so inconsiderate?'

'Why am *I* being so inconsiderate? Pepper could have drowned. We were convinced he had. It happened at Laybridge. I am shaken. Very, very shaken. I was there when they found him. It was horrible, Bruno, utterly horrible. He was crouched in a corner in the old turbine house by the weir, where they keep the fish food. He was wet through. We don't think he actually fell in because he can't swim and he would undoubtedly have drowned. But it was raining and he probably slipped and got a shock and went to hide in the turbine house. They had all the equipment there to drag the river. You had only to look at it to know how potentially horrific the situation was. And, of course, although no one came right out and said it, they were about to re-enact exactly what happened when Guy and Daisy drowned. When your brother drowned.'

'I wasn't around. I didn't see it.'

'So it's as if it never happened, is it? Just because you weren't there. Your own brother, Bruno. Hugh was more of a brother to him than you ever were.'

'Bit late to start taking that high moral line, isn't it? You never came out with any of this rubbish when you were cheating on Hugh. If I wasn't much of a brother to Guy, what kind of a wife were you to Hugh?'

'Well, at least I made a commitment to someone and I did stick by Hugh to the end.'

'That's because I never asked you to leave him.'

'Well, since you never asked, how do you know what I would have done? And you never asked because you don't even know the meaning of the word commitment. You can't understand that I love Pepper and I am too upset by the thought of what might have happened to him just to drop everything and devote my attention to you. I don't think you've ever loved anyone in your entire life, Bruno. Sometimes I think you're completely selfish.'

'What *is* all this? How dare you say I've never loved anyone? What do you think you and I have been about all these years?'

'Sex,' said Victoria simply, astounding herself that she could admit it aloud so abruptly when it had never even crossed her mind before.

'Oh, that's great. You're saying you've never loved me. You've just thought of me as a good fuck.'

'And what about Orlando? Pepper's his godson. He's in a terrible state. I can't go away and leave him now.'

'He's thirty years old. He's not a baby. Anyone would think you were his mother, the way you fuss about him. You always have. It's ridiculous. Anyway, he's got Lindy.'

'No, he hasn't. That's the point. She's gone.'

'Lindy's gone?'

'She was down here that weekend. It was all her fault. She was supposed to be watching Pepper and she let him wander off on his own. She was so obsessed with her work, I imagine. When she found out what she'd done, she didn't stay and face the music. She went straight back to London and Orlando hasn't seen her since. He can barely bring himself to mention her name. I've spoken to her, told her Pepper's OK. She's called me once since. It was very late at night and she was practically incoherent. She kept on saying there was no way she and Orlando could ever be together now this had happened, how it had all been her fault, how she was totally wrong for him. I couldn't talk her round. She'd convinced herself she was doing the right thing.'

'Did you want to? I had the feeling you didn't much like Lindy, even though she did wonders for your career.'

'I just didn't see how she would ever make things right for Orlando. He's so sensitive and she's so ...'

'She's a control freak. I knew it the minute I met her, when she picked me up at the station that first weekend. She struck me as being one of those people who just assume everything is going to go their way. Pepper nearly drowned, it was her fault, she fucked up and, worse, she got caught. That's what she can't handle. That's why she's flipped and run off somewhere. Nothing to do with Orlando. I love the way you say you tried to talk her into going back to him and then you tell me you can't see how she would ever make things right for him. You're such a romantic, Victoria. Even about me. Sex, indeed. You're in love with me. You always have been.'

'I was. Maybe I do still love you but I don't like you much any more, Bruno. You haven't been exactly supportive about my career for a start.'

'Your what?'

'My writing. I'm a successful writer now, just like you.'

'So?'

'So why don't you understand that I need to stay here and get on with my book instead of running off on holiday with you?'

'Wait a second. I thought you weren't coming because of Pepper's accident. When did your book become part of it?'

Victoria wanted to scream. This was typical Bruno. He was always catching her out. Winding her up, or whatever the dreadful expression was.

'Oh, go on your bloody holiday, Bruno. Go off to America on your fifteen-city book tour, or whatever it is they're sending you on. I'm going to stay here and keep an eye on Orlando and you can make as many snide remarks about my mothering him as you want. He had such a bitch for a mother it's a miracle he turned out as nice as he is.'

'You're right there.'

'I thought you liked Daisy. I thought you and she … years ago …?'

'Oh, you guessed about that, did you? It was years ago and anyway it was more or less a one-night stand. I loathed her. As you said, she was a complete bitch. Oh, why did you have to go and remind me about her? She was so scrawny. Her ribs dug into me when I was on top of her, I can still remember. Her hip-bones, too. Her fingernails were like claws. Long red talons. She smoked throughout sex. She was never still, she never stopped talking. It was like fucking a microphone. But I had to have her. Men get like that sometimes, did you know that, Victoria? They see someone, they find her repellent but nevertheless they have to fuck her. I imagine it must be a kind of power thing.'

Well, you would know, thought Victoria bitterly. She

was disgusted by Bruno's outburst. He was such a strange mixture. He could be quiet and tender but there was another side to him. Brutal, forceful, power-hungry. And the truth was that it was the combination of the two that attracted her to him. One without the other would be unbearable, the former boring and the latter overpowering. We can never be wholly satisfied with a man, she thought. They've always got a bad side and it's usually that side that attracts us to them in the first place, however much we might witter on about wanting a sweet, considerate man who really understands us.

Plus she had learned more about Daisy in the last few seconds than at any other time.

'Don't tell anyone I said this,' Bruno went on, 'but it's one of those blessings in disguise that she drowned. It's just a shame she took poor old Guy along with her. God knows what would have happened to that marriage if she hadn't died that night. She'd have ruined everyone's life somehow. It was what she was born to do.'

'Oh, she did. She ruined –'

'Ruined what?'

'Nothing.'

'Come on. I always thought it was bizarre the way the inquest found it to be an accident. Why did you say Pepper's accident was like Daisy and Guy's drowning? Were they found there? Up by the weir? I always thought they were found by The Cottage.'

'They were. They were.'

'The weir was involved, though, wasn't it?'

'Leave it, Bruno. It was a long time ago and, as you say, you weren't there. Let's meet when I come up to London for Pepper's birthday party and talk about this – about you and me, I mean. Or come to Laybridge for a few days. We'll thrash it out.'

'And waste a perfectly good holiday booking? You're joking. I'm going away even if you won't join me. I need a break. Isn't it about time you understood how much I loathe the bloody country? That's the difference between us. Bury yourself down there, if you want, but don't drag me down with you.'

Victoria had felt wretched when she put down the phone.

What did it say about her that she yearned only for tranquillity and order in her life and no longer craved the excitement of Bruno? And what did it say about her when she could admit to herself that she missed her old dead gardener more than her lover?

Orlando had insisted that Lily have Pepper's party in his house so that the children could run out into the communal gardens, even though it was freezing.

Orlando looked terrible when he opened the door. 'She's going to New York.'

Victoria proffered her cheek to be kissed and received a glancing peck. 'Who is?'

'Lindy. She's going to America for a while. That dreadful Delia called to say she's going to be in New York for a week or two because she's landed some new scouting job for Rubinstein and Rose. Who the fuck are Rubinstein and Rose?'

'I hope by the time Lindy's finished with them they'll be my new American publishers. They've been sniffing around after my books for a year or so now.'

'Well, as long as somebody's happy.'

'Stop feeling sorry for yourself and take me to the action. God, what a noise. I hope there's a sinful birthday cake I can gorge on by way of consolation.'

Lily was sitting at one end of the long kitchen table with her hands over her ears. Children were tearing round the room. The table was laid for about twelve. Paper hats. Crackers. Jellies. Twiglets. Smarties. Tiny sandwich triangles. A little neatly wrapped present in each place. And in the middle Pepper's birthday cake. Chocolate with three candles and bunnies running round it. At the other end of the table Pepper sat, spooning jelly into his mouth.

'Lily, this is wonderful but I don't know how you stand it.' Victoria kissed her on the cheek. 'Why isn't Pepper joining in?'

'He's a bit overawed. He doesn't really know what to do. He's never been to a birthday party before. This is the first I've had for him.'

'But surely he's been to other children's?'

'They don't ask him.'

'Oh, don't be absurd.'

'I'm not being absurd, Victoria.' Lily was quite angry. 'That's the way it is. It's the parents. They don't like having deaf children in their houses, they don't want to be responsible for them. For any disabled child. It's awful. I had no idea till I had one of my own. They'll always send over their rowdy, undisciplined kids to rampage all over my house but they won't have quiet, undemanding Pepper in case he says something they don't understand and they don't know what to do.'

As she sat down beside Pepper and gave him a hug, for one awful second Victoria wondered if it might have been better if he had drowned.

22

How many other rich men ever wonder what it would be like if they'd been born poor? Orlando thought, as he drove to work on a wet March morning. Was he the only one? Was he completely nuts? Wouldn't other men be thrilled to be part of a family that had so wisely invested their money that the youngest heir apparent could buy himself a photographic agency to play with?

But that was the problem. He didn't take the running of the agency seriously. He only went there two or three times a week. To him it really was only playing and the more he thought about it the more he realised that that was why he was less than happy. He ought to be devastated because his marriage appeared to have fallen apart but he was more worried because he knew he would have to face up once again to deciding what he wanted to do about his life.

He had to make more of an effort. Was that why he had been attracted to Lindy, because she was so dynamic? Because she made things happen in a way that he couldn't? Or was he just trying to make the wrong things happen for him? He had no great desire to rush to work at the agency every morning but on Fridays he was always desperate to get down to The Cottage. And it wasn't just because it was a weekend retreat. It was where his heart lay. It was the only place where he knew exactly who he was. Where he had confidence in himself. And, if he was honest, that was why it had gone wrong with Lindy. Could they have ever grown to love each other deeply? He doubted it. They approached life from two different angles. Lindy had never got the point of The Cottage or Laybridge and he had never got the point of her work in London, which meant so much to her (or his work in London for that matter). Neither of them had ever understood the thing that was most important to the other. Did that mean that they just didn't understand each other? Probably, sad though it was.

As he drove into the courtyard in the remote part of the city where his agency had its offices in a converted Victorian warehouse, he watched three women arrive within minutes of each other, picking their way across the slippery rain-soaked cobbles. One was Vivienne, who acted as his associate and who did most of the work. Orlando followed them in and slumped down on a sofa in Reception to read the paper. It was always complete bedlam first thing but he hoped that if he got himself caught up in the action it would inspire him to put more effort into running the place.

It was a narrow Dickensian building with one room on each floor. Patsy, the junior, and Steph, Vivienne's right hand, went to work the minute they walked in. There was the post to open, messages on the answering machine to listen to, faxes to be dealt with. Vivienne climbed the spiral staircase to her office on the next floor to hang up her raincoat. Patsy turned up the volume on the answering machine so she could hear the messages.

'Hi, it's Steve from Motordrive. Just ringing to confirm that you need the motorhome next week for the trip to

Camber Sands. Someone's pushing me for a second option. Give me a bell soon as you get in. Cheers.'

'Hi, this is Bill calling in from New York. I just got here from San Francisco. Is that job for CK still on for the end of the week because if not *Marie-Claire* want me for a four-page editorial? I'm at Lucy's ...'

'Steph, it's Fred. I need an assistant for Thursday, and do me a favour, get me someone who knows one end of a Polaroid from the other this time.'

'Steph, Patsy, anyone, help! Urgent! It's Jeff. I want twenty rolls EPR 120, two twin packs Polacolour and two packs AA batteries for Lighthouse Studios at ten o'clock this morning.'

'Steph!' Vivienne called down.

'Okay, I'm on to it. Patsy, call KJP film suppliers and order all that and have it put on a bike to get round to Lighthouse Studios. Go on! Jump! Do it now!'

But before Patsy could pick up the phone it rang. The front door opened, a courier walked in and dumped twenty model books on her desk.

'From Marks and Spencer,' he announced cheerfully. 'Who's gonna sign for them?'

'Oh, shit,' said Steph. 'They're for that casting this afternoon. Patsy, you sign for them and then make us all a cup of coffee. I'll call KJP.'

'We're out of coffee and looks like the milkman's not been this morning neither.'

'And we've got twenty girls coming in for this casting and I don't suppose there's any biscuits left. Patsy, you'd better get out to the shops while I start going through these faxes. It's going to be one of those days.'

An hour later it was worse.

Patsy had locked herself in the loo. Jeff had shouted abuse down the phone at her when his film had still not turned up at Lighthouse Studios by eleven. There was a very simple reason. Steph had forgotten to make the call to KJP but it was Patsy who had taken the rap. Orlando could hear Steph trying to coax her out.

'I'm sorry, Patsy. Please, Pats. It's my fault. I'll call him and tell him. Please come out.'

'Tell me when she surfaces, then send her upstairs with a cup of coffee. I'll calm her down.' Orlando began the long climb up to the top floor of the narrow building to what they called the executive office. He knew that when he wasn't there they used it as a changing room for the models when they had castings and who could blame them? He was always finding stray lipsticks, tights and, once, even a pair of knickers under his desk and having to have a word with the cleaner. Besides the three stark black telephones and the equally stark black table that served as a desk, there was a sofa, a fridge, a full bar, a giant television and a VCR.

As he went up the stairs he heard Vivienne shouting, 'Patsy, all five lines are going. Will you please get down here and answer these phones. You can take him his coffee in a minute.'

'I'll get it,' he shouted down. Might as well make himself useful.

'Orlando's'. He had never quite got used to the fact that the agency was called after him but they had assured him it was a good name. 'Orlando's. Hello.'

'Hi, this is Atlanta from the Janey Hardman Agency. You've got a first option on Michelle for makeup for that trip your photographer's doing in St Lucia in May. Can you confirm for me, please?'

'Which photographer?'

'It was Damien.'

'Damien McIntyre?'

'Yeah, can he confirm on Michelle?'

'Well, I'm not sure. I'll have to call you back.'

'So do you want the option on Michelle, thirteenth to eighteenth May, yes or no?'

'I'm not sure, I'll have to ask –'

'Oh, for Christ's sake, I'll take that as a no.'

Orlando groaned. It was always like this. Non-stop aggression. No one bothered to be charming or pleasant any more. It was a done deal or a fuck-you. Was that how all women in offices sounded? Did Lindy shout at people like that? Surely not. Was all the claptrap true that he read in newspapers and magazines about glass ceilings having to be shattered by women acting as tough as men?

Just before lunch, while he was standing waiting for a fax in reception Steph called the Janey Hardman Agency. 'Hi, it's Steph at Orlando's. Just want to confirm Neville needs to be at Click NS2 at nine tomorrow morning for the Wella job with David.'

'Over my dead body,' came the reply.

'I beg your pardon?'

'You seriously think we're going to give you a hairdresser after that git from your office tells us he's going to have to get back to us this late in the day?' Steph had the phone on the voice box so the whole office could hear. Orlando stood staring at the wall as Steph waded in. 'We haven't got a "git" working in this office. Who the fuck d'you think you're talking to? I'm calling to confirm Neville for tomorrow morning.'

'And I'm telling you, you stupid cow, that it was only ever a second option and you're not having him or anyone else from this agency as of this minute. *Adios*, Orlando. *Finito*. Call someone else.'

It wasn't just a flash-in-the-pan spat. When Vivienne rang Janey Hardman herself – Vivienne stayed at Janey's villa in Majorca every summer and they went to Henlow Grange together twice a year – Janey confirmed everything.

'Whatever you said to that agency,' Vivienne told Orlando, 'it's cost us our relationship with them. Not for ever, we'll make it up in a few weeks' time, but it's done a lot of damage. They have the best hair and makeup artists in the country. Our photographers only ever want to work with their people. And, worst of all, we don't have a hairdresser for the shoot at Click NS2 in the morning. Tommy the photographer's flying in from Milan tonight. He's going to go apeshit when he finds out he hasn't got Neville.'

Orlando decided there and then. He wouldn't come back after lunch. There seemed little point. In one morning he appeared to have ruined his own agency's key relationship with another without having the faintest idea how he'd done it. All he'd done was ask, politely, if he could get back to them. Everyone spoke a foreign language as far as he could make out. What was the point of staying in London to run a business he simply didn't understand any more and in which he had never been much involved anyway? He had only bought it because he had been attracted to photography and, years ago, his mother had given him several introductions. But this fashion stuff was a waste of time, as far as he was concerned. It didn't interest him in the slightest. If only he had paid more attention when he had bought the agency, if only he hadn't rushed into it – like he had rushed into his marriage.

Maybe he shouldn't be rushing away from everything either, but as soon as he arrived back at Elgin Crescent he began to feel better. He had made a decision. He would sell the agency. He scanned the list stuck to the side of the fridge for the Farleys' number.

'Rose? I'm coming down to The Cottage. Will you get everything ready?'

'Of course. Will you be down Friday night or Saturday?'

'Tonight. In a couple of hours.'

'Right. How long are you staying?'

'For ever. I'm going to come and live at The Cottage.'

At last, thought Rose, and began to make a shopping list.

She stocked the fridge at The Cottage with all his favourite snacks and then lay on her bed and waited. She heard the crunch of wheels on gravel at about eleven and looked out to see his car turning off the lane.

She left it until past midnight before she crept down the narrow staircase that divided her bedroom from Peg's and let herself out of Farley Cottage. She'd wrapped a raincoat over her nightdress to ward off the crisp night air.

Orlando was already asleep when she shrugged off the raincoat and climbed into bed with him. She infiltrated her way into his arms without waking him.

In the morning she would move things in.

23

'What are you doing?' Peg asked, standing at the door to Rose's bedroom.

What does it look like? Rose was tempted to reply as she pulled nightdresses and underwear out of her drawers and stuffed them into a holdall. 'I'm moving my things next door.'

'To Orlando's?'

No, on to the main road. 'Yes.'

'He wants a live-in maid now, does he?'

'I'm not going as a maid, Mum.'

'Are you not? Going to be his secretary as well as Mrs Hissey's?'

'Mum, I'm moving in there to be with him. As his friend.'

'Has he asked you to?'

Rose was glad she had her back to Peg. Why was her mother always so direct? How did she manage to hit the proverbial nail on the head and focus on the very thing Rose had been avoiding? No, Orlando hadn't asked her. That was the bad news. Not that there was much good news as yet. She was taking a mega gamble moving in her kit. She knew she was the one making all the running but when would she ever have another chance? Only last week she'd read a piece in a magazine about how vulnerable men were when they split up with their other halves, about how women survived so much better on their own than men, how men invariably remarried, didn't like being single whereas women sometimes found they relished it.

'He's another woman's husband, Rose. Has this been going on long?'

'No,' said Rose truthfully. 'Anyway, you know Lindy's gone. Actually, she's in America so I hear. And she was never down here with him. They were sort of living apart in any case.'

'But they're still man and wife. What do you know about their marriage? What are you doing, interfering? Marriages survive when husbands and wives spend time apart. Sometimes it's better that way. Your father and I –' She stopped abruptly.

'Oh, yes, I know, you and Dad, you were the golden couple, cooped up here in Farley Cottage in marital bliss.'

'If you really want to know I was going to say your father spent a great deal of time on his own, away from me, mucking about with his trout stews, doing God knows what, and I never made a murmur. I let him do what he wanted and we got along fine.'

'I thought he spent all his time down at the Laybridge Arms. I thought he died of drink, his liver ...'

Peg sat down on the bed.

'How do you know that? You were only a girl when Charlie died.'

'People talk, Mum.'

'Yes, they do, and they'll wag their bloody tongues loose if you move in with Orlando Manners.'

'I don't care. I'm in love with him.'

Peg was staring out of the window.

'I know, love. You always were. And I loved your father.'

Rose saw that she was on the verge of tears. She sat down beside Peg and put her arm round her.

'I know you did, Mum. I was never suggesting anything else. If I think about it I can see that you and Dad lived different lives. You were up at Laybridge half the time. He was at the stews. You were both too knackered to summon up the energy to even talk to each other, I shouldn't wonder. I'm young but I know enough to realise that after the first few years it isn't all candlelight and romance. Yet Orlando and Lindy had barely been married for a second. They ought to have been all over each other still. Mum, why did Dad drink so much?'

'He didn't.'

'Just enough to kill himself. Come on, Mum, was he unhappy?'

They'd never talked about it. Ever. Somehow with Harold sitting there at the supper table every night Rose had never liked to bring it up. Harold had been the great silent keeper of the peace. It was as if his withered old bulk had stood between mother and daughter's pent-up emotions like a referee at a boxing match. Conversation at mealtimes had always been perfunctory because of Harold. And, Rose reflected, what she had said about her father now applied to her. She and her mother were barely at Farley Cottage together long enough to have a proper conversation and even though they both spent the day up at Laybridge they could hardly have a heart-to-heart in front of Victoria. But why did Peg spend so much time at Laybridge? Rose had never thought about it before. Was her mother trying to escape from something? Was there something about Rose's father that her mother did not want to confront? Harold was gone now. It was as if a screen had been removed and Rose could see Peg clearly as she never had before: a woman old before her time, a woman who kept herself so busy she never allowed herself to face up to the demons in her past. For Peg had demons. Rose could see them in her sad eyes as she sat in a huddle on the bed, wiping them and drying her hands on her apron out of habit.

'Mum, what's up? If you don't want me to go to The Cottage, I won't, not if it's going to make you so unhappy. But you'll have to tell me the reason.'

'You do what you want. You're a grown woman now. If you won't listen to me there's nothing I can do. I've had my say.'

But you haven't, thought Rose miserably. There's something bottled up inside you and it's choking you.

When Rose returned, Orlando was sitting at the kitchen table nursing a large mug of black coffee and looking decidedly gloomy. Embarrassed, she tried to hide her holdall behind the fridge. He saw it and looked at her, but he didn't say anything. Well, what did she expect? 'Oh, great, you're moving in with me. Just what I've always wanted.' At least she didn't get 'What the fuck do you think you're doing?'

But this gloomy silence was unnerving.

'You're sitting at the kitchen table, minding your own business and a ravishingly beautiful princess walks through the door and says, "Give me fifty million pounds to save my kingdom or I shall disappear in a puff of smoke and you'll never see me again." What do you do?'

This was a variation of the game they had played as children, only then it had been more along the lines of 'The Bluebell Walk is crammed full of snarling crocodiles and any minute Peg will walk right into them on her way home. What do you do?'

'Your wife has left you, you can't run your own business, you're thirty years old and a complete and utter failure. What do you do?'

'Stop feeling sorry for yourself for a start,' said Rose. 'Look upon it as a chance to make a new beginning.'

'Of what?'

'I don't know. Life.' She wanted to say 'us' but she didn't dare.

'Life in the Country. Sounds like a Merchant Ivory film.'

'A what?'

'Oh, forget it!'

'No, go on, tell me. I might not be sophisticated like your smart London friends but I'm as good as them any day. Just don't patronise me. Tell me.'

'Oh, God, Rose, what on earth induced me to come down here for a bit of P and Q with a feisty little bunny like you on my doorstep? Why do you always get so furious with me? When I showed you how to do something when we were little you used to fly at me. You will not be told, will you?'

'That's just what I'm trying to say. You should tell me about things instead of expecting me to know everything and then saying, "Oh, forget it," when I don't. I want to learn.'

'Oh, Rose. Now you tell me something. What am I going to do about Lindy? Should I try and get her back?'

'Why are you asking me?' He was missing the point. What did he think last night was all about? What did he think she had in her holdall? Her homework?

'I'm asking you because for some bizarre reason I was under the impression you cared about me and what happens to me.'

'I do.'

'Well, then?'

'I think you should let her keep on leaving you.'

'Let her keep on ... Yes, I think I know what you mean. Any particular reason?'

'She's not right for you.'

'Why not?'

'I don't know. She just isn't.'

'Thank you, Rose. That's exceptionally helpful. "She just isn't." You sound like a thwarted child.' He saw her face. 'No. I take that back. Don't get into a fury again. You didn't like her, I take it. Not many people did, it seems. I really made a mess of things bringing her into my life. But then my life was a pretty fucking awful mess anyway. The only place I seem to function reasonably well is down here, the one place my mother loathed more than any other, the place that killed her.'

'It didn't kill her.'

'All right, it didn't actually kill her but she died here and yet I'm happy in this house.'

'Well, what's wrong with that? Come and live in it.'

'You always see everything in black and white, Rose. It's not as simple as that.'

'Why not? It could be. I don't understand why people like you run a mile from anything that's simple. Why do you always have to make life hard for yourselves? You grew up down here, you loved it, you went to London, you got all confused, you married the wrong woman, you came back here to where you're happy and you start complicating matters by questioning the simple truth.'

'Oh, Rose, you're such a baby.'

'I am *not* a *baby!*'

She couldn't see that Orlando was smiling.

'You're sitting there at the kitchen table and a great big beautiful babe walks in and starts screaming the simple truth at you. "*I am not a baby!*" she goes. What do you do?'

'Well, I'm not, you always treat me like –'

'What you do is you gather her up and rock her in your arms like this.'

He tried but he couldn't quite manage it at first. She was all furious flailing arms and legs but finally he got her on her back on the sofa in the next room.

'Pervert!' she hissed, thoroughly enjoying it. 'Child-molester. My mum's walking past the window right this minute on her way to cook lunch for Mrs Hissey. She's going to call the police to come and arrest you. What do you do?'

He rolled her on to the floor. 'Get you down here where she can't see you, lie on top of you and press myself into all your orifices so you can't yell for help. Then when you're well and truly stuffed I'm going to start tickling you.'

'*No!*'

You call me a baby, thought Rose, as she lay in his arms afterwards, but you're just a big kid yourself, Orlando. The number of times we rolled around tickling each other as children. Nothing has to change – if only you'd realise that.

*

A few weeks later Peg popped her head round the kitchen door as Rose was just about to make some herb breadcrumbs.

'Your uncle Mick's just rung. He's going to be passing through here later on this afternoon, early evening. Got to see a customer in Salisbury tomorrow. Wants to pop in. I expect he'll want to see you. Come over to us if you don't want him coming round here, upsetting your fancy lifestyle.'

Rose winced but said nothing. These days, it seemed Peg never missed an opportunity to have a go at her. She knew her mother was not happy about her arrangement with Orlando. She understood Peg's unease. It was just that she, Rose, was of a new generation. Things were different now. It might still be a case of 'them' and 'us' but it was possible for a Farley woman to broaden her horizon a little, to make something of herself, in a way that it hadn't been when Peg was young. Why couldn't Peg accept that and be pleased for her instead of sniping away with resentment?

'What's that you've got there? Looks dangerous.'

'It's a food processor, Mum. Victoria's got one up at Laybridge. Don't tell me you've never used it.'

Rose checked her measurements. Orlando was in London for the day. She was making him a surprise dinner: 50 g breadcrumbs, 25 g parsley, a sprig of thyme and rosemary, a clove of garlic, 50 ml olive oil and a pinch of salt. She mixed everything in Lindy's food processor until it was green, adding the olive oil slowly.

'You shouldn't call her Victoria.'

'Why not? She asked me to.'

'To her face?' Peg was horrified.

'Of course. Now, Mum, I've got to concentrate. Where are the eggs? I'm going to need size three. What are those, Mum? Can you check?'

'They're from your grandfather's chickens. How am I expected to know what size they are?'

'Oh, never mind. And a vanilla pod. It says bring the milk, cream and vanilla pod to the boil. OK, here we go. So what does Uncle Mick want?'

'He didn't say. I didn't tell him you were living with Orlando. I thought I'd leave that to you.'

'Thanks. You make it sound as if it might be a problem.'

'He'll hit the roof, Rose. You heard him at your grandfather's funeral. It's as if he's got one of Harold's blessed bees stuck in his bonnet as far as that family's concerned. You'd better have a pretty good explanation for him when you come over.'

'I won't be coming over, Mum. I'll have too much to do here and in any case I'll want to welcome Orlando home. He's gone to London for the day. I'm making him a surprise feast. You can give Uncle Mick the good news.'

'Just don't go getting your hopes up. It's not right.'

'What isn't?'

'Cohabiting.'

'Gossiping in the village, are they?'

'Yes, as it happens, they are, and I don't like it. What if she comes back?'

'Who? Lindy? Well, she'll find me here, won't she?'

'Is he getting a divorce?'

'Mum!'

'So he isn't.'

Rose poured her *sauce anglaise* mixture over the creamed eggs and sugar, returned it to the heat and stirred, looking down, avoiding Peg's question. Damn her. She was right, of course. Orlando had said nothing about a divorce.

After her mother had left, Rose spent the rest of the afternoon preparing her feast for Orlando but while she was confident in the knowledge that her new culinary skills were a match for any London dinner-party hostess, Peg's words nagged at the back of her mind.

What no one had ever understood, least of all Peg, was that she had always known exactly what she was doing with Orlando. She had always had a goal and that goal was now in sight. What she did not know was how long it would be before Orlando fell in love with her.

She wasn't stupid. She knew he did not take her seriously. Not yet. She knew he was ashamed of himself, that he thought he was using her to help him come to terms with the loss of Lindy, and to a certain extent he was. She knew he liked fucking her. He liked having her cook for him and look after him. But, as Rose very well knew, Orlando liked having anyone to look after him. He had assumed that Lindy would look after him and when she didn't – at least not in the style to which he was accustomed – he had turned automatically to Rose. Yet Rose knew he thought her beautiful. She caught him looking at her now and again when he thought she didn't know he had come into the room.

She laid the table for two and went upstairs to have a bath and change. Lindy had left all her beauty products behind and Rose was working her way through them. She cleansed her face with Clarins Lait Démaquillant Herbes des Alpes and smeared it with Masque Hydratante. She poured a ton of Floris into the bath and soaked herself. She wondered if Orlando had noticed that she had been wearing some of Lindy's clothes. When it came to scent though, Rose drew the line. No point in reminding him of Lindy in the most obvious way.

By nine thirty he still hadn't turned up. At nine forty-five he called and said he was just leaving London. He'd been having a drink with a friend. He didn't say if it was a man or a woman and Rose didn't ask. She abandoned the meal she had spent all day cooking for him and went to bed in tears. She could hear his voice mimicking hers: 'I am *not* a baby.'

The next morning he was so hung over he couldn't get out of bed. Rose crept out of The Cottage and trudged up to Laybridge. Victoria was away in London and Rose was relieved that she did not have to face more interrogation from that quarter as to her relationship with Orlando. She wondered how Victoria had taken the news. In a way, if things turned out as Rose hoped they would, Victoria would become her mother-in-law. She was the nearest thing Orlando had to a mother.

Rose checked herself. Peg's words reverberated around her aching head: 'He's another woman's husband.' It was nothing but the truth and so far she had no evidence to suggest that Orlando viewed her as anything other than a convenient lay.

She spent the day ploughing through Victoria's filing. A filing clerk! How could such a minion expect to replace the executive Lindy?

She worked late and returned to The Cottage disgruntled and tired to find Orlando still in bed. The kitchen smelled like a transport caff that had catered to all the truckers on the M25 wanting breakfast at once. Orlando seemed to have used every pan he could find. He'd taken the television up to the bedroom and was watching *EastEnders*.

'That Cindy's a bit of all right. Rose, I've been thinking. You were not wrong. This is the life. Keep it simple. Get us a beer and come and give us a cuddle.'

She went downstairs to get it.

'Sorry about the washing-up. Had a fry-up for lunch. You only have to stack it in the dishwasher, don't you? Simple.'

'I haven't touched it.'

'Why not?'

She didn't answer.

'What's for supper?'

'Last night's leftovers. That you couldn't be bothered to come home for. I didn't have time to go to the shop. I was working.'

'The Laybridge Arms might have something we can take away. Why don't you pop down and see?'

Rose stood up and kicked the bed.

'Why don't *you* "pop down and see"? I'm not your bloody skivvy.'

She didn't even look back at him as she left the room.

Rose stumbled along the Bluebell Walk in the darkness, not quite sure where she was heading but knowing that eventually she would arrive at Laybridge and that maybe Victoria would let her in, calm her down. Victoria. Not

Peg. It was not her mother to whom she turned instinctively.

There was a light in the old moss-covered turbine house. Candlelight flickering through the window. The moon must be nearly full. Rose could see quite clearly the white froth on the churning waters of the weir beside it. She hadn't been near the hut since the night Pepper had been found in it. Was someone in there? She ought to check.

It was a precarious route in the dark across the narrow plank above the seething waters but she made it. She pushed open the door of the hut and screamed.

Her father was sitting there, drinking a cup of tea just like he'd always done when she'd visited him to feed the fish.

'Give over, Rose. What's the matter with you?'

'Uncle Mick! You looked just like – I thought you were my –'

'Charlie? Don't be daft. Here, have a cup of tea from my flask. What's this I hear about you and Orlando Manners?'

'That's my business. What are you doing sitting here in the middle of the night?'

'Because this is where it all started, isn't it? This is where the trouble began with that family you're so determined to get yourself mixed up with.'

'This is where *what* all started?'

'ROSE! Where the fuck are you?'

Mick looked out the window. 'It's your poncey knight in armour come to get you.'

'Orlando?'

'Rose, come back.'

It was terribly romantic. They stood on opposite sides of the riverbank and looked across at each other while the water thundered through the weir beside them.

'I'm sorry,' shouted Orlando. 'I was behaving like a real shit. Please come back. I've made dinner. I've found a tin of *foie gras* and we can have it with toast. I've laid the table. I'll light the candles. I'll open a bottle of champagne.'

'Will you wash up afterwards?' Rose shouted, and when he nodded she ran along the bank to the narrow bridge. It was slippery and you had to put one foot in front of the other, literally, to get across. You also had to look to make sure your feet were safely on the bridge each time. It was a hazardous journey even in broad daylight.

Now it was pitch black and Rose was looking at Orlando.

She had only taken two steps before she missed her footing and toppled over into the waters below.

24

Victoria had always hated the word bonk. A good old Anglo-Saxon word like fuck was fine, and rather erotic. But bonk was just plain ugly. And so childish. Like snog. How could anyone call a kiss a snog? I really am getting old, she thought, objecting to the language of the young.

Then there was the way everyone now talked about their 'partner'. Nobody appeared to have wives, husbands, girlfriends or boyfriends any more. They had partners, as if they were working together in a law firm. She saw the point of the word. She could hardly describe Bruno as her boyfriend. Women of her advanced age did not have boyfriends. They had lovers and sometimes it wasn't really appropriate to talk to a complete stranger about someone being your lover. She could see how the word partner might be useful. But she would never use it herself.

Not that she had much opportunity these days. She had no idea how things stood between her and Bruno. She had hardly been surprised when he had called back shortly after their last disastrous conversation when she had told him she would not go on holiday with him. He always had to make sure she wasn't angry with him, that she understood she had been the one who had said he should go away without her. She wouldn't be able to blame him for anything. It had been her choice.

If only he could see how much he was widening the gap between them now that she had come to terms with all the flaws in his character. If she were honest, she knew she didn't really miss him as she once had. It was extraordinary how, as she had grown older, other things in her life had begun to take priority over Bruno. Now that her writing career had started to flourish she knew that if she had to make a choice she would choose that without hesitation over marriage to Bruno. Living with Bruno would be a nightmare and totally detrimental to her work as a writer even though he was one himself. Bruno was after money and celebrity. There was nothing wrong with that. In any case she never felt in competition with him. She relished being away from the 'action', as he called it. Providing that somebody bought her books she didn't really care who they were, just so long as she was left alone to write them. No, Bruno as a live-in 'partner' would be a nightmare. He would be understanding one minute and demanding the next. She could see that now.

But what would happen if Bruno suddenly turned up? Hadn't she been just as rational about his place in her life before she had run into him in Kensington Place? And look what had happened then. She had accepted an invitation to go waltzing round the world with him at a moment's notice and if it hadn't been for Pepper's accident she'd have gone.

Then, of course, there was her garden. It wasn't only her writing that occupied her, these days. Bruno might accuse her of burying herself in the country but when the garden was open the public came in droves and she had only to walk outside to find people to talk to. She opened a drawer in her bureau and brought out some drawings she had been working on recently with a view to redesigning the laburnum tunnel with a new walkway and some colourful plants. The public did love colour! Mercifully spring was on the way: the daffodils would be out soon and, of course, the bluebells.

Rose!

She had promised Orlando she would go down and see Rose.

'I think she did it deliberately,' Orlando had said on the phone the night before, 'to make me come to my senses.'

'Why do you say that?' Victoria could hardly bear to think of what might have happened to Rose. It was too soon after Pepper's accident. Here she was worrying about what to do with the garden that summer when she ought to be thinking about fencing off the turbine house and the weir. Thank God it was out of bounds to the public.

'Because,' continued Orlando, 'I spent all night thinking about how I'd have felt if I'd lost her. Not that there was any real danger. It's not as if Rose can't swim. When I jumped in to save her she was almost at the bank. But Rose and I used to swim in that pool all the time when we were kids, older than Pepper, of course. It was a bit colder last night. That's why I've insisted she spend the day in bed. Don't want her coming down with something.'

'Orlando, stop waffling on. How would you have felt if you'd lost her?'

'Completely devastated. She's why I love this place, Victoria. I've been trying to figure it out. It's where my parents were killed and yet I love it. And it's because it's where Rose is. She knows me better than anyone. She's the only person apart from you with whom I can be myself and I can't pretend that's not important. I'm fed up pretending, Victoria. London's not for me. I don't fit in there. I belong here. With Rose. I love her.'

Would they marry? And if they did, would it be this year and could she get the garden ready in time, Victoria wondered, as she went down the Bluebell Walk to The Cottage. Only as she reached it, her plans for the wedding progressing apace, did she remember that Orlando was married already.

'She's asleep,' said Orlando, when he let her in, 'but come in and have a cup of something.'

'What was she doing up there in the middle of the night anyway?'

'We had a row. Please don't ask me to tell you any more, Victoria.'

'No, sorry, none of my business. Let's change the subject. I've been thinking of redesigning the laburnum tunnel. Actually I've spent all morning wondering what to do with the garden.'

'Herringbone brick,' said Orlando.

'I beg your pardon?'

'Herringbone brick. It'd look great going all the way up the path.'

'You're absolutely right. So what else am I to do with it? If I'd known laburnum grew so quickly I'd never have suggested it to Harold. We'll be fighting our way through it, come the end of May.'

'I'll go and take a look. Put a bird bath at the end. It needs some sort of focus. And you need to plant something either side of the path.'

'I know I do, Orlando, but what?'

'Veronica. White veronica. Yellow and white are wonderful together.'

Perfect! Now, I'm in despair about my delphiniums.'

'What about them?'

'Well, the stakes are so ugly.'

'Hazel twigs. You have to catch them before they become hazel bushes but they look fine. I'd like to come and get some willow cuttings if I may. I want to make a willow trellis along the side of The Cottage for my clematis this year. What do you think?'

'I never realised you knew anything about gardening, Orlando.'

'I grew up here, didn't I? I used to spend a lot of time wandering round the gardens with Harold. Hang on, that's the loo flushing. Rose must be awake. Want to take her up a cup of tea?'

Rose was sitting bolt upright in bed. She looked wan but her eyes were burning.

'He knows. Uncle Mick knows. I thought I was the only one but Dad told him.'

'What does your uncle Mick know? Have you seen him?'

'He was up at the turbine house last night. I was on my way to see you, after my row with Orlando.'

'What did your uncle say?'

Rose looked away. 'Oh, nothing.'

But there was something. Mick Farley, his late brother Charlie and Rose had all known something, something that scared Rose. But Rose wasn't going to be drawn. Victoria looked out of the window to the river Lay, to the place where Daisy Manners had drowned. If Rose married Orlando one day, Victoria would have to tell her about The Visitors' Book. What would she do with Daisy's second volume with all its tawdry revelations? And why did she have this terrible feeling that Rose might be able to throw some light on the last section that led up to the night on which Daisy had died?

'I know what you all think about me moving in with Orlando,' Rose said suddenly. 'Sometimes I'm astonished myself at what I've done. But I'm not going to un-do it. Mum's going to have to get used to it, and so are you, Victoria.'

Rose had asked Victoria if she could call her by her first name and Victoria had said yes, of course she could, but it always sounded odd. Victoria knew that if she had worked in an office everyone would call her by her first name but she just couldn't get used to it. She dreaded to think what Peg would say. They were two of a kind, she and Peg, both reluctant to adapt to the new world in which they found themselves. At least I don't have a child to contend with, thought Victoria. But in a way she did. In fact she had two: Orlando and Rose. Not her *biological* children – it made them sound like a washing powder – but they were the closest thing she would ever have to the real thing.

'I think I can get used to you and Orlando.'

'Can you?' said Rose, clearly surprised.

'Certainly. You'll be very good for him.'

'Was Lindy wrong for him?'

'Are you right for him? That's what you really want to know, isn't it? Was Lindy wrong for him? Actually, no, I don't think so. In many ways Lindy was right for him in the same way that you are right for him. Yes, Rose, you are.'

'How?'

'You must remember that Orlando is desperately fragile. He went through a terrible ordeal as a little boy. He's such a warm lovable extrovert we forget how vulnerable he is underneath. We write him off as being hopeless – well, maybe you and I don't but lots of people do – but we forget that he doesn't have the confidence in himself that others have. Hugh and I tried to do what we could as parental substitutes but I used to watch him as he was growing up and I knew he was suffering. Orlando needs someone strong, someone who can lead him. That's why Lindy was good for him. She led, he followed. The problem was he didn't realise he liked following. He resisted her leadership, resisted the fact that she was stronger than he was, objected to her working as hard as she did. He should have let her have her head, then she would have stayed.'

'And what about me?'

'You're strong, Rose. You can lead him. You can look after him. And I think you do really love him. And … and I think he loves you.'

'And if Lindy decides to come back, then what do I do?'

'I don't know. But why don't you cross that bridge if you have to? In many ways Orlando is just a child. He has never really grown up. You, Rose, are far more grown-up than he is. You've made far more of your short experience beyond Laybridge than he ever will. You've assimilated the information you've gathered working for me, going to London, and you've put it to use so that it fits in with who you are and how you live down here.'

Rose was listening to her, drinking it all in.

'We're none of us what we seem to be, Rose. I probably come across as a supremely confident older woman to you, someone who knows exactly who they are, but inside I'm actually coming a bit unstuck. I'm not old, yet I feel so much older than everyone else. I'm irascible and arrogant. I shout at my publishers and I know they think I'm rude and difficult but I can't help it, I can't pretend any more. I have to say exactly what I think – otherwise I feel I'm letting myself down. They're all so much younger than I am and they see things differently. There's no one around any more who sees things my way and it makes me feel so lonely.'

'I see things your way, Mrs Hissey. At least, I try to.'

It was the way she'd known exactly when to say Mrs Hissey instead of Victoria that made Victoria realise just how special Rose was.

It came to her as she was walking back to Laybridge. The young man whom she had hired to attend to the gardens, the person she had thought might ultimately take the place of Harold Farley, had proved less than satisfactory. He was from London and this in itself had spelled trouble from the outset. The local people resented him. And now, Victoria realised, so did she. Although resent was the wrong word. She liked his ideas but they were not right for Laybridge.

When she reached home she decided to wander round the gardens. She stared dispiritedly at the simple path of stepping stones he had created, sunk into the soil and flanked by a dwarf box hedge and the ornamental lily pond. It was all too twee for Laybridge. This young man did not see things on a grand scale. He was behaving like a frustrated cottage gardener. Yet she liked him and she did not want to admit defeat by dismissing him too soon. Then she came up with an idea that might just work – might even be the perfect solution. She would relaunch the plant centre and put him in charge of it. He could combine his London-style salesmanship with his knowledge of plants and at the same time be relieved of Laybridge itself.

The more she thought about it, the more she wanted to offer Laybridge to Orlando, put him in charge, under her supervision, of course. He wouldn't really be a gardener like Harold had been, but he would be in charge of the design and planting, relaying his ideas and her own to others.

I'm not a wife, thought Victoria, and I'm not a mother but I may turn out to be a plantswoman, after all.

That evening she was feeling so cheered by her brilliant solution to her problem and Orlando's that she decided to call Jessica in New York for a chat. Too often Jessica caught Victoria when she was feeling low. Now would be a good time to show her that she was capable of being on top of things.

Two minutes into the conversation Victoria wished she had never picked up the phone. Jessica seemed determined to focus on the one subject Victoria had planned to avoid: Bruno.

'What do you mean you haven't seen him for ages? Is this a relationship or not, Vicky? Every time I speak to you he seems to be doing a brilliant impersonation of the Invisible Man.'

'That's not true. He's busy.'

'Doing what?'

'He's on holiday.'

'Is that what he's calling it?'

'Jessica, why are you always so down on Bruno?'

'I'm not. He just doesn't seem particularly supportive of

you. He swans about the place doing exactly what he wants. He picks you up and puts you down as and when he feels like it and I think it must be awful for you. I mean, when did he last do something really wonderful for you?'

'He asked me to go on holiday with him. I was the one who said they couldn't go. It was around the time when Lindy left. Orlando needed me.'

'There's always something, isn't there, Vicky? Either you're a complete pushover or the man's a bastard. You have to face up to it.'

'He's not a bastard. He has his faults and I'd be the first to admit it. He's vain and he's not terribly supportive of my career, it's true. But he's supportive of me – even though you don't appear to recognise it. You're always carping on about how wrong he is for me. As a middle-aged married woman, I'm not sure it was the best idea in the world for you to have had that affair with your child's paediatrician but I didn't bang on about it. I just let you get on with your life. Just because I can see quite clearly what's wrong with Bruno doesn't mean I've fallen out of love with him.'

As she said it Victoria knew it was true. She had fooled herself for a second that she had become immune to his charms but she wasn't. Nor did she want to be. 'No man is ever going to be perfect, Jessica. I want to be in love with Bruno. I choose to be in love with Bruno. I am happier loving him than not loving him. I have worked out in my own mind what kind of man makes me happy and it's Bruno. There isn't a DIY kit called How to Fall in Love. It just happens.'

'So you're fine about the fact that he's thinking of moving back to New York?'

Bruno moving back to New York. What on earth did Jessica mean?

'Vicky?'

'You've got it all wrong, Jess. He's away on holiday. There's been no talk of him moving back to New York to live. He'll be there for a book tour in a week or so.'

'He's been here for two weeks already, Vicky. I saw him in a restaurant last Friday. He said he was thinking of moving back. He's your man but he hasn't even mentioned it to you and you don't even seem to know where he is. What was it you just said? No man is ever going to be perfect. You said it, sweetheart, not me.'

25

Bruno had let himself go.

He looked at himself each morning in the bathroom mirror. He had a revolting paunch. He had bags under his eyes, and even though he told himself they were sexy, he knew they weren't. He had a surfeit of chins, and broken blood vessels on his nose and cheeks. He was overweight, he smoked far too much and his drinking had increased. Worst of all, he had given up exercise. He hadn't been near the gym for months, and his exercise bicycle now served as a clothes horse.

It wasn't even as if he could blame success for the change in him. His book had been a dismal failure and it was time he faced up to it and did something about it.

He blamed Victoria.

He had been in a state of rage for weeks. Try as he might, he found himself unable to be indifferent to Victoria. When she had announced she would not be accompanying him on holiday he suddenly found that he no longer wanted to go. He had leafed through his address book countless times searching for substitute women to invite and to his amazement he had found himself dismissing name after name as unsuitable. There was the minor problem that many of the women were married and a plausible explanation would have to be found for their husbands as to why they were flitting off on holiday with a known womaniser. But it was the sudden lack of appeal of the rest that surprised Bruno. Younger than Victoria, firmer than Victoria, livelier than Victoria, altogether more desirable than Victoria. On paper. For three hours. After several drinks. But when he was hung over – or even sober – in need of intelligent conversation or, to put it more accurately, a good listener, it was Victoria's company he wanted. He didn't have to pretend with her. She was the only person who knew the real Bruno. She was the only person with whom he could really relax. And that was what he felt like doing these days: relaxing.

He was slowing down. The failure of his last book had shaken him considerably. And if you set yourself up to be a bestselling commercial writer commanding huge advances, you were only as good as your last book. It was a competitive business just like any other. Never mind that he knew his new thriller was a cracker, something his fans would relish. First he was going to have to overcome that huge barrier that stood between authors and their readers known as The Book Trade. And before he even thought of wooing them, he had to find a new publisher. Fuck Charlie Rose for abandoning him at the first opportunity. Fuck Bruno's so-called hotshot agent for not fighting harder for him. But money talked loudest in the book business just as it did everywhere else. Never mind that he had a two-book contract, they had found a way to dump him. Well, Rubinstein and Rose would be sorry. OK, so they'd lost a ton of money on his Balkans thriller – but if only they could be made to realise they could earn it back on this new book.

This was one of the reasons he'd come back to New York: to kickstart his flagging career. But now he was propping up British Airways' excuse for a bar in their Club World lounge and murdering Bloody Marys while waiting for his flight back to London to be called. He smiled. Victoria hated that expression. 'I could murder a Bloody Mary / hot bath / holiday in the sun ... whatever', something you said when you really wanted something. Somehow it irritated her, along with God knows how many other expressions. She couldn't stand it when someone said, 'We must have that drink soon.' 'What drink?' she always asked. She always took everything so literally. She was so real all the time. If she said something, she meant it and she expected everyone else to be the same. That's what he loved about her. Loved. Suddenly he longed to hear her say she loved him. More than that, suddenly he longed to tell her he loved her. She would be gobsmacked. No, she wouldn't. She hated that expression too.

He was on his way back to London for a week or so. His excuse was that Orlando had invited him to The Cottage for the weekend – which meant there was a good chance of seeing Victoria. His pride wouldn't allow him to pick up the phone and call her, ask her if he could stay at Laybridge. She had turned down his offer of a holiday. He wasn't about to start begging to see her.

But it would be nice to run into her and take it from there.

He hated airport lounges. Grey plastic affairs full of pseudo-business types wittering away on the telephone, trying to look important.

Women on their own were rare so when she walked in he wasn't the only man to watch her progress as she dumped her carry-on luggage in the open closet provided, gathered up a few newspapers, helped herself to a cup of coffee and some biscuits before collapsing on to one of the grey sofas.

'Lindy?'

She jumped, nearly spilled her coffee. 'My God! Bruno!'

'Can I get you a drink? A real drink, I mean. Bloody Mary?'

'Oh, OK.'

'You tell me what you're doing here first and then I'll tell you,' he said when he returned. He handed her her drink and sat down beside her. She hadn't changed much. Shiny mousy bobbed hair, expensively cut; sturdy little back, short legs, nice smile. He couldn't help but admire this girl. She had nothing going for her other than her determination to succeed, and that she'd got as far as she had before she was thirty was impressive. They wouldn't appreciate it in England. She'd be dismissed as one of Thatcher's pushy children. Brash and on the make. She epitomised Victoria's most hated expression: 'Go for it!'

'I'm here because I'm about to get on the overnight flight to London. I've been travelling round America and I wound up in New York. Everything's worked out just as I planned. I met with Charlie Rose and now I'm Rubinstein and Rose's new scout. I've persuaded them to buy Victoria's new book and I also talked to them about you. Hope you don't mind.'

'Why should I mind? Depends what you said.'

'Well, now I have to come clean and tell you I've read it. Caroline Calder slipped me an early copy, bless her. Bruno, it's absolutely fantastic. That's what I told Charlie Rose. I told him, I said, "Charlie, I know you've taken a real bath with Bruno Manners' last book but this one is really worth taking on.'"

'And he believed you?'

'Why wouldn't he?'

'No reason. No reason at all.' Bruno felt her enthusiasm literally bouncing off her as he sat beside her. He had a sudden impulse to take her into his arms and kiss her. She must truly think a lot of his book to risk talking it up to a publisher who was trying to dump him. Bravo, Lindy, out there fighting for me – unlike a certain woman who is never by my side when I need her. 'You deserve a bottle of champagne for your efforts. Hold on a sec.'

'So what about you?' she asked him, when he returned.

'London. Same flight as you I imagine.'

'BA 174? Club?'

'Absolutely.'

'I'm treating myself to Club for the first time. You're slumming it a bit. Don't you normally fly First?'

'Why would I do that? Club's a treat for me too, actually. You look surprised.'

'Well, you are a bestselling writer.'

'Correction. *Was* a bestselling writer, although if I stick near you I might have another shot at the big time. Lindy, what you have to understand is that things are rarely what they seem. People with high profiles invariably have another side to their life that's just like anyone else's. We all have to make our money somehow unless we've inherited wealth like Orlando and we all have to keep on making it to keep up the profile. We all go to the same restaurants, we're all seen in the same places in public in various cities around the world because those are the places to be seen in. It's where we all come together, if we're the sort of people who think image is important, and you and I definitely fall into that category. The word image as we know it doesn't even exist in Victoria's vocabulary. But when we're not out in public, not on show, those of us who might be a little down on our luck are indistinguishable from any other person trying to make a buck. The problem with you, Lindy, is that you're too obsessed with your station in life. You were trying too hard that first weekend at The Cottage. You would have achieved more if you'd just been yourself. People would have seen the real you and liked you more.'

Why was he going on like this to this girl? He knew the answer. In some perverse way he was attracted to her. He always had been. It was a case of it takes one to fancy one. He'd never have thought of having such an intense conversation with her anywhere else. Airlines didn't know it but anonymous places like airport lounges were perfect for soul-searching conversations. Pour it all out to a passing stranger, then they'll be on their way and you'll never see them again.

'I assume you've heard about me and Orlando. I've left him. They're probably all delighted. Nobody really liked me much down there, did they?'

'Well, I did, but then, I saw the real you. You were just someone trying to get themselves a better life. Nothing wrong with that. But you're quite capable of earning yourself a good life. You don't need to marry someone like Orlando to get it. You'll be all right without him. You won't have The Cottage and you won't have the fancy townhouse in Elgin Crescent but soon you'll be able to buy a place of your own. That's the type of woman you are, Lindy. Face up to it. Many women marry a man to achieve security, a place in society, a conventional life but you're not one of them. You're more interested in your working life at the moment and there's nothing wrong with that.'

'Bruno, don't you see? It's all part of the same package. I spent my childhood growing up in a dreary suburb of London watching television and going to the movies and reading books and magazines and newspapers and knowing there was an exciting life out there. I was determined to be part of it. But it didn't just mean a career that would take me places and enable me to meet all sorts of people I wouldn't find in West Norwood. Can't you understand that just as I had to grab any work opportunity that came along, I also had to sit up and grab Orlando when he wandered into my life? He was the fairytale handsome prince but he was also sweet and kind. I fell in love with him, Bruno. Maybe initially it was just the idea of him but I did feel something for him. Don't you think I love him?'

'You think you do. Maybe you really do. If that's the case then you'd better go home and fight for him. How do you feel about Rose moving in there so soon?'

'I beg your pardon?'

'Didn't you know?'

'I hadn't a clue. What's happened? And how do you know?'

'Rose called me the other day, tracked me down here in New York via my agents. She knows everyone in publishing these days, probably more than you do. She told me she'd moved in with Orlando. She said they'd had something brewing for some time. She wanted me to come for the weekend at Easter.'

'Her first weekend,' murmured Lindy.

'What did you say? You don't sound particularly surprised that she's with him.'

'Well, don't you see what she's doing? She's establishing her position there just like I tried to do. It always comes down to those blessed weekends at The Cottage. She was always in love with Orlando. I saw it immediately. Are you going?'

'That's why I'm flying to London tonight. They just called our flight, by the way.'

'But you'll stay at Laybridge? With Victoria?'

'No, I think I'll stay at The Cottage.'

'Is there a problem between you and Victoria?'

'The only problem I have with Victoria is not a million miles removed from the one you have with Orlando.'

'You love her but you don't want to bury yourself in the country?'

'Something like that. I think if I stay at The Cottage I might bring her to her senses.'

'I can't see Victoria living in New York.'

'It doesn't have to be New York. I'm going to tell her I'd be prepared to spend more time at Laybridge if she'll only compromise and live with me elsewhere as well. Up to now I've always lived by my own stupid rules. Keep them wanting more, never commit to one woman because there's always another one round the corner. Well, there always is but I've discovered I no longer want any of them. I want Victoria.'

'And you're ready to make a full-time commitment? Marriage? The whole bit?'

'The whole bit. That's why I want to stay at The Cottage. I want to walk up that wretched Bluebell Walk to her at Laybridge and propose. Lindy, what's the matter?'

Lindy's eyes had filled with tears.

'Bruno, I'd never have guessed. You're an old softie. I've never heard anything so romantic.'

'Of course I'm an old softie. Hard-bitten scaredy-cats like me who never commit are always the most romantic of the lot. We know that if we settle down with someone it's the end of romance. But now I'm ready to settle for whatever Victoria wants. It's just a question of realising I'm happier with her than I am without her. Easter proposal, June wedding, how romantic can you get? Put it in your diary.'

'Who says I'll be invited?'

'I do. Now, what about you and Orlando? Are you going to fight for him? Go down there and oust Rose? Claim your prince?'

'Would it be easy?'

'Depends how much you want to. I have a feeling Orlando loves you both in your own way. It's like a role reversal of two swains fighting over the fair princess. Do you really want Orlando back? You're not an old codger like me. I'm prepared to spend time at Laybridge if it makes Victoria happy but from what I can make out you're far from ready to knuckle down to life at The Cottage. You've got years of London life ahead of you, office life. You go back to Orlando and you'll be gone again within the month.'

'I just want to see him again. I left under a cloud after that Pepper incident. You left under a cloud too the first time, Bruno, when Hugh died. And you had to go back, didn't you?'

'Yes, but at least I waited a decent interval to give Victoria time to work things out.'

'But if I leave it too long Rose is going to plant her feet even more firmly under the table. Is she really living there? Sleeping in our bed?'

'Well, I didn't exactly ask that question but that seems like the general idea. It's your competitive spirit coming out, isn't it, Lindy? If Rose hadn't moved in on your patch I doubt you'd bother going back for quite a while, if at all.'

'That's not true. I care about Orlando.'

'Of course you do. Well, when are you going down, then?'

'I'll have to pick my moment.'

'You know he's living down there full time now, don't you? No bearding him at Elgin Crescent. You'll have to fight for him in front of Rose.'

'Well, she's hardly likely to invite me.'

'I could take you down with me.'

'For Easter?'

'Well, not for the whole weekend but I could say I was bringing someone and arrive with you and you could take it from there.'

'You'd pretend I was your date?'

'Now that would really start them talking. And, believe me, I can think of worse people. But I'd have to ask for separate bedrooms, first stages of the affair, etc., etc. It's a shame we couldn't get together. We're two of a kind. I'm too old for you but I understand you. You're a girl in a hurry, you remind me of myself when I was younger. I doubt you'll find the right man for another ten, fifteen years. You'll have false starts like Orlando and you'll dump them. If I'm still around when you're ready, come looking for me. We speak the same language. We ought to be together. Funny how it never seems to work out that way. When two people are ideally suited they hardly ever fancy each other. Matchmakers work overtime with men like me, trying to fix me up with girls like you, and it never goes anywhere.'

'You mean you don't fancy me.'

'I never said that. I'd be delighted to take you down to The Cottage at Easter but only so you can get your foot in the door with Orlando. I've already told you what my own plan is. We'll be on the same mission. It's not that I don't fancy you – listening to you rave about my book made me want to pounce on you there and then, and I've always liked the way your hair is so glossy ...' He reached out to stroke it and for a moment her head rested on his shoulder. 'Come on,' he whispered, 'they've called our flight twice now. Final call, I'll help you with your bags.'

The drink had made her woozy. He had to put a hand under her elbow to steady her. Do her good to lose control for a second, he thought. God, he was tired. Well, he could sleep all the way to London.

The plane was fairly empty. Lindy was a few rows behind him. They shared another glass of champagne after take-off then Bruno went back to his own seat.

'Liqueur for you at all, sir?' was the last thing he heard the stewardess say before he sank into a deep sleep.

He was awakened by Lindy, her face very close to his own, asking him: 'Do you really fancy me?'

She was in the empty seat next to his. The movie was over. The cabin was dark. He nodded sleepily.

'Well, then, let's do something about it. I fancy you rotten, Bruno. It's just dawned on me. You remind me of

Orlando, your looks, or maybe he reminds me of you. But I want someone mature like you. Orlando's like a child and I'm just not motherly. I'm damned if I'm going to let him go without a fight now Rose has insinuated her way in there but in the meantime, Bruno, please, come here ...'

He knew what was going to happen and he did nothing to stop it. Her mouth was brushing against his and her tongue was trying to prise open his lips. He fumbled sleepily with the buttons of her jacket, reached inside and ran his hands up under her sweater and over her breasts. Her nipples were rock hard. Her tongue was exploring the inside of his mouth now. He was enjoying it. They kissed for minutes on end.

Then he felt her hand between his legs. He shifted in his seat, gently pushed her tongue out of his mouth.

'I can't.'

'Why not? I won't tell Victoria. I won't tell anyone. It'd do us both good.'

'It wouldn't. It's the last thing we want. It'd be like incest. Because I'm rather drunk and sleepy and because we're thirty five thousand feet above the ground and no one can hear us, I'm going to tell you this, Lindy, but you mustn't tell a soul. If you were anybody else I'd undo my seat belt and make you come so loud you'd wake everyone up. But it won't work. I can't. I'm your father-in-law.'

26

Victoria sat at her desk, digesting the news.

She knew Rose had not intended to give her a shock. Indeed if she hadn't called Rose to ask her why she hadn't come up to Laybridge to work she would probably never have found out. Rose was in a state. Victoria had heard it in her voice. Orlando had invited people for the weekend and Rose was going to play hostess for the first time. It was understandable that she was nervous, that she was preoccupied with planning her weekend rather than helping Victoria sort out chapter five of her new book. And it was nice of them to ask her to dinner. She'd be delighted, she'd replied, which was when Rose had told her Bruno would be there. Rose said she had personally tracked him down in New York – why did everyone seem to know Bruno was in New York except for her, Victoria wondered? – and invited him. Then she dropped her bombshell. Apparently he'd called since and asked Orlando if he could bring someone.

A woman.

Well, this was it. In just a matter of weeks he'd met someone else. She'd always been prepared for it and in a way it was something of a relief. She didn't belong with him anyway – hadn't she been telling herself that for ages? She was not part of his world.

The world is divided into two kinds of people, she

reflected, abandoning the troublesome chapter five, those who want a quiet life and those who don't. I do. Bruno doesn't. Yet we came together and I don't regret it. On the face of it we were totally wrong for each other but if I had not had my affair with him, there would have been a side of me that would have remained undiscovered. I am not boring and safe and timid even though I live in the heart of the country. I am brave and curious and through Bruno I learned this about myself. I do not have to go right into the thick of things like he does. I can imagine it all without ever having to leave Laybridge. Bruno needs to keep on living on the edge for as long as he can and no doubt he's found someone who'll keep up with him. Millions of people out there like that. But Orlando and Rose, they're different, thought Victoria. They're like me. They don't need the outside world. They have everything they need right here. She only hoped they realised it.

As for Bruno, it was better if it ended now. She never wanted to be in the position of having to say she didn't love him any more. After all, it was far sadder to fall out of love with someone than for someone to fall out of love with you. No one ever understood that.

It would be a turning point in her life. She would find a new love. She was optimistic about that. He would be nothing like Bruno. No one could be. Bruno had been dangerous. And necessary. Now she could look forward to the next stage.

Two important men in her life were gone: Harold Farley and Bruno.

One remained.

Orlando.

Let nothing happen to blight his new life with Rose, she prayed silently.

The next day Peg sprinkled finely chopped parsley into a white sauce for a fish pie she was making for Victoria's lunch, aware that her brother-in-law was watching her.

'She eat like this all the time?' Mick asked her. 'Fancy fish pies and that for her supper every night?'

'What's it to you?' Peg was irritated by his sudden arrival. Expected her to put him up without a moment's notice whenever he was passing through. Never used to come near them in the old days. Now he'd gone and lost his job. Laid off. She wondered what brought him down here, what he was up to. No good, more than likely.

'Rich, is she?'

'She's successful. She wouldn't be able to keep that place on if she wasn't.'

'Or you.'

'Or me. Now, get out of here, Mick, I want some peace and quiet. Take yourself off to the Laybridge Arms and don't come back till closing time. Shouldn't be too hard for you, judging by your track record.'

Peg was depressed. She didn't know where she was in the world any more. She hadn't been this unhappy since her husband had taken to the drink. It hadn't been him starting to drink that had upset her. Men drank. It was a fact. You dealt with it. So long as they didn't turn violent on you there was no point interfering. But she hadn't known the reason Charlie had started drinking. She still didn't know and it still bothered her. She had loved Charlie. He'd been quite a catch when she'd married him, the best-looking man in the valley and happy in his work at Laybridge. What had happened to change him? What had made him so unhappy? Most disconcerting of all was that Mick obviously knew more than she did. Why had Charlie confided in Mick and not her?

She wondered what Charlie would have had to say about the latest turn of events: she was going back to cook at The Cottage at the weekend just like in the old days but this time it was their own daughter who would be giving her her orders. One thing Peg knew for sure: if Harold were still alive he wouldn't have stood for it. He'd have put his foot down. What would Mrs Hissey say? She was expected there for dinner Easter Saturday. Well, Rose couldn't expect her mother to wait at table. She'd cook the food and leave it in the oven. It was bad enough having to discuss menus with Rose. She'd been summoned by her own daughter to be round at The Cottage at ten o'clock the following morning. Peg had a good mind not to show up.

'I thought we'd keep it simple, stick to French,' Rose announced, 'just some nice *carré d'agneau* for dinner on Saturday night followed by a *tarte aux pommes*. I'll get some *pâté de campagne* to begin when I'm in Salisbury at that new deli. We'll have *crudités* with drinks.'

Peg couldn't be doing with Rose's sudden obsession to say everything in French.

'Roast lamb. Apple tart. You get the starter. Raw carrot sticks with drinks. What about Easter Sunday? Don't you want your roast then so you can curry it about for your lord and master on Monday? He likes a nice bit of mutton curry.'

'I don't curry things about, Mum.'

'Pardon me.'

'I want to break with tradition. We'll have pasta for Sunday lunch. Lasagne, maybe.'

'That's not French. Thought you wanted to keep it simple and French. Suppose I could make a béchamel sauce, that's French, and shove it on some layers of pasta. That do you? Who's coming to your fancy weekend, by the way? Important guests, I expect.'

'Mum, stop it. I just asked you to help with the cooking. If you don't want to do it that's fine but can't you understand that I'm nervous? I've always been the one in the kitchen. If I'm still there they'll go on treating me as if I'm the cook.'

'You're the cook's daughter, ducky, and you always will be. Don't you forget that. You be yourself and they'll respect you all the more. You're behaving no better than that silly Lindy on her first weekend down here. She put on airs and graces and look where it got her. Of course you're a bit nervous and I'll be here to help but why can't we do it together? Show 'em what a great team we are. Now for the last time of asking, who's coming? How many will there be?'

'Bruno's coming down on Saturday, in time for lunch. Orlando said he was bringing a guest, didn't say who. Lily and Peter McGill will be arriving around tea-time like they always do. Victoria's coming to dinner.'

'Well, Mr Bruno won't be staying here, will he?'

'Don't call him Mr Bruno, Mum, please.'

'Why ever not? I've always called him Mr Bruno.'

'It's just not appropriate any more. Can't you understand that?'

'Well, we'll see.' Peg wasn't going to give in right away. 'But you didn't answer my question.'

'No, he's staying here. I think that's what Orlando said. Here he is, I'll double check. Orlando, you did say Bruno was staying with us and not Victoria?'

'Yes, something odd going on. He's bringing someone. A woman. Didn't give her name.'

'Well, I'll put them in the best guest room. Lily and Peter won't mind.'

'How do you know they'll be sharing a room?' asked Peg.

'Oh, Mum!' Peg saw Rose look to Orlando for help.

'Don't look at me. I haven't a clue. I don't even know if they're an item. To be totally honest, I don't even know if she's staying the night. Bruno just asked if he could bring her for Saturday lunch.'

'Well, what time are they arriving? What shall I give them for lunch?'

'Rose, what's the matter with you? You, of all people, you know what it's like here on Saturday afternoons. Everyone turns up when they feel like it and eats whatever's there.'

'Mum and I are going to do a double act in the kitchen,' Rose told him, not looking at Peg. 'I was thinking of her. We'll be seven for dinner, right?'

'Eight,' said Orlando.

'You, me, Lily, Peter, Victoria, Bruno and his surprise bit of fluff. Seven. Don't tell me you've gone and asked someone else without telling me.'

She sounds more like Lindy every minute, thought Peg.

'No, I haven't but you've forgotten someone,' said Orlando.

'Have I? Who?'

'Your mother. If she's going to be slaving away in the kitchen with you it's only fair that she should come and eat with us. Times have changed, Rose. You're the one who's always telling us that.'

'You're a real gent, Orlando,' said Peg, not looking at Rose.

27

'They're not coming,' Rose said flatly. 'They know it's going to be me looking after them and I'm not good enough for them.'

It was Saturday afternoon, after five o'clock and getting dark outside.

'It was always you looking after them,' Orlando pointed out calmly. 'I never noticed Lindy rushing around making up the beds and putting out clean towels and if we'd relied on her efforts in the kitchen everyone would have lost an awful lot of weight. So can I lay my pieces out all over the table now?'

They'd nearly had their first serious row when Rose had asked him to move his jigsaw off the table so she could lay lunch. They'd reached a compromise whereby he was allowed to use half the table.

'Who's Bruno bringing?' Rose asked, for the umpteenth time.

'I don't know. I didn't ask but whoever it is I'm sure they'll be charming. Stop flapping.'

Rose glared at him. Orlando never flapped and it was beginning to irritate her.

'Go and check the bedrooms, rearrange the flowers or whatever it is you've been doing all morning. Can I have some of that cottage pie your mother made or are you going to keep it for posterity?'

Peg had cooked lunch and left it in the oven and on the dot of one Rose had placed it on the table.

'It'll be really welcoming for them to have a nice hot cottage pie on the table when they walk in.'

She'd heard Orlando trying to reason with her about the likelihood of people undertaking two-hour car journeys from London arriving dead on time, but she didn't care. She was going to welcome people in her own way.

'Anyway, you know I told everyone to arrive when they felt like it. You're the one who's got it into her head that they'll all be arriving for lunch. I, however, am hungry so I'm going to tuck in. Go upstairs and calm down and if anyone arrives I'll offer them cottage pie and say it's high tea, a new feature at The Cottage.' There he was, trying to get a rise out of her again. Well, it wouldn't work.

They both heard the car.

Rose grabbed the cottage pie. 'It's stone cold. I'll heat it up.'

She collided with Lily coming through the front door and dropped the pie dish, which broke. Cold mince and potato spread all over the floor. Peter, following Lily, unwittingly stamped it firmly into the impractical but expensive cord matting with which Lindy had insisted on covering the hall floor.

'Oh, what a mess. How awful. Sorry, Rose. You must have bumped into Percy.'

'Percy?'

Lily pointed to her stomach. There was a slight bulge.

'We call him Percy, don't we, Peter? Might be a little girl, of course, but for now he's Percy. Orlando, didn't you tell Lindy about Percy?'

Nobody said anything. Rose thought she was going to scream.

'Oh, I mean Rose. Sorry. I'm always doing that. I call you Orlando sometimes, don't I, Peter?'

'No,' said Peter. 'Come on, Rose, I'll give you a hand scraping this stuff off. I always said to Lindy she should never have put down this matting. Must have set you back an absolute fortune, Orlando.'

'And it marks so easily,' said Lily. 'Now, haven't you noticed who's missing?'

'Bruno,' said Rose. 'He's bringing someone down to meet us. They'll be here soon.'

'No. I meant Pepper. You'll have to forgive me if I keep on using your telephone but this is the first time I've left him with someone else for more than a few hours. Peter says he'll be fine and I'll have to get used to it but I can't help worrying. Peter insisted I needed a bit of rest on my own away from him.'

'That's not strictly true, Lily. You didn't want to bring him down here because of what happened last time we ...' Peter stopped. 'Sorry ... I didn't mean ...'

'Well, try not to have the baby this weekend, Lily,' said Orlando. 'Remember that weekend you came down here when you were about to have Pepper?'

'And did,' said Lily. 'Now, Rose, what can I do? Shall I peel some potatoes? I'll make us all a nice cup of tea. Peter, do you want a sandwich or something? I wouldn't let him stop on the way down like we usually do. I told him we must get down here early to give you a hand. Orlando, toast?'

'Yes, please. Marmite.'

'It's all right, Lily. Go and sit by the fire. I'll make tea.'

Rose scraped up the last of the hapless cottage pie and deposited it in the rubbish bin.

'All right, you do tea and I'll begin the vegetables for dinner. How many are we? What are we having? Shall I lay the table?'

'Lily, for Christ sake leave me alone!' Rose couldn't help it. 'I've been preparing meals in this house for years now. Just give me a break. Better still give yourself a break.'

Rose regretted her words immediately. A deep pink flush began to creep up Lily's neck and face.

'I'm really sorry, Rose. I don't know why I go around driving everyone potty but I always do. I just need to feel useful all the time or else no one will want me around. Having so much to do for Pepper has made me feel a little more fulfilled. I sometimes wonder if he wasn't born deaf deliberately, so I'd have someone to help all the time.'

'Of course he wasn't. All babies need help.'

'I know, I know. I'm always making excuses. It's just that everyone's so competent, compared to me. Look at you, the way you run everything.'

'But everyone always thinks you're so efficient, Lily.'

'Do they? Do they really?'

'Of course. "Where would we be without Lily?" I hear it all the time. How's Pepper?'

'He's fine.'

Rose wanted to ask, 'Will the next one be deaf too?' It must be preying on Lily's mind. Instead she handed Lily the tea tray.

'Could you do me a favour, Lily, and take this in? I'll make Orlando's toast.'

Rose heard the front door slam and looked out of the

kitchen window. Bruno was getting out of a taxi. He and his guest must have come by train to Salisbury. Why hadn't she thought of that and gone to meet them? More to the point, why hadn't Bruno told them?

Rose peeped through the kitchen door to sneak a look at the woman Bruno had brought. When she saw Lindy with her arms round Orlando's neck she couldn't move until she felt Peter pushing her aside.

'Rose, what's the matter with you? Can't you smell the toast burning?'

Lindy had an agenda.

She'd worked out how it was going to be as she sat opposite Bruno in the train. Rose would be completely thrown. She'd have to get her on her side. Somehow the fact that she knew about Bruno being Orlando's father while Rose didn't gave her a sense of power that made her feel she had the upper hand even though Bruno had forbidden her to mention it.

'Daisy was such a detestable woman. It's not as if I loved her or anything. I'm not sure I even fucked her more than a few times. It wasn't worth rocking the boat by telling everyone he was my son.'

'You mean you didn't want the responsibility?' said Lindy shrewdly.

'He was better off thinking Guy was his father. Can you imagine how horrified I was when I found out Guy and Daisy didn't sleep together? She taunted Guy all the time. It made you feel very uncomfortable being anywhere near them. I never discussed it with Guy. I couldn't bring myself to, especially when I found out about Orlando. The awful thing is that Guy must have known who the

303

father was. I didn't believe Daisy when she told me. I was under no illusion that I was the only man she went to bed with. It could have been anyone. But she insisted it was me, said she hadn't had any other lovers around that time. It was only when Orlando grew up that I knew she'd been telling the truth. He looked so like me. No one else ever commented because he also looked like his father. I mean Guy. But you have to promise me, Lindy, you can't go raking it all up now. Keep it to yourself because I warn you, if you do go shooting your mouth off I shall deny it.'

Lindy went into the kitchen and embraced Rose. 'Don't look so shocked. Did Orlando forget to tell you I was coming? Typical.' Lindy knew perfectly well that Bruno had deliberately kept quiet about her coming. 'Well, we know what he's like, don't we, Rose? Nothing ever matters with Orlando, does it? I bet I can imagine the kind of afternoon you've had. Jigsaw all over the table. Lunch getting cold because we weren't here to eat it for the simple reason that Orlando failed to ask us to lunch. Then Lily arrives and drives you bananas. Don't tell me, she wanted to make tea, dinner and Sunday lunch within five minutes of walking through the door.'

Rose laughed. 'She's a nightmare. But she means well.'

'They're the worst. Listen, you're not to worry about my being here. I know I should have called and cleared it with you but —'

'You're his wife. You've every right to be here.'

'Well, yes, I am but you're with him now. It had been going wrong between us for quite a while as I'm sure he's told you. But when I walked out it was a bad moment. All that mess with Pepper. I had to come back and face up to what I'd done. I couldn't end our marriage on that note. I had to talk to him, clear the air. You understand that, don't you? And I knew he wouldn't let me come if I called and asked him. Sneaking down with Bruno was the only way.'

'If you say so,' said Rose.

'Oh, Rose, don't be like that.'

'Well, how do you want me to be?'

'You have nothing to worry about.'

'I'm not worried.'

'Well, that's all right then. Now, which room have you put me in?'

'Is the futon OK?'

'It's perfect. You're so wonderful, Rose. I've always adored you. Friends for life?' she clasped Rose to her.

'Have a cup of tea.' Lindy couldn't help feeling awkward when Rose disengaged herself in embarrassment.

'Don't believe a word she says,' warned Peg, when she came over to help prepare dinner and Rose filled her in on the surprise guest.

'No, Mum, she wants to be my friend. You've got it all wrong.'

'No, I haven't,' said Peg firmly.

Victoria was reading The Visitors' Book again.

She was drawn to it like a festering wound whose scab itched and demanded to be picked at. Daisy's second volume. To Victoria this was the real Visitors' Book, the only one that counted. To her own intense irritation Victoria often reflected on what it must be like to be a woman like Daisy Manners. A woman who could manipulate men and act as a magnet, pulling them to her as and when she wanted them and holding them, often against their will. While she had no desire to be someone like this, Victoria often envied their power over men.

It was the last few pages of The Visitors' Book that most sickened Victoria. The repellent details about Daisy's final lover. Victoria often wondered if Daisy had fancied herself as a writer. Her diary entries were more than just a quick record of the day's events. Towards the end the prose became violent and melodramatic, clearly written for effect.

He hates me. He was almost in tears today when he came. He hates me and he is angry with me and his anger makes him more passionate, forceful. When he fucks me he is hungry and crazed. He is out of control. I have control of him now.

He is out of his depth with me. He does not know how to handle me except in sex. I want to fuck him. He wants to kill me. It's the same thing.

It plagued Victoria that she knew who the man was. For some reason he was never mentioned by name, but various references made it obvious.

It was quite a cool evening but at least it wasn't raining. Victoria decided she would take the Bluebell Walk to The Cottage but she couldn't find a torch in the boot cupboard where she usually kept it.

Then she remembered.

Rose had bought her one of those new-fangled contraptions you plugged into the wall to recharge the batteries. Now, where on earth had she inserted it?

She checked all the sockets in the hall, the breakfast

room and the kitchen before she found it in one by the toaster. By which time she was late.

Yet still she dawdled. It had been on her mind all day. Should she or shouldn't she? If she did it now while she was in a hurry then it would be done and she could go out and forget about it, be distracted by dinner at The Cottage.

She went upstairs to her bedroom. The fire was still burning. She moved the guard to one side and retrieved The Visitors' Book from her bedside locker. She placed it on the fire, waited until the embers flickered to life and the flames began to devour the leather binding, then she put back the guard and left.

Now she could keep Daisy's secret to herself. No one else would ever need to know.

She went downstairs, feeling surprisingly calm. Bruno's woman would undoubtedly be a brash New Yorker considerably younger than himself. Considerably younger than her, too. Well, there was no use fighting it. She had walked in that time Orlando had invited that model, Nona something, and Bruno had ignored her and attached himself to Victoria. Things were a little different this time, of course, because he had brought the woman himself. But in a way it made things easier for Victoria. She wouldn't have to keep worrying about what was going to happen. It had all been decided, taken out of her hands. She could mourn Bruno in private and in public she could sit back and enjoy Rose's cooking.

Or would it be Peg's cooking? What had Peg said? Something about having to work for her own daughter.

Victoria picked up a cashmere throw that someone had given her and tried to toss it around her shoulders. Maybe it was meant for narrower shoulders. No matter how many times she tugged at it, it never seemed to sit right. In exasperation she grabbed an old quilted anorak and, plunging her hands into the pockets for warmth, she set off down the Bluebell Walk.

As she passed the weir, Mick Farley, sitting in the turbine house, saw her go by and slipped out to follow her.

Victoria never knew what made her go round to the kitchen door at The Cottage instead of ringing the front-door bell.

She could see immediately that Rose was terribly upset. Peg wanted to put the pâté on the table as a starter and Rose had just realised she had forgotten to go to the deli in Salisbury as she had promised. They had no starter.

'I've got some smoked salmon up at Laybridge but there isn't very much,' offered Victoria.

'Let me go and get it, Mrs Hissey,' said Peg, 'I'll pick up some of our eggs and we'll have smoked salmon and scrambled eggs. Now, give her a boost while I'm gone. You've got to stand your ground,' she told Rose. 'Don't let her get near Orlando. He doesn't want her, he wants you. Doesn't he, Mrs Hissey?'

'Who's she? Who doesn't he want?'

'Oh, Mum, stop going on. Victoria, you mustn't worry but Bruno has turned up with Lindy.'

'Lindy? Lindy's the woman he's brought down here?'
'Yes.'

'He's taken up with Lindy?' Victoria couldn't believe it.

'No, that's what you have to understand. He's brought her down to help her get Orlando back. That's what he thinks he's done anyway. But she's been really sweet. She says she just wants to end it with Orlando in a civilised fashion.'

'Don't you believe a word of it,' reiterated Peg. 'She's after something.'

'Or someone. Bruno, I shouldn't be at all surprised,' said Victoria, and to her intense fury felt a sudden urge to burst into tears.

It was a funny thing about champagne, Victoria reflected half an hour later, it really did lift the spirits. Bruno hadn't left her side since she'd walked into the room. In fact, it was more worrying to see Lindy clinging like a limpet to Orlando.

Poor Rose. Maybe Peg had a point, after all.

In true Cottage tradition, Orlando, Bruno and Peter sat down one side of the table with Rose, Lindy and Lily opposite them. Victoria sat in splendour at the head of the table and Peg's place was at the other end, handy for the kitchen.

No atmosphere could remain tense for long when Lily was present. She was so idiotic, Victoria thought, that everyone always wound up barely able to control their laughter.

'I rather thought,' Lily said, as Peg brought in plates of smoked salmon and scrambled eggs, 'that we might have an Easter egg hunt in the garden tomorrow morning. In honour of Pepper — in his absence, so to speak. I've got some chocolate bunnies. I could go and hide them in the bushes and we could look for them.'

'It'll be damp and wet and a complete nightmare,' said Lindy.

'Well, I think it's a sweet idea. Mum and I will help.' Rose sprang to Lily's defence. 'We'll do it for Percy. Lily's baby,' she explained hurriedly, to everyone else. 'When's it due, Lily?'

'End of September. What about you? Christmas baby?'

'You're pregnant!' It was Lindy who spoke. She had gone quite pale. It could have been you, Lindy, thought Victoria, if only you'd listened to what I had to say.

'Who's pregnant?' Orlando hadn't been listening. 'Someone else besides Lily?'

'You are, by the sounds of things,' said Lindy.

'Rose?' Everyone was staring at her. The scrambled egg was quickly becoming cold and congealed on their plates.

'How did you know?' Rose asked Lily.

'Oh, how awful,' squealed Lily. 'You mean you haven't told anyone yet? Maybe it takes one to know one. I just knew. I sensed it almost the minute we arrived. You are, aren't you?'

'I'm late,' Rose confessed.

'How late?' Orlando could barely speak.

'Two months if I don't come on soon.'

Victoria noted the look of pure devotion that had come over Orlando's face. Peg's fears had been groundless. If Lindy had once wanted Orlando back, now she didn't have a prayer.

Peg was up and around the table before anyone could say anything else. 'Oh, my love, why ever didn't you tell me? It's what I've always said — when someone dies you often find someone's about to bring a new life into the world. This little babe is going to be born for your grandfather. It'll bring his spirit back into the world.'

'That's a load of tosh, Peg. If we want anyone's spirit back in this valley it's your husband's.'

Peg turned and screamed. Rose put out a hand to steady her. 'It's all right, Mum. It's because he's standing in the shadows and you can't see him clearly. It's not Dad. What are you doing creeping in like that, Uncle Mick? Giving us all a scare.'

'He's drunk,' said Lindy in disgust, as Mick slumped down beside her. 'Get him over to the men's side of the table before I'm overcome by the fumes. For once I'm in favour of this ludicrous tradition of separating the sexes.'

'Get out, Mick. Don't come in here causing trouble, I'm warning you,' said Peg, clutching him by the arm. 'Look at you, drunk out of your mind, bringing disgrace on the Farley family.'

'Why do you think Charlie drank, Peg? Don't you want to know? I know what happened that night right outside that window. I know why Charlie drank himself to death. Now I can walk out that door and you'll never see me again and you'll never know what happened. Or I can stay and tell you. Which is it to be?'

'Sit down, Uncle Mick.' Rose pulled up a chair beside her and Victoria shivered at the sight of their unnervingly similar profiles: the same sharp straight nose, the same prominent cheekbones with their high colour, the same unruly gypsy hair. 'Orlando, he can stay, can't he? You may be drunk but you loved my dad and that's good enough for me. I don't know what you're going to say but I saw something that night that I've never been able to bring myself to talk about. Maybe now I can face up to it.'

Victoria decided to keep her counsel, at least until she

had found out how much he knew, how much he was going to say.

28

'Just in case there's anyone who doesn't know,' began Mick, 'I'm Peg's brother-in-law. I'm Charlie's brother. I've been coming here for years but they never let me near you, Mrs Hissey. Ashamed of me, see. Because I left the valley. Made something of meself. Didn't want to stay around here and vegetate like my dad, boring old fart. Why'd you have to go and interfere and have his funeral up there? I wouldn't come. I went to the church. But I wouldn't come up here. I said to myself: "If she didn't invite me before I'm not going now."'

'Well, you would have been very welcome, Mr Farley,' said Victoria quickly. There was no way of knowing where this was going. There was an edge to the man's voice, something that said he could turn nasty – violent, even.

'Oh, I would have been welcome, would I? Lord knows why I've bothered to come here. You Hisseys have been the ruin of us Farleys. You think just because my father was employed up there at Laybridge as head gardener, or whatever he was, and just because you allow Peg to cook your meals and you give her a home to live in, you think that makes it all right, do you? Well, do you?'

'Makes what all right?' Victoria was aware that everything he had said so far seemed to be directed at her.

'Makes it all right for my brother to drink himself to death. She ruined him, didn't she? She –'

'Wait!'

So Mick did know. Victoria had to stop him. She would have to think fast. She had thought she could get away with it, that she could burn The Visitors' Book and never have to reveal its contents. But Mick knew and now he had begun his revelations he wasn't about to stop.

Orlando couldn't learn the truth about his mother from a drunken weasel like this. Nor could Rose ... nor Peg ... But Mick was off again.

'And because she ruined him, she ruined everything for Dad and Peg. They needed Charlie. With me gone, Dad only had Charlie to share his love for this godforsaken neck of the woods. It destroyed my father when Charlie died so young. I don't suppose you ever stopped to think about that, did you? Too busy starting up your stupid plant centre, easing him out to pasture to make way for your fancy new ideas. And how d'you think Peg coped? You Hisseys, you never made up for the income Farleys lost when Charlie died. Brought in someone new to look after the trout stews, gave Charlie's whack to him, never thought about what Peg did to make up the shortfall. She needed Charlie's money, did Peg. She needed it more than she needed him, I've often thought. You shut him out, Peg girl. All your fault. That's why he spent so much time up with his trout stews, in that turbine house. She used to visit him there. That's where all the trouble started. I couldn't believe it when he first told me about it. I was always the flashy one, trying to get ahead with women. Charlie was better-looking, granted, but he was the quiet one. That's the irony, that this scandal, call it what you will, should fall to him. All he wanted was a quiet life with Peg – looks like the back end of a bus, sorry, darling, you do, but he loved her – and look what he got.'

'Who used to visit him?' Rose interrupted.

It's just what I was thinking. Victoria looked at Mick with a mixture of pity and revulsion. Some of us want quiet lives, others don't.

'Well, who do you think it was, Madonna? I can't believe I have to spell it out for you. It was –'

'That's enough, Mr Farley.' Victoria was on her feet with a hand out to stop him going any further. 'I know you're upset about your brother but he was also Peg's husband. And Rose's father. And ...' Victoria hesitated. It had to be said and she didn't want Mick to blurt it out. 'And she was Orlando's mother.'

'It's all in that book isn't it?' said Peg suddenly. 'The one you've burned. You shouldn't have done that, Mrs Hissey. It had some glue inside it or something, it was burning away, making a terrible smell, when I went back just now to get the smoked salmon. I went up to see what it was.'

'And you tried to read it?'

'Oh, I've read it before now. The Visitors' Book. You didn't hide it very well, Mrs Hissey. I'm ashamed of myself, I shouldn't have done it. It was him she was writing about, wasn't it? My Charlie. Is that why he drank himself to death? Because she died? Did he love her that much?'

'No, Peg,' cried Victoria. 'If you read The Visitors' Book you know it wasn't like that. He hated her.'

'What are you all talking about?' Rose was nearly screaming now. 'What *is* this Visitors' Book?'

'I know,' said Lindy. 'I've got one, it's –'

'Be quiet, Lindy.' Victoria was sharper than she had intended to be. 'Yes, you have got one but I hope to God you haven't filled it with vile material like Daisy did. The Visitors' Book,' she turned to Orlando, 'is something someone gave to a French woman who use to live in this Cottage.'

'Oh, I know all about her,' said Orlando. 'That was your father-in-law's mistress. Wonder what happened to her. She left once she realised she was never going to be mistress of Laybridge.'

'I don't know whether or not they have Visitors' Books in France but this woman didn't know what to do with it so she used it as a diary and left it here. Your mother found it, Orlando, and she went on using it as her diary.'

'I've got it in London. You gave it to me, Victoria,' said Lindy, looking rather smugly at Rose.

'I gave you the first one but I kept the second. The vital one. The one where Daisy chronicled all her lovers. I'm sorry, Orlando, but now it's come out you'd better hear the truth. Better to hear it among family.'

'Yeah, and better Peg and Rose hear about Charlie from family too. No, let me finish.' Mick was not to be stopped from saying what he felt he had to. 'Charlie told me all about it. He had to tell someone. It was choking him up. Here was this hard-as-nails glamorous bitch who'd taken a shine to him. She lived for sex, she used to tell me, and that husband of hers obviously didn't give her anywhere near enough.'

Lindy shot Bruno a look but he ignored her.

'Charlie said she was like a dog, a regular bitch on heat except she went sniffing about looking for it. He said she used to lie in wait for him in the lane outside The Cottage as he walked up to the trout stews. She used to flirt with him and ask him if he'd like to come in. Well, he went in once and she took his hand and put it straight on her titties without even asking. With the boy playing in the next room.'

Victoria knew she ought to stop him but she couldn't help it, she had to hear it all. She was fascinated. Repulsed, but fascinated.

'Then she started going to the turbine house. He'd made it all nice in there, radio, camp bed so he could have a kip when he felt like it, kettle and stuff for making cups of tea, probably even had a bottle of something stashed away to keep out the cold. She started it, make no mistake. Told him she'd had her eye on him since they first started living at The Cottage. She threw herself at him, walked in there one night when it was pouring with rain and took all her clothes off. Said she'd come in to get dry on her way home. Stood there naked and started fondling him.'

'He told you all this ... this detail?' Victoria was appalled but she couldn't stop him now. She glanced around the table. It was sordid stuff but they were adults. And Mick knew more than she did. She would only ever have been able to tell them what she had guessed to be the truth. Mick could explain to Rose in her father's own words. No, thought Victoria, it would be wrong for me to halt this now.

'We were very close, Charlie and me,' continued Mick. 'That's why I'm here now. I'm useless, I'm unemployed but I loved my brother. He understood why I went off.

He understood what I was trying to do – didn't want it for himself but knew I needed it. When he gave me all these … details, as you call them, it was because he was so shocked at what he was doing. It was like if he confessed everything to me each time he saw me it would make it all right. She had to have him on the floor with the waters of the weir rushing through the sluice only inches below them. He was terrified, see. She said she'd tell Peg, tell you, tell everyone if he didn't "service" her. That's what she called it, so he said. Servicing. Like a gas station. You want to say it's like that *Lady Chatterley's Lover* business, don't you? But it's not. That John Thomas or whatever his name was, he wanted Lady Chatterley. Charlie didn't want it with Mrs Manners. Oh, he wanted "it", he couldn't help it, but he didn't want her.'

Victoria almost smiled. It sounded as if Mick Farley thought Lady Chatterley and John Thomas were real people.

'Well, anyway, he lost her, Mick, didn't he? In the end.'

'You say that, Mrs Hissey. You say that. And you're right. But it made it worse and I don't know why.'

'How do you mean? Made it worse?'

'The night Mr and Mrs Manners drowned. They had a dinner party. Charlie told me all about it afterwards. He walked past The Cottage on the way to the turbine house and he looked in and he saw them all having dinner. You had the nipper up at the house and they'd asked people over and there they all were, sitting at the table, the men down one side, the women down the other just like you are tonight. Some stupid tradition she was always telling him about. She looked up as he was going by and she saw him. He said it was after midnight when she came to him.

She was drunk. She'd stripped off all her clothes as she went up the Bluebell Walk and she'd left them strewn in the mud. She said all her guests had gone and her husband had retired – that's the word she used, apparently, retired. But he hadn't. Well, he'd gone upstairs but he'd looked out the bedroom window and seen her waltzing up the lane throwing all her clothes all over the place and he'd rushed out and followed her.

'When he walked in on them Charlie was lying on his back and she was sitting on top of him, pumping herself up and down. Her husband yanked her off and went for poor Charlie. Charlie took fright and ran out of there, buttoning up his flies as he went. It comes close to making me laugh, that bit. Like some old silent movie. Charlie running home to Peg, doing up his trousers as he goes. Well, that was it. Mrs Manners followed her husband home and the next thing we hear about is that the two of them were washed up on the banks of the river like drowned sheep. Presumably her old man was so angry he threw her in but that doesn't explain how he came to drown too. And it doesn't explain why Charlie took to the drink. I could have understood it if he'd started drinking while it was still going on, pressure of having to keep it from Peg and all that. But once they'd drowned he didn't have anything to worry about any more. He was safe from her. But there's no doubt about it. From that day on he went downhill. It's like they drowned and he drowned right after them only it was in the booze instead of the river. He didn't give a monkey's for her. I just couldn't understand it.'

'Why did you feel you had to come and tell us all this?' asked Victoria.

'It's not what you think. It's not blackmail. It's like Charlie had to tell me. I've got no one to talk to about it and it's been driving me crazy. I'm drinking like Charlie was. It preys on my mind. What happened to him? I've got this secret about him that I'm carrying around with me and he must have had an even bigger secret he was carrying around after they drowned. I can't talk to Peg. I can't talk to Rose. I've tried raising it with them a few times but Peg's put it behind her and Rose gets hysterical if I mention her father. Or, at least, she used to. Looks like you've changed, Rose. I know I said what I did about your family being the ruin of ours, Mrs Hissey, but then you're not one of them, are you? You're an outsider. You married old Mr Hugh. I don't know, I just had a few drinks and I was sitting in the turbine house thinking about Charlie and I saw you go past. I followed you. I've been standing outside wondering what to do. Then I decided. Get it off my chest. I'm sorry. I'll go off now. I'm no use to anyone. Lost me job. Useless. Except ...'

He looked up at Rose.

Rose reached across the table to hold Orlando's hand. She said, 'I always used to wonder if I was imagining things. I've never forgotten that night when your parents drowned. Two people drowned, they said, but I saw three people right outside here from my bedroom window at Farley Cottage – it looks out over Orlando's garden. I used to watch him in it. I could see right down to the river. Your parents, Orlando, and a third person – it must have been my father – down by the riverbank. She was naked. I saw her run after Dad. I saw your father try to pull Dad away. I saw your mother clinging to him. They were all three fighting each other. I see now that Dad was trying to get away but, of course, it didn't look like that to me that night. But he did get away and your mother leapt on him again. She wouldn't let him go and he had to fling her away from him to get rid of her. That's when she was thrown into the river and your father jumped after her, trying to save her. Who knows what happened? They were swept away, pulled down by reeds, but they were lost.'

'And Charlie didn't try to save them. He saw a chance to be rid of them for ever and he took it. It was only afterwards he realised what he'd done, that he'd taken the coward's way out, that he'd more or less killed them. No wonder he took to drink.' Mick was on the verge of tears.

Victoria sensed she had to say something. 'What you said earlier, Mick, was quite right. The Hisseys' actions have been the ruin of the Farleys in some ways – but what we have to remember is that all that can change. We have to rise above what's happened and look to the future. You've suffered too, Mick. I can see that and I'm sorry. But try to remember Charlie for the man he was before he met Daisy.'

'Daisy Manners was a real cow,' said Peter suddenly, 'I always despised her when I was a kid. Condescending bitch.'

'Peter, that's the strongest thing I've ever heard you say,' said Lily 'She was Orlando's mother don't forget.'

'Sorry, mate,' he was looking at Orlando, 'but I've been wanting to admit what I thought about her for years. Hands up anyone who actually has a good word to say for her.'

'It's all right,' said Orlando quietly, taking them all by

surprise. 'I know exactly what she was like. It's extraordinary that Rose remembers as much as she does. She was only four years old then, but it was her own father she was watching that night. She's stored it up in her mind all these years. But I was *twelve* when my mother was drowned. I know I've always pointed that out to prove that I could remember how wonderful she was. I had to keep pretending she was wonderful because I couldn't face up to the fact that I'd had a bitch for a mother. And the fact that she drowned. Death by drowning is so horrible. It sickens me that the woman who gave me life – however unpleasant she may have been – died like that. Have you ever stood under the shower with your face up and suddenly you're struggling for breath. Every time I take a shower I think of her. Her eyes must have bulged. It would have distorted her beauty. Because I do remember her beauty. I've always known about her. I think the real reason I married you, Lindy, was because you were her total opposite. Nobody understands how much children see the truth. Just as I've always known about you, Bruno, even before you told me.'

'Even before he told you *what*?' asked Rose.

'I know,' chipped in Lindy.

'Shut up, Lindy,' said Bruno sharply. 'I told Orlando that night I came here when you were first married, when I first met you. You went to bed, we sat up talking. But it's between him and me and if he wants to tell other people, he will, in his own good time.' He reached across the table and squeezed Lindy's hand. 'Sorry to snap at you. You know what I mean.'

'Of course.'

No one else saw it. Only Victoria saw the look that

passed between them. She knew Bruno. He'd looked at her like that in the past.

'You and Orlando, you've got so much baggage to bring to your relationship,' Lindy told Rose.

'Baggage!' Victoria was positively spitting. 'I absolutely loathe that expression more than you can possibly know.'

Bruno smiled. 'You're such an old bat. Come on, let me walk you back up to Laybridge unless you can salvage whatever's burning in the oven, Peg?' This time he reached for Victoria's hand. And held on to it.

'Oh, my God, the lamb.' Peg and Rose flew into the kitchen.

'My guess is that they'll stay in there for quite a while and we should let them,' said Orlando. 'Mick, why don't you join them? After what we've all just heard, I imagine a Farley family conference is long overdue. Help yourself to a glass of something on the way, and make it a large one. Ask Peg to bring in what's left of the lamb when she can but tell her to take her time. Did Rose really say she might be having a baby?'

'It's not confirmed,' said Lindy. 'I've been late many times and I've never been pregnant.'

'No, Lindy,' said Orlando, 'you never have.'

29

At two in the morning Rose slipped the latch on the back door of Farley Cottage and let herself out. It'd been a marathon session but she was relieved it was all out in the open, about her father and Orlando's mother. Lindy had been right. She and Orlando had a fair amount of baggage in common but it could only bring them closer together.

The evening's revelations had been horrifying but also cathartic. She'd helped Peg up to bed and left Mick sprawled in an armchair by the stove. They were a family again. Mick and her mother had made their peace, drawn together by their loss, their love for Charlie. It should have happened years ago.

It was cold for Easter. Without a coat, she shivered as she walked back to The Cottage. The river was very still, barely a ripple. Trees were reflected in the moonlit water. She could almost see the marsh marigolds and wood anemones. She stopped for a second and listened to the rustling in the wooded banks either side of the Bluebell Walk. Night creatures. Easter bunnies. She giggled.

She let herself into The Cottage and was about to tiptoe upstairs when she heard a sound. She stepped back and peered into the darkness.

Orlando was lying on the sofa and in his arms was Lindy.

Rose lay awake for nearly an hour before Orlando joined her. 'I saw you,' she whispered in the darkness.

'Saw me?'

'With Lindy.'

'It isn't what you think.' Orlando raised himself on one elbow to look down at her. 'I saw a spider. You know how terrified I am of spiders. She killed it for me.'

'And you leapt into her arms?'

'It's an old joke between us. We were just saying goodbye, Rose.'

'Your marriage is over?'

'No. Well, not exactly.'

'What does that mean? Exactly?'

'Don't get all het up, Rose, please. Our marriage isn't over because it never began. That's what I was explaining to Lindy. I knew I'd have to tell her one day. Lindy and I were never legally married out there in the West Indies. It was just some hocus-pocus ceremony performed by some ex-hippie on a beach. Which leaves me free to ask you to be my wife. I really think it would make Victoria's day if we opted for a June wedding.'

Rose never went to sleep.

She eased herself out of bed and pulled back the curtains so that she could watch the dawn come up over the river. It looks the same from here as it does from my window at home, she thought. But, then, why should it look any different? A river doesn't change because it's flowing past a more upmarket home. And it's my home now. I must remember that.

It was going to be a misty morning. She climbed back into bed and dozed until eight o'clock. She heard rustling outside and sat up. There was a figure in the garden. Back at the window Rose saw Lily running about in her dressing gown and slippers, hiding chocolate bunnies behind bushes.

Another sound. A car.

Rose turned to the other window where she could look out to the Bluebell Walk. A taxi was drawing up outside the house. Rose watched as Lindy came out of The Cottage with her bags. Lindy was leaving. From the minute she had arrived she had never fitted in. As she watched the taxi disappear from view Rose felt a twinge of something she had never experienced before. What was it like to be Lindy? What was it like to have a life outside this valley?

She placed her hands protectively on her stomach and wondered about the person she would bring into the world. Would they grow up to be someone like her and Peg or Orlando and Victoria, content to remain here and lead a quiet, peaceful life? Or would they be like Lindy or Bruno, someone who would leave her behind to follow their ambitions and a life she knew nothing about?

I might not be leaving Laybridge but I've outgrown the life my mother envisaged for me. How much further, Rose asked herself as she looked down at the sleeping Orlando, will our child go?

30

'I'm gutted, Victoria, I really am.'

'I loathe that expression. I immediately think of your lower alimentary canal. Is that what you want? Right after sex? What's the matter now?'

'It really is outrageous,' said Bruno, pouring himself a glass of whisky from a decanter he had placed beside the bed before he and Victoria had made love.

'What is?' She was drowsy, warm and peaceful, lying against his chest with her eyes closed.

'I traipse all the way down to the bloody country for what I imagine will be a cold but at least peaceful weekend with some good food and a decent claret, only to walk straight into a family crisis. Burned grub. Not enough booze. Yanked back to a bedroom stinking of some singed glue. Still, in spite of all this I've decided to go through with it.'

'Through with what?'

'Proposing marriage. You and me.'

'Out of the question.'

'What did you say?'

'No.'

'No? Victoria, I'm asking you to marry me.'

'I know. I heard.'

'But why won't you?'

'Why didn't you tell me you were Orlando's father?'

'Stop trying to change the subject, Victoria. I love you. I'll live down here with you, if that's what you want. I want to marry you. Please will you marry me?'

'I love you too, Bruno. But it's too late. I don't want to be married to you. I've come to understand that now. It doesn't mean I want to stop seeing you. You'd never be happy at Laybridge. I'd never be happy in New York or London or whichever city you choose to live in. I could marry you but I wouldn't want to be with you all the time and it wouldn't be fair because that's what you'd expect.'

'So what do you want?'

'I want us to go on as we are. We love each other. We see each other from time to time. We live the lives we want to live and we have each other's love to keep us going.'

'In other words you want me on your terms. It's pretty unconventional, what you're suggesting.'

'The only thing that's unconventional is that I'm suggesting it and I'm a woman. Women have always had to fit in with men's plans in their relationships. Now I'm saying you're going to have to fit in with mine. Take it or leave it but hurry up because I'm falling asleep.'

'OK. All right. I love you, I'll take it, for Christ's sake. On one condition.'

'What's that?'

'I'm allowed to propose to you every Leap Year.'